BLACK SITE, BLACK MOTHER

RYAN RENNIK

TREPIDATIO
PUBLISHING

ISBN: 978-1-68510-134-3 (tpb)
ISBN: 978-1-68510-135-0 (ebook)
Library of Congress Control Number: 2024945774

First printing edition: November 22, 2024
Published by Trepidatio Publishing in the United States of America.
Cover Design and Layout: Don Noble / Rooster Republic Press
Edited by Sean Leonard
Proofreading and Interior Layout by Scarlett R. Algee

Trepidatio Publishing, an imprint of JournalStone Publishing
1400 North Wood Road
Murphysboro, Illinois 62966

Trepidatio books may be ordered through booksellers or by contacting:
JournalStone | www.journalstone.com

Praise for
BLACK SITE, BLACK MOTHER

Black Site, Black Mother is a terrifyingly crafted vision of a man questioning not only his own morality, but that of his co-workers, his country, and their enemy, all the while failing to take notice that beyond man's inhumanity, something monstrous lurks in the darkness, waiting to take advantage of the pain and madness. Ryan Rennik's slow burn novel of personal apocalypse is steeped in the lore of Lovecraftian Horror but is more than capable of standing on its own, and sets Rennik in the same class as James Moore, Brian Keene, and Mary SanGiovanni, carving out a new and distinct cosmic horror mythology. —Peter Rawlik, author of *The Cthulhu Heresy and Other Lovecraftian Sins*

So much of *Black Site, Black Mother* feels dangerous, perhaps even forbidden to read because of Rennik's frightening ability to place the reader in such close proximity to the horrors on the page. Arresting and utterly original, Rennik's novel is a blistering portrait of war, surveillance, and transformation. —Eric LaRocca, author of *Things Have Gotten Worse Since We Last Spoke*

Ryan Rennik has given us a relentless and propulsive cosmic body horror underpinned by unsettling anxieties about what the US has become in the post-911 world. The CIA agents and contractors trying to break the will of a high-value abductee at a black site somewhere in Poland, find themselves questioning who, or even what, is in control of their interrogations. And once that question is broached, the granular, concrete detail of a spy thriller that begins on the dusty streets of Peshawar, unravels at dizzying speed into full blown phantasmagoric catastrophe. *Black Site, Black Mother* is the very definition of nihilistic, hallucinatory pandemonium. It's like dropping that tab of acid you got from H.P. Lovecraft just before you settle down to enjoy your favorite Tom Clancy. —Robert G. Penner, author of *The Dark King Swallows the World*

Black Site, Black Mother is creeping dread with a dynamite finish. Part military thriller, part Lovecraftian horror, and all of it uncomfortably believable. Rennik writes like he's seen things the rest of us—luckily—haven't. —K.L. Young, author of *The Secret Language of Spiders*

Black Site, Black Mother deftly balances various genre conceits—it's a found document novel, a claustrophobic military thriller, and a Lovecraftian work of cosmic horror. Lean, expertly paced, and teeming with hypnagogic visions of weird grotesquerie, this is a freakily compelling read. —Mike Thorn, author of *Peel Back and See*

Black Site, Black Mother is a novel that intertwines several genres: spy thriller, horror, and what I guess I'd call CIA procedural rather than police procedural. The story takes place at a black site in Poland where CIA agents are interrogating terrorists post-September 11. With one terrorist, they discover something worse than a dirty bomb. It felt like I was watching a very good extended episode of *The X-Files* while an elder god whispered Lovecraftian nightmares in my ears. Calling it creepy doesn't do it justice. A solid read. —Charles Allen Gramlich, author of *Razored Land*

Brilliant. Mark Romero used to be a captain in the US Army. Now he's a CIA operative, fully committed to the War on Terror, his dedication to preventing another 9/11 making strangers of his family. He cannot tell them about his latest assignment to remote forest in Poland, for it's a black site. The man known within Al Qaeda as 'The Engineer' used to be a microbiology student at Virgina Tech. Now he's an important asset, tasked with working on the next terrorist outrage. But he cannot tell his Brothers of the one who truly guides his actions, for she is the Black Mother. When their paths meet, Romero must try all he knows to break through the Engineer's web of evasions and cryptic clues. But will he unearth a planned biological attack? Or is something far darker and far more terrifying coming ever nearer? —Mark N. Drake, author of the *Jack Glennison Darkisle* novels

To Bob
I think you would have liked this one.

BLACK
SITE,
BLACK
MOTHER

It is a terrifying thing to fall into the hands of the living God.

—Hebrews 10:31

April 2, 2004
Peshawar, Pakistan

THE ENGINEER LEFT his safe house for the first time in two weeks. He was growing concerned that the Americans were closing in, but had been finally driven outdoors by the simple necessity of running out of food. He waited until well past nightfall, when the streets would be relatively empty and he could easily spot any watchers. He began walking in the direction of a store only a few blocks away that he had purchased some staples from previously. He knew he could get there quickly, grab enough food to tide him over for a few more weeks, and get back to the apartment with no one the wiser. He passed a few people on the street, all of whom seemed to avoid his gaze as they scurried past on whatever inscrutable errands they were engaged in. To them, he was simply a middle-aged man wearing ill-kempt clothes, occasionally muttering to himself. Certainly no one to pay any attention to. He was also a man with a $10 million bounty on his head.

One woman dragging a child behind her caught the Engineer's eye as they approached each other on the sidewalk. He grinned at her—rakishly, he thought, though she would have described his look as maniacal—and she hurried past him, shrinking as far away as possible. His smile fell; then he ignored her as she slipped past. He could hear occasional traffic noise in the distance, but it was faint, part of another world to him. Nothing mattered but his mission. His mind turned and twisted over the intricacies of what had been revealed to him, what he must do later when called upon. For now, he was simply awaiting that call.

Night had fallen, and while there were still a few open businesses, there were almost no streetlights in this part of the city. It was dark and quiet, just how he liked it. The heat of the day had dissipated, and he found that he could breathe much easier outside than in the stuffy rooms he had been confined to for weeks. No one was around to bother him, and despite the urban environment, the only evidence of other people were rows of parked cars on the street and an occasional driver zipping home. He was startled by a police officer suddenly stepping onto the sidewalk in front of him, putting a hand on his chest, demanding his papers.

The Engineer was confused, mumbling to himself more than the cop. Where had the cop come from? He wasn't there a second ago, did he step out from between the van and the car in front of him? *I was just walking here and thinking about...* His reverie was broken by the cop once again asking for his papers, more insistently this time. He fumbled in his pockets, pulling out his identity card, almost dropping it. The cop studied it a long time, squinting in the darkness, trying to read it by the little light that was available. The Engineer couldn't take his eyes off the man as he pulled out a cell phone and made a call, murmuring something into the phone.

Without warning there was a titanic bang from somewhere nearby, and the Engineer vaguely felt hands grabbing him, pulling him inside the white van that he had been standing next to. The door was open and there were men inside, the policeman pushing him into the men's arms, then he was being dragged up and into the van via brute strength. He flailed his arms, tried to gain purchase, but one of the men slapped him across the face, hard, harder than anyone had ever hit him. He was disoriented long enough to be shoved face down on the floor of the van, his arms wrenched back and zip ties or some other bindings wrapped tightly around his wrists. They put a hood or sack over his head, and once the drawstring at the bottom was pulled tight, he could see nothing, though he could still breathe through the fabric. He had been starting to hyperventilate, his chest tightening almost unbearably, but the hood seemed to help a little. One of the men crouched on top of him, the man's weight preventing him from moving. He felt strange movements, then realized the men were cutting his clothes off, slitting them up the back and down the arms and legs, twisting and pulling them off his body. The Engineer was limp, dead weight, as they did this. He was soon completely naked, the van's metal floor ice cold on his skin and genitals. He could hear the rustle of a plastic bag as they stuffed the remains of his clothes into it.

The Engineer's hands were bound tightly, inescapably, behind his back, and his ankles were likewise secured. He thought he might have pissed himself a little from sheer terror as they dragged him into the van, though they had cut off his clothes so quickly that he couldn't tell if he had shamed himself by squirting a hot jet of urine down his leg, soaking his *shalwar kameez*. He wasn't sure if his nose or cheek were broken or not from when the man slapped him. His face still felt like it was on fire.

He started to say something, ask a question, but at the first utterance, one of the men slapped him again, this time on the back of the head. His face slammed back down into the metal floor of the van, bringing a renewed wave of agony. He immediately fell silent.

He could sense the man who had slapped him crouching or sitting next to him. He couldn't feel or see or hear him, but he knew the man was there, ready to cause him agony again. The other man climbed into the driver's seat, started the van, and peeled out at a high rate of speed.

The men still hadn't said a word to him.

April 2-3, 2004
Peshawar, Pakistan to Kabul, Afghanistan to Szczytno-Szymany Airport, Poland

THE VAN DROVE the Engineer for what seemed like forever. At one point it stopped, and he heard the rustle of the bag with his clothes being handed off to someone outside the van, then they were speeding off again, the entire exchange taking only a few seconds.

Eventually the van stopped and the driver once again rolled down his window and talked quietly with someone outside the vehicle for a few moments. Then they drove onward, more slowly now, then came to a stop once again. The man in the back of the van cut whatever was binding his feet together. The driver came back into the body of the van and both men grabbed the Engineer by the arms and pushed and pulled him until he was standing, then they swung the van's side door open. *Ah*, he thought, *that was the loud bang I heard when they first grabbed me.* He still couldn't see anything through the hood. His breath had created condensation inside the hood, but he could breathe just fine, though the air was stale with his own foul breath. He struggled to recall what the men who had abducted him looked like. They were white, Americans almost certainly, or Europeans working for them. Both had dark hair, but that was mostly all he could remember. It had all happened so quickly, and when the man had slapped him he had become disoriented, focused only on the pain and what they were doing to him in the moment.

The men helped the Engineer gingerly step down from the van. His weight mostly rested on them; with his hands still bound behind him, he had few other options. They walked forward, perhaps a hundred or more steps, and were met by others, who murmured to his captors. He was aware of the absurdity of how he must look—naked, hooded, hands bound behind him, shivering in the night air, his genitals shriveled from cold and fear, strangers all around him, staring at him, touching him. He wanted to vomit, but his mouth was too dry and he feared choking on it inside the hood. Would the men help him, or would they just let him choke to death on his own bile and vomit? He forced down the impulse.

They walked him farther into a building, though where he was he had no idea. He could feel cold, smooth concrete beneath his feet. Then they stopped him, and he was made to stand still for a minute or so. The hood was jerked off his head quickly and he blinked repeatedly to clear his vision. They were inside what looked like an aircraft hangar or some other large, open structure. He was surrounded by half a dozen men, all of whom wore hoods, though unlike his, theirs had eye and mouth holes. He didn't want to move his head around too much, afraid that it would bring a beating, so he tried to track the men with his eyes and peripheral vision only. One man, perhaps a doctor or some kind of medical person, shined a light in his eyes, ears, and nose. When the man said, "Open your mouth and stick your tongue out," in English, it was the first speech that had been directed at him since he had been abducted. The man proceeded to use some kind of swab on the inside of the Engineer's cheek.

The man then donned a pair of plastic gloves and squirted something onto his right glove. The man told him to bend over and walked behind him. The Engineer started to protest and shook his head, so two of the men grabbed him and bent him over, practically folding him in half. The doctor stuck first one finger, then two, then perhaps more inside his rectum, wiggling his fingers around inside for a long while. *Are they going to rape me?* he thought, starting to hyperventilate again. He felt the man's hand withdraw, then reenter him. It felt like the man shoved something deep inside him, then the fingers withdrew again, though they left behind a feeling of fullness within him. After a few moments, the men pulled him upright again. The Engineer knew his face must be bright red from the shame of it. He had never been so violated in his entire life. Despair flooded him when he realized that undoubtedly many more such violations, perhaps even worse, were coming.

The Engineer hadn't wanted to face it until now, but he knew that his life was over. There was his life before the men grabbed him and threw him in the van, and then his life after the van. And that new life would undoubtedly be short and filled with pain and torment and, after they had extracted everything they could from him, death. Eventually, he knew, he would pray for death, maybe even beg the men to kill him. That was probably what they wanted. He resolved to hold out as long as he could, no matter how much they tortured him. That was what his friends in Al Qaeda had told him he must do. He must hold out at least a day—two or three would be better, because by then they would know that he had been taken, and all the brothers could be moved. After a day or two, the information he knew about where people and things were wouldn't be valuable anymore, it wouldn't compromise anyone. They wouldn't know something had happened to him until tomorrow morning at the earliest, he was certain. Saad would be coming by at noon, but only if he adjusted the upstairs curtains in a certain way. So Saad would know immediately that something was wrong when that didn't happen. Alarm bells would start ringing. Phone calls would take place. The brothers would be warned. They would take action. He just needed to hold out as long as he could.

Two of the men grabbed his upper arms and stood next to him while a third took photos. They seemed to pose with him, and he imagined that they must all be proud of having caught him, a big fish in Al Qaeda. He almost wanted to smile at the camera to see what the men would do, but he didn't dare—a beating, or a rape, might ensue—and he couldn't muster the wherewithal to try to defy them in even this tiny, petty, meaningless way.

The men cut off the ties that bound his hands, though they retained a firm grip on his arms. He brought his arms around from behind his back slowly, tentatively, unsure if this small luxury was permitted. The doctor handed him a white bundle of something, which he took instinctively. He looked at it puzzled, never having seen something quite like it. The doctor took it from him impatiently, shook it out, motioning for him to put his legs through the holes in the thing. *A kind of diaper*, he thought. Another humiliation for him. It made crinkling sounds as he shifted. When the diaper was on him to the men's satisfaction, another man thrust a kind of overalls at him, and he slowly donned it while the men hovered all around him. The diaper made a thick, heavy bulk under the overalls. When he had finished donning the garment, they handcuffed him, this time with his hands in front of his body, and shackled his ankles. They then placed a hood over his head again, and his world shrank with the darkness and closeness of it on his face.

Two men took his upper arms again, handling him with firm grips—the Engineer was under no illusions that he could fight them off or shake them off for even an instant—but they weren't rough, just forceful. Only the men in the van had slapped him; he hadn't yet been beaten again, though he knew it could come at any time, and expected it, and far worse things to come. They told him to start walking, which he did, as fast as the shackles would allow him, which was much slower than a normal walking pace. The concrete of the hangar floor remained cold on his bare feet. As they left the hangar, the sound of engines nearby grew loud. They walked him out onto the tarmac a ways, then up a flight of stairs, which was hard to navigate in the shackles, but he managed it without falling or stumbling more than a few times. He entered what he assumed was an aircraft because they forced him to duck at the top of the stairs and he could feel industrial carpeting under his feet.

They had him sit and then lie down on something, and then strapped him in tightly with restraints across his limbs and chest. The shackles, handcuffs, and hood remained firmly in place. By this point, despite the stress and strain of his abduction, or perhaps because of it, the Engineer felt himself starting to grow drowsy. His thoughts began to fray around the edges, becoming hard to hold onto. He could hear the murmur of voices around him, but couldn't make out what they were saying, and couldn't really even force himself to care. He was in the hands of Allah and the Mother now.

He vaguely felt the aircraft take off a while later—how long after, he knew not, because his perceptions had drifted off again. He thought of nothing in particular, just vague wisps of thought that came in softly and flitted away almost immediately. The plane landed somewhere, which shook him out of his reverie slightly. They remained on the ground a while. The Engineer remained tightly bound on the stretcher. At one point, someone pulled the hood up a bit and they thrust a drinking straw in his mouth. He was extremely thirsty by this point and didn't care if they fed him poison. It just tasted like water though, and then the hood was pulled back down. Again, some time later, the aircraft took off, but he was fully asleep by this point, in a dark dreamless state. At some point they woke him and let him drink something else, this time a kind of milky, chalky liquid. He had never tasted anything quite like it, but he had little choice but to swallow or resist, which would undoubtedly result in a beating and then still being forced to drink the liquid, whatever it was. He could tell that they remained in flight for what seemed like many hours. He felt the need to relieve his bladder and tried to hold it in for as long as possible, but eventually he gave up and felt the warmth of the urine in the diaper. He passed out again and thought little of it after the initial embarrassment and discomfort. The second time he felt the need to urinate, he didn't try to hold back, but simply urinated as soon as he became aware of the need. He worried that it would soak through the diaper, but it didn't seem to. It was hard to tell.

At long last, the plane landed again, though he had no way of telling how much time has passed. After a while, he could hear more men boarding the aircraft.

One of the men crouched over him. He could smell the man's breath—sour, oniony—even through the hood. He could hear the man's breath, a slight whistle in his nose as he breathed. The man leaned over him, speaking in a harsh whisper right next to his ear. "Wake up, asshole. I know you speak English. You're in deep shit now."

April 4, 2004
Stare Kiejkuty, Poland
CIA Site LAPIS

Mark Romero Diary

WHY AM I beginning this journal? Is this a journal? I haven't kept any sort of diary since I was a kid, and that never lasted long before fizzling out. What's the point of it? I'm probably just going to burn this thing when my time here is up and I'm sent home. If nothing else, it would be too classified to keep with me. Well, for now, I'm going to try my hand at keeping a journal, out of sheer boredom as much as anything else.

I'm the new guy, just arrived with the new High-Value Detainee (HVD), who used to be considered a High-Value Target (HVT) until, well, he was detained. Most people would just call him a prisoner, but you learn immediately that just like the military, the CIA has its own lingo for everything, and none of it is what normal people call things.

My name is Mark Anthony Romero. I'm 34 years old. I grew up in East Aurora, New York, which is a nice little suburb of Buffalo, and went to school at Syracuse University, where I majored in political science and communications. After college I was commissioned into the U.S. Army (Hooah!) and was there for eight years, as a Ranger for most of that time. I was medically separated from the Army as a captain because of a knee injury I got in a training accident. Theoretically my knee is almost as good as new since I had a couple surgeries and a lot of very painful PT to fix it. I'm fine now, but that wasn't good enough for the Army. Not that I'm bitter or anything. Actually, my last unit in the Army sucked and I hated it there. Terrible, terrible leadership all up and down the chain of command, and I was kind of glad to be out of there. Other than the months and months of pain and the surgeries and all that. So yeah. I wasn't really ready to transition to the civilian world, so a buddy of mine suggested that I contact the CIA because they were always looking for paramilitary officers and my background was perfect, yada yada yada. I didn't have a lot of other options and didn't want to get stuck behind a desk for the rest of my life after being a Ranger, so I threw my hat in the ring. Lots and lots of interviews and tests and the security clearance took forever, despite already having one in the Army, but almost a year later I started at the CIA in the Directorate of Operations (the DO, the cool part of the Agency) in late 2000. Then a year later, well, you know what happened. Things all of a sudden got really, really busy and have been basically insane for the last three years.

I have a wife named Jessica and an eighteen-month-old little girl named Katie. My wife and I got married a few months before 9/11. Jessica is an accountant for a defense contractor, and her dad was in the Navy, so she kind of gets it, but things have been tough since 9/11, not going to lie. I've had a lot of deployments since then, almost constantly, and it's even harder for her because she has no idea where I am or when I'm coming home, unlike the Army, when things were a little more predictable and she had a stronger support network of the other wives and all that. She didn't exactly sign up to be a single parent, but that's kind of how things have turned out. But it's not like I have a choice, or that what I'm doing isn't important or building a better future for our little girl.

My parents are still around; Dad runs a car dealership, and I've got an older brother, Steve, and a younger sister, Lauren. I never see any of them—the last time I did was right after Katie was born—but Jessica keeps my mom in the loop when I'm deployed. I'm not incredibly close with any of them, with the possible exception of Mom, so...that's okay. Not a big deal. Dad is one of those emotionally detached types, just watches football and baseball on TV when he's around, and kind of grunts at you if you try to talk to him. Steve was always kind of an asshole. He works with Dad at the dealership and is a classic salesman type. Always smiling, but you know it's fake, and he's one of those two-hand handshake guys. Christ, I hate that. Needless to say, I don't think I would buy a car from him, friends and family discount or not. Lauren is off being a new mom (yes, I am an uncle with a niece and nephew I think I've seen maybe twice each) and outfitting her home in Schenectady with her husband. She's prim and proper now and doesn't seem to want much to do with the rest of us, despite being passed around the football team back in high school, so I guess we all grow up in different ways. Enough about them.

So where am I and what am I doing here?

For now, I'm stationed at LAPIS, which is near Stare Kiejkuty (I think I've got that spelled right, I know about six words of Polish and those mostly consist of the words for please, thank you, and beer). Near as I can tell, that means "Old Kiejkuty." Don't ask me what "Kiejkuty" means because I'm not even sure I'm spelling it right. That's the name for both the village that's nearby and the Polish intelligence base that's located a few miles down the road. I haven't been to the base yet, but it's supposedly an intelligence training center, probably like their equivalent of the Farm in Williamsburg.

The airport is 10-15 miles south of here. That's where I flew into yesterday along with that HVD I mentioned earlier. He's a Very Important Person, or Very Important Asshole to be more precise, because we think that guy—Omar Abu Khattab, a.k.a. "Muhandis" (which means Engineer)—runs Al Qaeda's biological program. We think. We don't know enough about him yet, but we know he's a big fish, and very highly placed. I was involved for the better part of the last four months with helping track this guy down. Now that we've got him, we're going to sweat him and see what he knows and what we can get him to tell us. If there's an AQ plan to use BW against the homeland, or a plot like that underway, well, he's the guy who set it up and the one best positioned to tell us all about it. This was a real coup for us, and for me in particular. This is a Really Big Fucking Deal. The biggest thing I've ever been involved with since I've been at CIA, and hell, when I was in the Army too.

Okay, enough writing for one day. Dinner time. Starting to get hungry and at least I can say that the old ladies they've got to make meals for us are pretty good cooks. It's mostly just Polish peasant food, but there's always a lot of it and I'm hungry enough to eat a horse (which I suspect they would serve with lots of cabbage and potatoes).

April 5, 2004
Stare Kiejkuty, Poland
CIA Site LAPIS

Mark Romero Diary

OKAY, SECOND ENTRY. Is writing in this diary a habit yet? Maybe, maybe not, but it does relieve the evening time boredom. Lots more to say about what's going on here. I'm the newbie but already know enough to say that LAPIS is one weird place, and the people who work here are even weirder. Lots more to say about all that too.

But I learned something important in the Army (other than how to kill people and blow shit up): when you write something, you've got to use the BLUF principle: Bottom Line Up Front.

BLUF: We have not yet cracked the Engineer, surprise, surprise. He has got to be the weirdest guy I have ever met, and that's saying something given that I've been at the CIA for four years. They do not hire non-weird people, present company excluded of course. This guy is going to be a tough nut to crack. I am confident we'll learn what we need to in time, but it's going to be a struggle.

Anyway. Let me back up a step. So how did I end up in RDG, and here in a black site?

I've been assigned to the Counterterrorism Center (CTC) pretty much my entire time at the CIA. I requested the assignment when I joined in 2000 because I thought it seemed like a chance to kick some ass and do some good, probably in that order. But, of course, I, and everyone else, had no idea how much the counterterrorism mission would blow up after 9/11. To be honest, when I started it seemed a little like a backwater kind of assignment, with not a hell of a lot going on, but in hindsight that just seems absurd. How much can change in four years! So as a paramilitary guy, because of my time in the Army, I became part of the Special Missions Department (SMD) and did some work in Afghanistan starting in spring 2002. I wasn't one of the first guys over there (too new, I guess, and hadn't met the right people yet—CIA is all about who you know, unfortunately), but I did get there shortly after we were trying to form some kind of stable government while also chasing AQ around the countryside. I did that for a while, and then a stint back at HQ in Virginia, which was a nice change of pace and gave me some breathing room and a chance to decompress. Then I was eventually assigned to the Renditions and Detention Group (RDG) about a year or so ago.

Okay, so that's my history for the most part.

The goal is to stop the next 9/11 attack on the homeland and degrade or destroy Al Qaeda to the point that they can't mount any more attacks on the U.S. or any of our allies. And the way we do that is by going after the AQ leadership, wherever we can find them. Some of them are still hiding out in Afghanistan, a bunch have now fled to Pakistan—like our friend the Engineer—and a bunch more are elsewhere. Who really knows? They're scattered now, but every now and then they'll pop up, and we snatch or kill them when they do. It takes a lot of concerted effort to make that happen, and if I'm being really honest, a good measure of luck and waiting for them to fuck up. When we are able to find one (see: the Engineer), we'd ideally prefer to capture them rather than kill them. Sure, killing is nice and satisfying and that's the only way we can do it sometimes, but it's really much better to actually capture them. That gives you a chance to go through their stuff, including pocket litter (the stuff that's literally on their person), hard drives, etc., plus you get to interrogate them. But that takes a long time. It's not at all like in the movies where the detectives are able to break some hardened criminal with some clever wordplay and by sweating the guy for an hour. You've really got to get inside the guy's head and, more often than not, apply some strenuous efforts. Those are called "enhanced interrogation techniques" (EITs for short), though there are other nasty things some would call those techniques. More on that another day probably.

You've got to stage an elaborate operation to locate and capture an HVT like the Engineer. Let me tell you, that's a major effort. Dozens of people involved in various ways, and it takes forever, and lots of factors have to come together and work in your favor to even catch the guy. Then, once you do have him, you need someplace where you can work on the guy for a long time. Could be weeks, could be months. And, I suppose, could be years. Christ, I hope it's not years. You've got to have a place where you're not going to be disturbed, and questions won't be asked about "What goes on in that dark, windowless building where guys go in but they don't come out?" That can't be done in the U.S., and it's not going to be done in a place where there's a Western liberal media that can poke around, so you need a friendly regime where the rule of law is a little less strict. A lot less strict. Not that I think what we're doing here is illegal. No, sir. We're doing everything here by the book. It's just that it's not very pretty to look at. So that's why the first black site was in Afghanistan at a place called the Salt Pit, which makes sense because that's where we caught most of these fuckers at first, but then, well, some people got a little over-zealous and a guy died. He was a bad guy, so no one's losing sleep over it, but we needed a better process and more control over the environment, so they moved it to an air force base in Thailand, and now it's dispersed across other friendly places, including Poland, which leads us to our very own LAPIS.

So LAPIS is actually a pretty nice facility. It's certainly better than I had expected, and given that I'm likely to be stationed here for the foreseeable future, this is a pretty cush assignment. Well, logistically speaking, it's cushy, but knowing that you have the guy who heads up AQ's biological weapons program and there may be attack preparations underway but you can't get him to talk, well, that adds a little stress. I guess you'd call LAPIS a country estate or manor house. No way this place was built by the Communists, it's way too nice for that. If it's a big-ass concrete box, it was done by the Communists. If it's beautiful and old-fashioned and there are those little fixtures and trimmings in every room that have decorations on them, you know it came long before them. So probably some nobleman's villa out in the country, but you better believe that it was the vacation home for some Commie bigwigs during the Cold War. Now it's owned or run by the unimaginatively named Foreign Intelligence Agency (don't ask me to spell that in Polish, please), which is the equivalent to the CIA, and they've turned it over to us for the duration. Lots of room for all of us to spread out, and plenty of privacy. Place is secure too. There's a big security contingent of CIA people here, and the whole place has been retrofitted by a razorwire-topped chain-link fence, and there are surveillance cameras and sensors everywhere. No one's getting into this place without us knowing about it—and without being blown away long before they can bust our buddy out. We're maybe 20 or 30 minutes from that Polish air force base I mentioned before and about the same distance (different direction) from the nearest sign of civilization, such as it is, which is a not-so-big town with a bar, restaurants, shops, etc., but no real reason to go there. Fraternizing with the locals is not exactly encouraged. Only fraternizing with the locals I'm likely to be doing is with Michal, who is the local intelligence liaison officer. Seems like a good guy so far. I'm sure I'll get to know him better down the road. But we're here basically completely surrounded by what looks like some pretty dense woods. No one's going to bother us, you can't even see the place from the road, since you've got to head up a long driveway and pass through the gates and security checks.

So right now, it's just us, the Engineer, and a couple very low-level AQ guys who have been here for a few months. By this point, their intelligence value is nil—I'm not sure they ever knew much at all anyway—but no one really knows what to do with them. The interrogators have been mostly just left asking these guys to speculate about various hypothetical scenarios and report back to HQ. "What do you think AQ is planning? What kinds of targets do you think they might be interested in hitting next? Etc." These guys don't know shit. So LAPIS has been a backwater until now.

April 6, 2004
Stare Kiejkuty, Poland
CIA Site LAPIS

Mark Romero Diary

I'VE BEEN SPENDING the bulk of my time over the last few days with the two interrogators who are assigned here to LAPIS and am learning a lot from them. They're contractors, both ex-military, so not technically CIA employees, but the next best thing. It's not like the CIA had dozens and dozens of trained interrogators laying around. I guess I'll pick up a little bit of the interrogator skillset from them, not that I would want to be an interrogator or anything. I still have plenty of ass-kicking left to do. But I'm also not exactly ready to get back into the field because, let's face it, I've got to see how this whole Engineer thing works out. You don't dedicate months and months to find someone and snatch them and not stick around to see what happens when the guy cracks.

Back to the interrogators. Pete is in charge. Former Air Force, senior enlisted guy, where he did HUMINT (human intelligence) and picked up interrogation training there. Early forties, kind of a loudmouth, fast talker, asshole type. Thinks he knows way more than he does, but he knows how to work the system so he always comes out smelling like a rose. I can't tell you how many guys exactly like Pete I met in the Army. The other one is Deb, former Navy, roughly similar background as Pete, which seems common as my understanding is that a lot of these contractors are ex-military. Deb's probably late thirties, reddish hair, some freckles, too much sun on her skin in the past, so she's a little rough around the edges, but she's funny and doesn't put up with Pete's bullshit, which I appreciate. She's been showing me around, so she seems like good people so far.

Let's face it, the CIA hired me because of my background as a Ranger. They needed someone for paramilitary operations and I had the right skillset for that as a "gun guy" comfortable with living in rough conditions and surviving in the wild, so it was a match. And while I received a good amount of training at the Farm and on the job, there are big gaps in my knowledge, and interrogation is one of them.

Before I got to the CIA, I had the standard counter-interrogation training that Rangers get, and the CIA gave me a little more, though that was a cakewalk compared to Ranger training. But I never considered that I might have to be on the other side of the table.

My goal is to not get hauled before the Hague on some kind of war crimes charge when the war on terror is over and people start combing through the archives, so I thought it would be helpful to get a clearer picture of what we can and can't do. I'm here for results. We're all accountable for getting the Engineer to talk, but there are still things that are outside the lines, and I don't want to get anywhere close to that line. So I sat down with Pete and Deb and got them to walk through it, as they understand things, and show me what we can and can't do.

Here's what they told me (note that this conversation is being reconstructed from memory, but it will serve our purposes):

"How handsy can you get with detainees? I mean, I know we can't beat them, obviously," I asked, probably naively.

Pete: "So, we've got all the basics, little stuff. We can do an 'attention grasp.' Grab them by the collar and pull them close and talk right into their face. Nobody likes that, but it certainly does get their attention and ensures they know we mean business. You can grab their face with your hand. You can do what we call an 'insult slap.' You can't ball up your fist or anything, but you can slap them with spread fingers, holding your hand loosely. That's always good for catching them by surprise, or stunning them, or humiliating them."

Deb: "There are certain things, like a facial slap, that Muslim men find especially humiliating if a woman does to them. So Pete and I will trade off, and I might slap them for a while. That can be effective at breaking them down."

Pete: "Stress positions are also really good. You can force them to remain standing, or squatting, or something else like that. Remember, these guys are almost always handcuffed when they're out of their cells, so they can't usually use their hands to help with balance or fatigue, plus, they're always going to be sleep deprived. We'll typically make them assume a stress position as long as they can stand it, then we pick 'em back up when they collapse and begin it all again. We'll also make them assume a stance facing toward the wall, but keep them at a certain distance with their fingers just barely touching the wall and their arms outstretched. You'd be surprised at how exhausting something that simple is. We'll also 'wall' them sometimes when they're standing in front of a special wall. It's made to collapse back and make a really loud noise right behind them when they're pushed hard into it. It scares the bejesus out of them and makes it seem like we pushed them so hard we collapsed the wall behind them."

Deb: "There's also random shit, like insects and stuff—nothing actually poisonous or anything like that, but some of these guys are terrified of bugs, so if we find that out, we'll put them in a box or some other kind of confined space with a big freaky-looking insect. Abu Zubaydah was terrified of insects, and that helped break him. It can't hurt them, but they don't know that. Or, even without the insects, keeping them in dark closely confined spaces at times, coffin-like, can help. Then, of course, there's waterboarding. Have you ever seen a waterboarding session, Mark?"

I said no, so she went on to describe it. "The detainee is prone and strapped down tight, then a cloth is placed over their face and water is poured on the cloth. That forms a pretty tight seal over the mouth and nose and the detainee feels like they're drowning or suffocating. We just do that for twenty, thirty, maybe forty seconds max. Then we take the cloth off, let them take a few full breaths, then the cloth goes back on and we do it all over again. We could do it a couple times or a dozen or more. That all depends on the detainee. Sincere cooperation means that the process stops. Fake cooperation just means we're going to keep doing it."

"Have you guys ever had that done to you?"

"Sure, Pete and I have both been waterboarded. Just a couple times, not, like, dozens, and as an interrogator it's a bit different because you know the process and what's going to happen or not happen. You know that nobody's going to let you die. But I'm not going to lie, it's rough. As your CO2 level increases, it definitely induces some panic."

Pete: "Okay, Mark, don't get too fixated on waterboarding, though. Deb's right; it's no fun, but it's not like it immediately cracks them wide open. I'll let you in on a little secret: Sleep deprivation is the key. It's our secret weapon. Not waterboarding or any of the other stuff. Everything hinges on sleep deprivation. We fuck with every aspect of sleep. Everything else follows. It's really that simple. Sure, some interrogators love waterboarding. It's satisfying, that's for sure, and it certainly produces results. But my money is on sleep deprivation every time."

Deb nodded in agreement.

"Okay, I'll bite. What's so special about sleep deprivation?"

Pete: "You were in the Army, you've been up for extended periods, you know how physically exhausted you get from having to operate for long periods without sleep. But it's the mental effects that are the key for us. We control every aspect of the detainee's life, when they get to sleep, how long they're allowed to sleep, when they get woken up, and all that. They never see clocks or watches. They never know what time it is. They have no idea how long they're sleeping. We wake them up after two hours and tell them that eight hours have passed. We immediately put them into stress positions so they can't sleep when it looks like they're starting to nod off, or we slap them awake. Now imagine that day after day. It affects their mood, their memory, they become more compliant, they would eventually do almost anything just to be allowed to put their head down for a little bit and get a good night's sleep. That will never actually happen, but they don't know that. They can eventually become completely disconnected from reality, even hallucinate because of prolonged sleep deprivation. It's all good stuff, bro!" Insert Pete's shit-eating grin here.

So yeah, interrogators. They're a fun bunch. I'm glad I'm not on the receiving end of this stuff, but then again, I'm not a fucking terrorist. Also had a couple (brief) meetings with the chief of base, Dave, who is theoretically in charge of everything that goes on in LAPIS. I say theoretically because I have been getting the distinct impression that he doesn't give much of a shit what goes on here and isn't actually in charge of much. So Dave is Senior Intelligence Service (SIS), which means he's a big deal at the CIA. He would normally be in charge of a big station overseas or a high muckety-muck back at HQ after a long and illustrious career, but here he is, which indicates the amount of importance they put on LAPIS.

I called one of my buddies back at HQ and asked him about Dave. He did a little digging and told me that Dave has had a long career, has spent a lot of time both in the Middle East and in Europe, especially the Balkans, and has by and large done some pretty cool shit. So that explains why they put him in charge of LAPIS. But that's all totally at odds with what I'm seeing here. He seems completely checked out. No real interest in meeting me, or hearing how the interrogations are going, or what we hope to get out of the Engineer, etc. etc. First day I showed up, he gave me about two minutes when I went to his office before telling me he was busy and we could talk later. Today I swung by again to update him in person on how things are going. I asked him if he plans to attend any of the interrogation sessions himself. He said no, said he'd read the transcripts or watch the tapes. Again, the guy waved me out after maybe five minutes max, said he had to make a phone call. I'm sure. I could literally smell the booze coming off him, though he struck me as one of those kinds of alcoholics who never slurs a single word even when they're shitfaced. The only way to tell they're wasted is to smell their decomposing liver being sweated out of their pores. So maybe it's a bad sign that he's here in charge of LAPIS. Maybe this really is a shit assignment.

I talked with Pete and Deb about Dave and they said he's like that with everyone. Said he's going through a nasty divorce but that he reads everything we produce and all that. We'll see. All the cable traffic from LAPIS back to HQ has to go through Dave and be approved, but they told me it's all pro forma and as long as we don't fuck anything up, Dave will leave us alone and approve any cables we need to send. Okay. I guess that will have to do.

Everyone else I've met here was mostly pretty friendly. Certainly laidback for the most part. We've got the comms shack, which is where all the classified messages are transmitted and received from. That's manned 24-7 and they've got the safes with all the classified records stored in there. The comms guys seemed okay. Also met a couple of the medical personnel. The main guy there is a Dr. Richards. Seemed all right, business-like, keeps to himself. He's always present whenever EITs are being used on one of the detainees. He gives them all a medical exam every day and ensures they're in good shape. It was a little cursory if you ask me—not what I'd be looking for in a physical—but better than nothing, I guess. Plus, there are a bunch of security guys. Seems like a mix of Polish guys manning the front gate plus some CIA guys, either actual CIA employees or contractors. Mostly all ex-military, and I see some of them out and about when I'm doing my PT every morning. Weird place, but there are a lot worse places to pass a month or two.

April 7, 2004
Stare Kiejkuty, Poland
CIA Site LAPIS

Interrogation Transcript: Omar Abu KHATTAB
Interrogation Session 07APR04-1
Attendees: Omar Abu KHATTAB (detainee), Peter DABROWSKY (lead interrogator, contractor), Deborah SULLIVAN (interrogator, contractor), Mark ROMERO (CTC/RDG liaison, CIA)

[excerpt]

KHATTAB is secured and seated across the table from DABROWSKY, SULLIVAN, and ROMERO in Interrogation Room 3.

ROMERO: "What were you doing in Peshawar when you were caught?"

KHATTAB: "Mr. Mark, I was there looking for work. I did not have a job or much money, so I was there to try to find a job. Any kind of job, maybe a job in a store or a business."

ROMERO: "Why did you travel to Peshawar? Who told you to go there?"

KHATTAB: "I heard that there was work there. Lots of people said there were jobs. But I looked and looked in Peshawar and had trouble finding a job. But I did not give up, I looked for jobs there all the time."

ROMERO: "How long were you planning on staying in Peshawar? Where were you going next?"

KHATTAB: "I was planning on staying in Peshawar for a long time, once I found a job there. I had no more travel plans, I wanted to make Peshawar my home as soon as I found work."

ROMERO: "Who arranged for you to live in the house in Peshawar?"

KHATTAB: "I was just asking around the city where there might be a nice place for me to stay and someone in a coffee shop told me about a house his brother had that was for rent, so I told him, please take me to your brother because I want to see the rental place and he did. It was nice and cheap, so I rented it from the man's brother."

ROMERO: "Where were you staying before you arrived in Peshawar?"

KHATTAB: "I didn't have a fixed address, I was moving around, looking for work. Always looking for work. I am a hard worker and willing to do work, but it is never easy finding a job, so I have to move around a lot."

ROMERO: "Where specifically were you living before you moved to Peshawar? What was the address of the place you were living?"

KHATTAB: "I was living in Quetta, which is a nice place, but then it was not so nice when my job ended, so I had to move. I am just looking for wor—"

DABROWSKY: [agitated] "This is going exactly nowhere, Khattab. You're feeding us nothing but bullshit, complete and utter bullshit. Everything you have told us today is a lie."

KHATTAB: "No, Mr. Peter, I—"

SULLIVAN: "You know what happens when you lie to us. You know it is always painful and uncomfortable and just gets worse and worse until you can't stand it anymore. You know what we're going to do to you every time you lie to us."

KHATTAB: "I'm not going to lie to you; ask me your questions, you will see that I'm not lying to you."

[SULLIVAN nods to ROMERO.]

ROMERO: "When was the last time you met with Usama bin Ladin?"

KHATTAB: "I have never met him. I do not know him...that man. He is not someone I know. I have said this before, many times. You have the wrong man. This is a case of mistake identity. I do not know any of the people you ask me about."

ROMERO: "What types of biological weapons did you help develop for Al Qaeda? What were you planning on doing with these weapons?"

KHATTAB: "I do not develop biological weapons or any kind of weapons for anyone. I am a man of peace. I am not interested in making weapons or using weapons."

ROMERO: "Who were you working with on the biological weapons?"

KHATTAB: "I have not worked with anyone on any kind of weapons. This is mistake identity. I came to your country a long time ago to receive education at Virginia Tech on biology and immunology. I earn bachelor's degree and master's degree. I only ever work on medical projects to find cures for diseases. You think I am some kind of bad guy, but I am a medical researcher. I want to cure diseases and help people."

DABROWSKY: "We know that you're the head of Al Qaeda's biological weapons program, Khattab, so let's cut out all the bullshit. We have you dead to rights. Quit stalling and answer the goddamn questions."

KHATTAB: "You certainly have a lot of questions for me. It doesn't sound like you know very much about me or anything else. What *do* you know?"

DABROWSKY: "Listen up, fuckface, we're asking the questions here. Not you. Do you understand me?"

KHATTAB: [KHATTAB nods.] "Yes, Mr. Peter. I understand. You ask me questions. I do not ask you questions."

ROMERO: "All right, Khattab, let's go back to my last question. Who were you working with on Al Qaeda's biological weapons program?"

KHATTAB: "I told you, Mr. Mark, I am not working on any biological program. I am a man of peace. I—"

DABROWSKY: [sighs loudly] "Okay, Khattab, that's it. We're going to go do what will soon become one of your favorite things: we're going to waterboard you now."

KHATTAB: [agitated] "Wait, no, Mr. Peter, I am telling you the truth."

[excerpt, transcript begins 18 minutes after end of last excerpt]

KHATTAB is now immobilized by being strapped to an incline board at an approximate angle of fifteen degrees downward. DABROWSKY, SULLIVAN, and ROMERO are now standing around KHATTAB. Dr. Arnold RICHARDS is also present, monitoring KHATTAB's vital signs. RICHARDS releases KHATTAB's wrist and nods his head while looking at DABROWSKY and SULLIVAN. SULLIVAN places a towel over KHATTAB's face.

DABROWSKY begins pouring water from a pitcher onto the cloth from a height of approximately eighteen inches for the next 38 seconds. KHATTAB immediately begins to splutter and unsuccessfully attempts to move on the incline board. His chest heaves and his breathing appears rapid. Sounds of distress continue.

SULLIVAN lifts the wet cloth off KHATTAB'S mouth and nose, though it remains draped over his eyes and forehead. KHATTAB takes three deep breaths in rapid succession, then SULLIVAN replaces the cloth and DABROWSKY begins pouring water on the cloth again.

This process is repeated another eighteen times over the next twenty minutes. RICHARDS checks KHATTAB's pulse briefly twice more during this period and nods his assent after both checks.

Eventually SULLIVAN exits the room briefly and returns with two security personnel, Michael BARDACH and Gilbert FLORES, who assist the others in releasing KHATTAB from the incline board, re-securing his handcuffs and leg shackles, and escorting him from the room. KHATTAB is unsteady on his feet and remains silent. His breathing is unsteady and his gaze remains downcast.

DABROWSKY: "We're going to resume our conversation in a couple minutes, KHATTAB."

April 7, 2004
Stare Kiejkuty, Poland
CIA Site LAPIS

Mark Romero Diary

I'VE SAID IT before and I'll say it again. What we're doing here is right. It's moral and ethical and is going to save countless American lives. I'm absolutely, 100% convinced that what we're doing is strictly legal and by the book and the president and George Tenet and the American people are 100% behind us and want us to be doing exactly what we're doing here. But it's hard work and it's *ugly* [underlined three times in original]. It's hard to watch. Really fucking hard.

So despite all that, what I'm about to write here is reason enough for me to burn this journal before I go back home or whatever godforsaken hellhole they send me to next. (Christ, Northern Virginia and strip malls and American food sure sounds better than fucking Pakistan again, doesn't it?) Anyway, today I witnessed my first waterboarding. We waterboarded the Engineer today. It was his first time being waterboarded and I guess it kinda sorta worked. I mean, it wasn't magic, it wasn't like he cracked immediately and started spilling his guts, but he was pretty upset and begged us to stop and said he was ready to start talking. I mean, they made it pretty clear that this was going to happen to him again (...and again...) if he didn't. I know that it's been a helpful technique with some of the other HVDs. It helped break KSM when we caught him last year. God only knows how many times he's been waterboarded, but eventually it worked on him, and the Engineer isn't immune to it either.

It's not like waterboarding is the first thing we do. It's part of a long progression of things. There's a lot that leads up to waterboarding—we try a lot of other things first, and it's not like we waterboard all the detainees. I don't think we've ever waterboarded any of the low-level AQ guys housed here at LAPIS. (I'm pretty sure, I've just kind of peeked my head in on a couple of their interrogations, but it's clear that they don't know anything.) There's a very clear set of requirements before we waterboard someone. The individual has got to have time-sensitive, critical information that would save lives that they're otherwise unwilling to reveal, and all other efforts to get them to talk have to have already been tried, and failed.

I've talked with Pete and Deb a lot about waterboarding, and even the (as far as I can tell) worthless Dave, the chief of base here at LAPIS, and the onsite physician, Dr. Richards. Everyone is agreed that the Engineer has got time-sensitive, absolutely critical information locked away in that creepy little brain of his, and if we can extract it, it will save American lives, both in the field and back home. He gets a medical exam every day, and Richards is convinced that waterboarding him isn't too much of a strain on the guy. I mean, he's not in amazing shape, but he's fit enough and just middle-aged; it's not like he's some senior citizen with a heart condition. He can take it physically, it's not going to kill him. It's not like we're actually going to drown him or let him choke to death or something. It's all just a simulation.

So was it worth it? Yeah, I think it probably was today. It felt like we made some progress and can build on that moving forward. He gave us a few names in the session after we waterboarded him, and we can check those out. He told us more details about his travels before he ended up in Peshawar, and some dates, and some partial addresses and things like that that we can check out. We can cross-check all of it and see how much of it he was telling the truth about. We wrote up the cable describing all the new information in detail— Dave didn't give a shit, didn't even say nice job, just looked at the draft for like 15 seconds, then said, "Okay, send it," and that was it.

No reward for good behavior around here. Story of my fucking life. I think I'm going to have some rum, jack off, and try to get some sleep. Big day tomorrow. Going to try to capitalize on the success we had today. Good stuff.

April 8, 2004
Stare Kiejkuty, Poland
CIA Site LAPIS

Interrogation Transcript: Omar Abu KHATTAB
Interrogation Session 08APR04-1
Attendees: Omar Abu KHATTAB (detainee), Peter DABROWSKY (lead interrogator, contractor), Deborah SULLIVAN (interrogator, contractor), Mark ROMERO (CTC/RDG liaison, CIA)

[excerpt]

ROMERO: "What are Al Qaeda's plans to use biological weapons in attacks against the United States or American interests abroad?"

KHATTAB: "We never had any plans to attack with biological weapons. It was way too early to even think about using them in any kind of operation. We didn't even have any workable materials we could use."

ROMERO: "How many resources has Al Qaeda put into developing or acquiring biological materials?"

KHATTAB: "ZAWAHIRI brought a little interest in biological weapons with him when he joined Al Qaeda, but we never had any real capabilities. There was interest, but no biological agents available. If we had wanted to use them, we would have had to make them ourselves. People sometimes talked about using anthrax or ricin, but those are very hard to work with, you know? Not easy. It was really hard trying to make a strain of anthrax or ricin that would be harmful to humans. I worked on it for a while but didn't make much progress. Very, very dangerous, you know? That stuff could have made me very sick, so I didn't like working with it. They were paying me, helping me get some equipment and set up a tiny lab, and they moved me around for a while and paid for my living expenses and gave me a little salary, but it was never much of an effort."

ROMERO: "What kind of biological weapons or materials did you have access to in Al Qaeda?"

KHATTAB: "They gave me some anthrax they got somewhere that had killed some sheep. It was a very weak strain, not really harmful to people. There were some castor beans I was trying to extract some ricin from. That was very hard. Much harder than people think. I never had much luck with it. That was all we had."

[excerpt]

DABROWSKY: "What name were you using and traveling under before you arrived in Peshawar?"

KHATTAB: "I used the name Muhammed Abu BAKR. Sometimes I would use the name Khaled ALHARBI. Sometimes I would just call myself Ahmed KHAN when I was traveling outside Pakistan, and I would just tell people I was Pakistani rather than Saudi. I only told non-Pakistanis that, just people who didn't matter, not officials."

DABROWSKY: "You had official identity documents for your Abu BAKR and ALHARBI and the KHAN one?"

KHATTAB: "Yes, I had different documents for those names."

DABROWSKY: "What kind of documents did you have for each of the names you were using?"

KHATTAB: "I used to have a Saudi passport for when I traveled as Muhammed Abu BAKR. I had a Saudi driver's license for that name too at one point. But those were taken from me when some wretched thief stole my bag on a train and caused me so many problems. I had to stop calling myself Abu BAKR then because I couldn't get new documents to replace the stolen ones. I had a passport for when I called myself ALHARBI. I had a Pakistani ID card in the name of KHAN, but no passport. I never crossed a border with that name."

DABROWSKY: "Where did you get the fake Saudi passport you used? Who made it? Who got it for you?"

KHATTAB: "I don't know who made it. I never met with the man who makes papers like that. My friend Mohammed in Jeddah got it for me. I told him that I needed it to travel, and he say, okay, I know someone who can make you one. I ask him, who is this man, how do I know I can trust him? How do I know this is a good document? And he tell me, don't worry about it, he very good at his job, he make good passports, you do not need to know his name. That's better for you and for him. You don't need his name. And I say okay."

DABROWSKY: "We'll come back to that. Now: where were you staying immediately prior to the house you were living in in Peshawar when we caught you?"

[excerpt]

ROMERO exits the room briefly and returns with two security personnel, Robert SAMUELS and Earl FOSTER. SAMUELS and FOSTER exit the room with KHATTAB. ROMERO, DABROWSKY, and SULLIVAN remain seated and begin speaking shortly after the door closes.

ROMERO: "So that was a pretty successful session, right, guys?"

SULLIVAN: "Yeah, I would say so. He gave us some aliases he's used, the names of a couple associates—though I doubt those will pan out for much—some details on his movements, dates and places, and some locations he's stayed. That's all pretty good, but some of it could just be bullshit or uncorroborated."

DABROWSKY: "Yeah, it was all good stuff, but I don't know. We'll have to see what ends up panning out, because there were a couple times I thought it was obvious he was choosing his words really carefully and deciding exactly what to tell us and what to leave out as he was talking. I want to go through the tapes again and take some notes on those places where I thought he was holding back."

SULLIVAN: "Definitely. That should give us a solid list of things to drill down into next time. We can ask him all those questions again and see what deviations we get, but I think it's going to be most important to focus on the things he hesitated on or was clearly holding back on."

ROMERO: "You guys believe him when he said that they had no actual biological weapons capabilities and therefore no attack plans on the homeland?"

DABROWSKY: "Hard to say. Probably impossible to know. Could be true. Could be that he's covering up the whole enchilada. I mean, without probing a lot deeper, a robust BW capability and specific plans for how to use them could be what he's trying to hide."

SULLIVAN: "I don't know. His reputation as some kind of badass, Western-trained biologist could all be completely exaggerated. A lot of these guys are like that. They're just running off their reputation, but when you actually meet them, there's nothing there, nothing to back it up."

ROMERO: "Probably too early to say then. But doesn't it seem like they were kind of parking him in Peshawar for some reason? I mean, from what we can tell, he traveled there alone and was just sitting there in the safehouse for a couple weeks. If they were close to developing usable weapons or an attack was imminent, wouldn't he have been with a lab, and a bunch of other guys who were helping him?"

DABROWSKY: "Maybe. Or maybe he already finished designing a weaponized strain of anthrax or ricin, and they've got all that they need already, so they're just stashing their guy somewhere safe until after the first attack, then he starts developing the materials for a second wave of attacks once they see what worked and what didn't."

April 9, 2004
Stare Kiejkuty, Poland
CIA Site LAPIS

Interrogation Transcript: Omar Abu KHATTAB
Interrogation Session 09APR04-2
Attendees: Omar Abu KHATTAB (detainee), Peter DABROWSKY (lead interrogator, contractor), Deborah SULLIVAN (interrogator, contractor), Mark ROMERO (CTC/RDG liaison, CIA)

[excerpt]

ROMERO: "Are you a pretty religious guy, Omar? Do you follow all the pillars of the faith, pray five times a day, and all that?"

KHATTAB: "Sure, I am faithful to Allah and omm Al shayateen. I pray every day, do the will of Allah and omm Al thalma. I am faithful Muslim."

ROMERO: "I know about Allah, but what does omm Al shayateen [mispronunciation] or the other one mean?"

KHATTAB: "I follow her will. She is as important as Allah. She helps guide me, gives me purpose, tells me what I need to do to serve her, how to be faithful to her."

ROMERO: "Never heard of her."

SULLIVAN: "If you're cooperative with us and answer our questions honestly, we can help you. We can get you a prayer rug and let you do your daily prayers the way you want. Would you like that?"

KHATTAB: "Okay. I have been honest with you already. Sure, I did not tell you everything right away, but I had to be faithful to Al Qaeda, I had to hold out a little while. You know how it is. Now I am telling you everything."

DABROWSKY: "Okay, well you need to think long and hard about how you can better cooperate with us. If you cooperate, we will be good friends and you can earn some small privileges and be treated well. You know what happens when you're not."

KHATTAB: "Okay."

DABROWSKY stands up, leaves room, returns two minutes later with two CIA security personnel, Gilbert FLORES and Robert LECKEY. FLORES and LECKEY escort KHATTAB out of the room.

DABROWSKY, ROMERO, and SULLIVAN all return to their seats after KHATTAB is taken out of the room.

ROMERO: "So what the fuck was that last part about? Who was he talking about? I don't know much about the intricacies of Islam."

SULLIVAN: "No clue. Maybe that was one of Muhammed's wives or daughters or something? Some kind of Islamic saint? Do they have saints? Women saints?"

DABROWSKY: "You've got to be fucking kidding me. You've seen how these assholes treat women. No way do they revere some female saint."

ROMERO: "Well, let's include it in today's report. We can try to sound it out for the cable and flag it for an analyst at HQ to take a listen to. I'm sure they can make sense of it and tell us what that was all about. Maybe it'll give us a religious angle to talk with him about."

SULLIVAN: "Sounds like a plan. It's your turn to write the first draft, right, Mark?"

ROMERO: "Shit. Yes."

DABROWSKY: "Good luck spelling that shit."

DABROWSKY, ROMERO, and SULLIVAN exit the room.

April 8, 2004
McLean, Virginia
CIA HQ

CABLE #RX347723-04

SUBJECT: Post-Detention Report on Omar Abu KHATTAB

DATE OF REPORT: 08 APRIL 2004

NAME: Omar Abu KHATTAB

ALIASES: The Engineer ("Al Muhandis"), Muhammed Abu BAKR, Khaled ALHARBI, Ahmed KHAN

NATIONALITY: Saudi

SEX: Male

DATE OF BIRTH: November 1, 1959

PHYSICAL CHARACTERISTICS AND DISTINGUISHING FEATURES: 5 feet, 9 inches in height. 154 pounds in weight. Black hair mixed with small amount of white/grey hair. Full beard and mustache, both with significant white/grey hair. Dark brown eyes. Minor scarring on upper left bicep and burn mark on right forearm.

MEDICAL HEALTH/HISTORY: Teeth in good repair; four metal fillings, wisdom teeth and two molars removed. No apparent current major medical conditions. Abdominal scar that corresponds with removal of appendix. Nail fungus under large toenail of right foot. Evidence of athlete's foot. Minor rash on left side of testicles and inner thigh.

BIOMETRICS AVAILABLE: Full DNA profile, full fingerprints, retinas, facial recognition.

KNOWN ASSOCIATES: Believed to know Al Qaeda's senior leadership, including Usama BIN LADIN and Ayman AL-ZAWAHIRI. Has other contacts within Al Qaeda, but specifics remain unknown.

KNOWN TRAVELS: Has traveled extensively throughout the Middle East, including Saudi Arabia, Afghanistan, and Pakistan, but likely has traveled to Sudan and possibly Egypt. Traveled to the United States and possibly Europe. Last known travel to the United States in 1984.

EDUCATION: B.S. in microbiology at Virginia Tech, Blacksburg, VA, in 1982. M.S. in microbiology/immunology at Virginia Tech, Blacksburg, VA, in 1984.

LANGUAGES KNOWN: Arabic (native), English (near fluent), Pashto (likely fluent).

BACKGROUND/BIOGRAPHY: KHATTAB was born to a relatively affluent family in Jeddah, Saudi Arabia. Third child of five (two older brothers and two younger sisters). Father was a senior administrator in city government. He was afforded a private education in Jeddah and then family arranged for him to attend college in the United States.

Traveled to the United States for the first time in 1978 to attend college at Virginia Tech. Started studies in biomedical engineering, but transferred freshman year into microbiology. Graduated with a bachelor's degree from Virginia Tech, then remained to continue graduate studies, earning a master's degree before returning home to Saudi Arabia in 1984.

He seems to have been employed as a medical researcher at various hospitals, clinics, and small biological sciences firms throughout Saudi Arabia, though he does not appear to have achieved any particularly notable professional successes. His name does not appear in any published scientific journal articles or patent application materials.

KHATTAB seems to have become radicalized at some point in the 1990s, and possibly met BIN LADIN briefly in Sudan in 1994 or 1995, and may have met ZAWAHIRI in Egypt in 1997 or 1998. It is not believed that he met with either man during their time in Jeddah in 1995-96.

Rumors of KHATTAB's role as head of the Al Qaeda biological weapons program began circulating in 1999 and became more prevalent in 2000 and early 2001.

KNOWN/SUSPECTED ROLE IN AL QAEDA: Believed to be the head of Al Qaeda's biological weapons program (multiple confirmations). If not actually directing the program, KHATTAB is confirmed to be highly placed within the program.

DESCRIPTION OF POCKET LITTER AT CAPTURE:

The following items were found on KHATTAB's person when he was captured:

- Small black faux-leather bound notebook, 3 inches by 5 inches. Contains notes handwritten in black ink, awaiting document exploitation.
- Scrap of paper #1, approximately 5 inches by 8 inches, folded in quarters, contains writing or symbols in unknown language, awaiting further linguistic analysis.
- Scrap of paper #2, crumpled, has black stain covering most of one side of sheet. Stain is slightly tacky substance, chemical composition unknown, awaiting chemical analysis.
- Pakistani identity card in the name of Ahmed KHAN, awaiting forensic analysis.

- A black piece of wood, exact species unclear, approximately four inches in length, 1.5 inches in diameter. Carved shape is vaguely human, with vague suggestions of a head, torso, and limbs. Surface is glossy and smooth. Unknown purpose/significance. Has been subjected to x-ray and is solid wood with no interior cavities.

DESCRIPTION OF MATERIALS RECOVERED FROM RESIDENCE IMMEDIATELY AFTER CAPTURE:

Contents recovered from the house that KHATTAB had been using immediately prior to capture:

- Cellular telephone, awaiting forensic analysis.
- Saudi passport in the name of Khaled ALHARBI, awaiting further forensic analysis.
- Personal diary/journal
- Laptop hard drive
- Document exploitation (DOCEX) is currently underway on personal diary/journal and laptop hard drive.

REPORTS OFFICER: John S., CTC

April 9, 2004
Stare Kiejkuty, Poland
CIA Site LAPIS

Surveillance Camera NV401-17 (LAPIS Staff Breakroom) Recording Transcript
Attendees: Mark ROMERO (CTC/RDG liaison, CIA), Deborah SULLIVAN (interrogator, contractor)

[ROMERO and SULLIVAN enter room at 9:07 PM (local)]

SULLIVAN: "Come on, Romero, it's Friday night. Got to blow off some steam, right?"

ROMERO: "Yeah, sure. I guess. I've got to get up early tomorrow for my PT [physical training] but...yeah, let's blow off some steam, sure."

SULLIVAN: "That's my boy. All right, well, we've got this six-pack here and some Doritos. Cool Ranch, got to love it."

ROMERO: [picking up bottle] "What the fuck is a 'Zubr' [mispronunciation]? Is this some kind of...buffalo-looking thing on the label?"

SULLIVAN: "It's just kind of a pale lager. You see it everywhere. I don't know what that thing on the label is supposed to be. There's a bunch of brands—Poles definitely love their beer—but a bunch of that shit is unpasteurized. You know, kind of sketchy. Can you imagine what Polish quality control is like in a brewery?"

ROMERO: [opening two bottles] "I don't want to know."

SULLIVAN and ROMERO: [both clinking bottles] "Cheers."

ROMERO: "Hmmm. That's not bad. Not great, but not bad. Inoffensive."

SULLIVAN: "Yeah, it hits the spot."

ROMERO: "So, yeah. Things have been pretty crazy around here, but it feels like we're making some good progress with the Engineer, don't you think?"

SULLIVAN: "Yeah, I'm hopeful about it. We'll have to see. You never really know when or if you're going to have a breakthrough with a detainee. Sometimes you do and sometimes there's just...nothing. Like the other ones we've got here.

ROMERO: "Yeah, but those are low-level guys, right? They never knew much to begin with. Not like the Engineer. I mean, he's a big fish. He could bust it all wide open for us. He could lead us to breaking up 9/11 Part 2, you know what I mean? He could tell us about attack plans that are underway, targets, maybe operational cells, all that stuff. This could be big.

SULLIVAN: "True. Could be."

ROMERO: "I have to say, I was surprised at how this place looks. I didn't know what to expect when I got here, but I was definitely expecting more of a...dungeony kind of vibe. I wasn't expecting shabby mansion on the outside and an antiseptic vibe on the inside."

SULLIVAN: [laughing] "Yeah, I know what you mean."

ROMERO: "Don't get me wrong, this place is still plenty weird. I mean, our 'guests' are hooded and shackled and handcuffed, and either naked or wearing an orange jumpsuit. That takes some getting used to."

SULLIVAN: "And the smell of the place. Don't forget the smell."

ROMERO: "True. It kind of smells more like a hospital or something, and not, I don't know, a prison or something. I assume prisons smell pretty bad."

SULLIVAN: "Yeah, probably. All the detention centers I've been in smell pretty rank. [pause] But, ummm, enough about work, right? We get enough of that during working hours, and it's not like we work a nine-to-five job. Duty calls and all that, but let's just relax a little."

ROMERO: "Okay, okay, let's make a pact: no more talking about work stuff. Sorry I brought it up."

SULLIVAN: "No, no, it's fine. Just no more work talk for a while. We have to spend all day with the HVD, let's not spend all evening talking about him too."

ROMERO: "Yep, I hear you. I definitely need to decompress. This place gets oppressive after a while."

SULLIVAN: "Tell me about it. Wait until you've been here as long as I have."

ROMERO: "Wait. How long have you been here?"

SULLIVAN: "Ummm...we're talking the better part of eight months."

ROMERO: "No shit?"

SULLIVAN: "I shit you not. So, anyway, tell me about yourself. What's your life story?"

ROMERO: "Uh oh, this is a dangerous question from a trained interrogator."

SULLIVAN: [laughing] "Don't be scared, you're a big boy, you can handle it."

ROMERO: "Okay. So, I think you probably know most of this. Army captain, Ranger, got out after eight years in, then I joined the DO at the CIA as a paramilitary officer and been doing that for four years. Been at CTC since before 9/11, and obviously since then things have gotten insane. Been deployed all over the place for months and months, and the last few on tracking down KHATTAB. This one was my big break. Haven't been home for way too long."

SULLIVAN: "I hear that. What does your wife think of all that?"

ROMERO: "Well...let's be honest. She's not thrilled. I mean, she knows how important this all is, she's from a military family so she kind of knew what to expect, but yeah, this hasn't exactly been good for my marriage if you know what I mean. I haven't even seen my daughter since she was an infant. She's a toddler now, she's walking and talking and everything else. I've missed all that. I'll never get that time back. All she knows is that Daddy is a voice on the phone."

SULLIVAN: "God, that sucks."

ROMERO: "Tell me about it."

SULLIVAN: "Where did you grow up? You're in Northern Virginia now, right?"

ROMERO: "Yeah. Grew up in a little suburb of Buffalo. Went to school there, played football and all that."

SULLIVAN: [laughing] "Oh, I bet all the little girls in Buffalo loved you."

ROMERO: "Nah, I was always a little shy around girls. Kind of a late bloomer."

SULLIVAN: [laughing] "Awww, poor Mark. Did they call you 'Romeo' instead of "Romero'?"

ROMERO: [laughing] "Maybe, maybe not. No comment. So what about you, Deb? What are you like when you're not interrogating a detainee at a black site?"

SULLIVAN: "Well, I enlisted in the Navy right after high school. I was ready to leave Ohio and the Navy sounded like the best way out. Got into an intel billet and loved it, signed up for whatever training they would give me. That was how I became an interrogator. Did my twenty years, then got out and then, well, 9/11, and got picked up as a contract interrogator. I have to say, the pay is a hell of a lot better as a contractor, and there's way less bullshit to put up with, you know what I mean?"

ROMERO: "I do. Truly. I got out of the Army mostly because of a fucked-up knee, but I was already at the point where the bullshit was piling up and I was ready to go. You got anybody waiting for you at home?"

SULLIVAN: "Nah, met a dude a long time ago while I was in the Navy, but we divorced forever ago. No kids, thank God, that would be terrible right now." [laughing] "No offense."

ROMERO: [laughing] "None taken."

SULLIVAN: "You know what I mean though. I can't imagine not being able to see your kids. No, it's just me and my mom, back in Columbus. My sister when she's around, which isn't very much. That's about it."

ROMERO: "Gotcha."

SULLIVAN: "Sounds like neither of us has an ideal home and family life, right?"

ROMERO: [laughing] "That's definitely true. This work has definitely left us a little...disconnected from friends and family; I mean, even more than military service did, you know what I mean?"

SULLIVAN: "Oh, definitely. Even my Navy deployments weren't really this isolating. I mean, sure, there was always classified stuff I couldn't talk about with people and all that, but there was enough other stuff I could. Plus, even though deployments always lasted longer than they said they would, you knew pretty much when you were going to be done and headed home. But now...well, it's all pretty fucking open-ended, you know what I mean?"

ROMERO: "Yep. The 'Global War on Terror' isn't going to end any time soon, is it? I mean, this is a generational challenge. I heard someone call it 'The Long War.' Our kids are going to be fighting this. I mean, if it doesn't end until the last terrorist dies, well..."

SULLIVAN: "Shit. You can't think about it that way though. What we're doing here matters. I mean, it's weird as shit, right, but it really fucking matters."

ROMERO: "Absolutely. I mean, you've seen the videos of what the chemicals and biological weapons they're working on do to people and animals. God forbid they should get a nuclear weapon. I mean, that's these guys' wet dream: taking out an American city with a nuke, or hosing it down with chem/bio."

SULLIVAN: "That's what it's all about. I mean, for all we know, there's an attack that's going to be launched tomorrow."

ROMERO: "Christ, I don't want to think about that. I used to have nightmares about AQ killing children, seeing those little faces..."

SULLIVAN: "Yeah."

ROMERO: "Christ, this is a depressing conversation!"

SULLIVAN: [laughing] "Yeah. I thought we had a pact on no work talk."

ROMERO: "It's hard not to."

SULLIVAN: "I know. How about beer? That's a safe topic."

ROMERO: "True."

SULLIVAN: "Okay, well, we'll have to try some other Polish beers some time. This one isn't bad, but I bet we can find some better ones. Have you tried any of the other local beers?"

ROMERO: "No, not really. I wasn't exactly encouraged to seek out the local night life and check out the bar scene here."

SULLIVAN: "Don't worry, you're not missing much. I went with Pete and a couple of the guys, plus Michal once or twice, but it's kind of weird. We're not really supposed to talk to the locals much, and they all know that they shouldn't be bugging us, so yeah...awkward."

ROMERO: "Yeah, I can imagine."

[end excerpt]

April 12, 2004
McLean, Virginia
CIA HQ

CABLE #RX348201-04

SUBJECT: Document Exploitation (DOCEX) Report on Possessions of Omar Abu KHATTAB

DATE OF REPORT: 12 APRIL 2004

ITEM 1: Cellular telephone

PHYSICAL CHARACTERISTICS: TracFone, standard model, prepaid no-contract mobile phone. Unit was purchased by reseller in Karachi, Pakistan. SIM card and phone battery had been removed from phone and were placed on top of the phone when recovered.

LOCATION: Table in kitchen/dining area in apartment he was using at the time of his capture.

CONTENTS: No saved contacts. Incoming/outgoing call logs have been deleted.

INTELLIGENCE VALUE: Only fingerprints on phone belong to KHATTAB. Phone history of calls links this phone with four other telephones, two of which were already known as low-level Al Qaeda logistical nodes/facilitators and two of which were previously unknown. The two known telephone numbers have been prioritized for further collection and the two new telephone numbers have likewise been prioritized for ongoing surveillance. It seems clear that KHATTAB was in regular contact with other known members of Al Qaeda, making approximately one call to these contacts each week. Additional collection efforts on KHATTAB's telephonic contacts ongoing.

ITEM 2: Faux-leather notebook

PHYSICAL CHARACTERISTICS: Small black faux-leather bound notebook, 3 inches by 5 inches. Notebook brand cheaply manufactured and distributed in at least 14 countries across the Middle East. Contains notes handwritten in black ink. At least some pages torn out, pen nib imprints from missing pages are unrecoverable.

LOCATION: Found in KHATTAB's left front pocket on his person at time of capture.

CONTENTS: 33 pages contain writing, remainder are blank. The bulk of these pages appear to contain either incomplete thoughts or sparse notes that are indecipherable without a clearer context. In several cases, there are number sequences written that could indicate telephone numbers or possibly location coordinates. Initial analysis of these numbers suggests that either they are random number sequences or they are written in code—no obvious telephone numbers have been found, nor do the numbers seem to indicate any particular geographic locations. List of these number sequences available separately. Six Arabic male personal names (no plus one information available for any of the names) have also been written at various places in the notebook, though context is unclear and no further information is available about any of these individuals. List of these names is also available separately.

INTELLIGENCE VALUE: Only fingerprints on notebook belong to KHATTAB. There may be a few names and/or phone numbers of possible associates concealed within the contents of the notebook; clarification and additional context by KHATTAB would be invaluable, and may spur additional lines of inquiry.

Image scans of notebook pages available upon request.

ITEM 3: Student composition notebook

PHYSICAL CHARACTERISTICS: Student composition notebook, 7 inches by 10 inches. Notebook brand cheaply manufactured and distributed in at least 23 countries across the Middle East, Latin America, and the United States. Contains notes handwritten in black ink and pencil.

LOCATION: Found tangled in bedsheets on KHATTAB's mattress on the floor of bedroom in apartment he was using at the time of his capture.

CONTENTS: 78 pages contain handwriting or drawings. All are done by hand in either black ink or pencil. Handwriting analysis (75% confidence) suggests that a single individual wrote all entries in the notebook, though poor penmanship and erratic nature of the writing increases uncertainty. No dates appear in the notebook, rendering unclear when any particular entry was recorded.

The exact nature of the contents of the notebook remains uncertain. Best analytic supposition is that this notebook may be a kind of dream journal or personal diary that records a mix of dreams/nightmares, sexual fantasies, religious beliefs/doctrine, and activity plans. In many cases, it is difficult to determine if an entry records a dream, a sexual fantasy, or a religious belief, or some combination thereof. Dreams and sexual fantasies are frequently violent or sadomasochistic; most are surreal or nightmarish in quality, and/or anatomically impossible.

One common element in many of the entries is one or more individuals referred to as "omm Al shayateen" (translation: mother of demons), "omm Al thalma" (translation: mother of darkness), or "omm sherreera" (translation: evil mother). Analytic consensus is that these monikers reference a single individual or figure, though there is a possibility that the different titles are significant and may reference more than one person. KHATTAB writes frequently about worshipping this person in a religious sense, and at other times writes about having sexual dreams or fantasies in which this person figures prominently. Use of the terms "Habib Albi" (translation: "love of my heart") and "Habibi" (translation: "my love"/"beloved") are often used to describe this individual. At least one poem entitled "Ya Rouhi" (translation: "[You Are] My Soul"/"[You Are] My Dear/Beloved") also seems to be about this individual.

In several instances, KHATTAB writes that he worships this individual, that she is a goddess, that she is above Allah, and that he follows her in the belief that he is helping her bring about her vision for transforming the world in her image. Note that Muslims would universally find these ideas abhorrent and would deem the author a heretic. These ideas are not consistent with known Al Qaeda or broader Salafist ideology or religious beliefs. KHATTAB would likely be sanctioned or killed as a heretic by his associates for expressing these beliefs if these are unauthorized ideas and not part of some Al Qaeda operational planning effort. On several occasions he notes that this individual told him where to go or what to do. On one occasion he notes that she told him to kill a man (name unknown) who was the worshipper of a rival deity (identity of deity unclear). On three occasions he writes that she told him to pass along her "black seeds" to others, though the locations, names of individuals, or dates of these transfers are unlisted, as is any further information about these seeds. At least some of these messages appear to have come to KHATTAB in dreams, or as part of his dreams; it is unclear if any of these messages or activities actually occurred.

INTELLIGENCE VALUE: Only fingerprints on notebook belong to KHATTAB. Dried bodily fluids found on notebook also match KHATTAB's DNA.

Psychological analysis of author suggests a highly disturbed individual who may be delusional and suffering from a major psychotic disorder. Symptoms likely include abnormal thinking and perceptions, hallucinations, erratic behavior, poor hygiene, among many others. Recommend additional psychological assessment.

Intelligence value is uncertain until more can be learned about the nature and identity of the various names noted above. Disentangling fact from fiction is impossible without additional context. If the titles noted above refer to one or more real people, then this could be a codename for a religious authority or Al Qaeda affiliate, perhaps even someone else involved in the Al Qaeda biological weapons program. Standard database checks on these titles have not yet turned up additional references, though checks are ongoing and could produce results in the future. These names have been added to all standard watchlists.

Analysts are split on the meaning of the entries in this notebook. The majority view is that these are delusional rantings and have no specific correlation with any actual events, persons, or activities. A minority analytic view is that this information may represent coded messages about some sort of intra-Salafist or intra-Al Qaeda rivalry, or perhaps a dispute between Al Qaeda and some other jihadist organization. If so, references to "omm" ("mother") may be a codephrase for Usama Bin Ladin or Ayman al-Zawahiri, though neither is known to have ever used a feminine codename among jihadis. If so, then KHATTAB may have been under orders to transfer biological agents or precursor materials ("black seeds") to others, and this would represent a plan to disperse biological weapons to at least three other individuals/sites.

Image scans of notebook pages available upon request.

ITEM 4: Laptop hard drive

PHYSICAL CHARACTERISTICS: 80GB hard drive. Standard operating system and other factory-installed software present on hard drive. Rudimentary commercial off-the-shelf (COTS) security software installed, no hidden partitions located.

LOCATION: On shelf in bedroom closet in apartment he was using at the time of his capture under pile of clothing that concealed the presence of the laptop.

CONTENTS: Internet search history primarily consists of searches for pornographic image and video files, news sites (various Western and Middle Eastern media outlets), and regular access of Hotmail personal email account. Search of Hotmail email account shows no emails sent or received, except for ordinary spam messages received. COTS security software had been used to clean up deleted files on hard drive; these were unrecoverable.

Data files on laptop: 37 GB of what can only be described as unusually disturbing pornographic images and videos stored in folder with additional images and videos that appear to depict either autopsies or surgical/medical procedures, or wounds. Pornographic images depict a wide variety of extreme sexual acts by men, women, children, and animals of various species. Note that the majority of these files are not widely circulated on the Internet, and at least some may be private files or files circulated within private group(s). Images and videos have been subjected to steganographic analysis, and no hidden messages have been located. Further analysis available upon request, though not recommended by analyst.

INTELLIGENCE VALUE: Only fingerprints on laptop belong to KHATTAB.

47 relevant files may have some intelligence value, though specifics remain unclear at the time of this report; analysis continuing. Files include some number sequences, though as

with the numbers listed in Item 2 (above), they appear to be written in code. List of number sequences available separately.

There are also several records of financial transactions that appear to have been downloaded from the Internet from various bank and other financial transaction websites that provide a list of the funds that KHATTAB appears to have had access to (total of $23,171.78 USD) housed in three separate bank accounts. In each case, a separate account made deposits into those three accounts. Financial monitoring of KHATTAB's three accounts is ongoing, though no transactions have been detected since KHATTAB's capture. Sending accounts were previously unknown, but are being monitored as well. No further transactions from these accounts have been detected since KHATTAB's capture.

No references to any of the "omm" names are found on the laptop.

Copies of files and list of files available upon request.

ANALYST NOTE: More context from KHATTAB is needed before definitive analysis of the contents of the documents discussed here can be attempted.

REPORTS OFFICER: Roger B., CTC

April 12, 2004
Stare Kiejkuty, Poland
CIA Site LAPIS

Surveillance Camera NV401-23 (LAPIS Conference Room 2) Recording Transcript
Attendees: Mark ROMERO (CTC/RDG liaison, CIA), Deborah SULLIVAN (interrogator, contractor), Peter DABROWSKY (interrogator, contractor)

[ROMERO, SULLIVAN, and DABROWSKY enter room and sit down at 8:02 AM (local)]

DABROWSKY: "Well, happy Monday, guys. I saw you were up pretty fucking early in the morning, Romero."

ROMERO: "You know me, trying to stay in shape. Got to do that PT every day. Don't want to develop a beer gut."

DABROWSKY: "You know the best thing about getting out of the Air Force? None of that bullshit anymore."

SULLIVAN: [laughing] "Yes!" [gives DABROWSKY high-five] "It sucked when I was in the Navy, and there was no way I was going to keep doing those early morning runs as a civilian."

[All laughing.]

DABROWSKY: "Okay, so let's go over this DOCEX report that came in. Now that we have that, we can assess if it sheds any light on anything or suggests any new avenues of attack to us. Have you guys got copies of this?"

[SULLIVAN and ROMERO nod and indicate in the affirmative.]

SULLIVAN: "They sure took their time writing this one up, didn't they?"

DABROWSKY: "Yeah, and per usual, there's not all that much immediately actionable."

ROMERO: "You guys have looked at a lot more of these reports than I have. I want to read through it more closely, but it's a little hard to see the exact value of all this. I can see that there's some potentially useful stuff here, but it's also all tangled up with junk."

DABROWSKY: "Yeah, that's fair. This is pretty typical. There's always a lot of 'on the one hand' and 'we're not sure what this means, it could be super important or it could be nothing.'"

SULLIVAN: "The good news is that we have him indefinitely, so we can work through all this stuff with him over time."

DABROWSKY: "True, but we have to prioritize and separate the wheat from the chaff. I don't want to spend a week with him on his jerk-off material when we could be asking him about specific associates and attack plans."

ROMERO: "Well, it looks to me like the number sequences and names are obviously important, right? If those are written in code, we can try to get him to decipher those for us, and we can ask him about the names."

SULLIVAN: "The bank account and financial transaction histories are good too. It's going to be hard to get a straight answer out of him, but I'd love to know why they were sending him so much money. What was he going to do with it?"

DABROWSKY: "Exactly. Was he traveling somewhere? Buying materials? Paying someone else for something? I mean, given what his living situation was, he wasn't exactly spending a lot on his housing arrangements."

ROMERO: "Okay, so the million dollar question: What do you all make of this psychological assessment and the uncertainty about his diary or whatever the fuck that thing is? I mean, we knew the guy was crazy, but...he's really crazy, right?"

SULLIVAN: "Yeah, pretty unstable. I think we can use that, but we also don't want to traumatize him to the point where he goes catatonic or has a psychotic break and loses all touch with reality. Then he'd be worthless to us."

DABROWSKY: "Yeah, there are definitely some psychological angles we can exploit here. We'll have to think hard on that and work up a plan to take advantage of it."

ROMERO: "The other thing we need to do is figure out what the deal is with this 'Black Mother' character. Is she a real person? Is she just a figment of his imagination?"

SULLIVAN: "Right. Obviously we've got to start hammering him on that and get to the bottom of it."

DABROWSKY: "I'm wary, but yeah, you're right. He could be just a crazy who's written a bunch of weird, fucked-up shit about some imaginary person or god or whatever, but if this is a codephrase for someone he's taking directives from, than we've got to know that."

ROMERO: "This whole 'black seed' thing worries me. Could be nothing, could be the whole enchilada."

SULLIVAN: "That's the heart of it. I mean, this all could be one big, giant wild goose chase. But if that was a dispersal of, say, bioagents to attack cells, then that's exactly what we need to know."

DABROWSKY: "I'm betting it's the ramblings of a madman."

ROMERO: "Yeah..."

[end excerpt]

April 14, 2004
McLean, Virginia
CIA HQ

CABLE #RX348916-04

SUBJECT: Transcripts of three telephone intercepts of Omar Abu KHATTAB

DATE OF REPORT: 14 APRIL 2004

ANALYST NOTE: Recent DOCEX of recovered telephone used by Omar Abu KHATTAB (see CABLE #RX348201-04) has enabled translation and analysis of several conversations between KHATTAB and unknown parties. Relevant portions of three of these conversations are noted below.

TELEPHONE INTERCEPT 1: Conversation between Omar Abu KHATTAB and Unknown Party 1, 02 MAY 2003, call beginning 09:03 PM local time.

[excerpt]

KHATTAB: "My brother, have I ever told you about omm Al thalma [reference unknown; literal translation 'mother of darkness']? She has changed my life."

UNKNOWN PARTY 1: "No. 'Darkness'? No, what does that mean? Who are you talking about?"

KHATTAB: "She is the one who gave birth to us. She creates life. She brought us forth from her holy womb, and wants to bring more life forth from her. She wants to make life blossom all over the world."

UNKNOWN PARTY 1: "Wait. Is this your mother that you're talking about? Who are you talking about?"

KHATTAB: "She is not just my mother, she is all of our mothers. She birthed us, gave us life. She plants her holy seeds and they grow."

UNKNOWN PARTY 1: "What do you mean? Allah gave us life. Who is this woman you are talking about?"

KHATTAB: "Yes, yes, brother. You must keep an open mind about what I am telling you. There are many things I can explain to you that you do not yet understand."

UNKNOWN PARTY 1: "I am not sure I want to understand. I do not want to be a kafir [infidel or unbeliever]. I am thankful to Allah for my life."

KHATTAB: "Oh, my brother. Your eyes and mind are closed."

UNKNOWN PARTY 1: "My mind is not closed, brother. But I am worried about what you are saying. Muhammed was the last prophet. Allah is god, there is no other god. There can be no other god, no other source of life. I worry that what you say is shirk [translation: unpardonable sin of polytheism]."

KHATTAB: "No, no. This is not shirk, that is not what I am saying. I am not explaining myself well and you are not listening."

UNKNOWN PARTY 1: "I am worried about you."

KHATTAB: "There is no need to worry. Everything is clear to me now, in ways that it was not before. I have purpose now, my brother. She has given me that purpose."

UNKNOWN PARTY 1: "I don't understand, but this is very frightening to me. Let us not talk about this anymore."

KHATTAB: "Very well, my brother."

[end excerpt]

TELEPHONE INTERCEPT 2: Conversation between Omar Abu KHATTAB and Unknown Party 2, 11 AUGUST 2003, call beginning 11:17 PM local time.

[excerpt]

KHATTAB: "Are you going to bring the seeds as a gift for the wedding with you, my brother?"

UNKNOWN PARTY 2: "No, one of my cousins is."

KHATTAB: "Is he trustworthy? These seeds are very valuable. We don't want to disappoint the bride. That would be a huge problem."

UNKNOWN PARTY 2: "Yes, I know, I know. That is no problem. My cousin will bring the seeds, he has done this many times before. He has never lost a present."

KHATTAB: "Okay. Let me know when you hear from him."

UNKNOWN PARTY 2: "I will. It will be a beautiful wedding. The bride will plant wonderful gardens, all over the world, with these seeds."

KHATTAB: "Yes, she will. I am so excited I could scream for joy. Your cousin knows how to find Ahmed? You're certain?"

UNKNOWN PARTY 2: "Yes, I have given him the instructions. It is no problem."

KHATTAB: "Your cousin is not one of us. He doesn't serve the mother."

UNKNOWN PARTY 2: "No, but that doesn't matter. He is very trustworthy. He doesn't have to serve her or know anything about the wedding presents to transport them safely and deliver them to Ahmed. You will see. Everything will be fine."

KHATTAB: "I am trusting you, my brother."

UNKNOWN PARTY 2: "You don't have to trust me. It is the mother's will."

[end excerpt]

TELEPHONE INTERCEPT 3: Conversation between Omar Abu KHATTAB and Unknown Party 3, 4 JANUARY 2004, call beginning 4:01 AM local time.

[excerpt]

UNKNOWN PARTY 3: "I'm worried, brother."

KHATTAB: "What do you mean? Why?"

UNKNOWN PARTY 3: "This is all taking so much time. It's not happening fast enough."

KHATTAB: "All in good time. You have to have faith. It will all happen according to the mother's will. Faith, brother. She will ensure that everything works out according to her plans."

UNKNOWN PARTY 3: "It is hard, my brother. I know that her time is coming, but..."

KHATTAB: [agitated] "Do not lose faith! We are too close. Have faith in her. In her, all flowers blossom."

UNKNOWN PARTY 3: "Yes, I know. I know. But what about the others, the ones who worship the abomination? They want to stop her and all her plans. They would destroy her gardens and prevent her seeds from ever blossoming. They would destroy all life, all living things."

KHATTAB: "Don't worry about them. They will be destroyed utterly. Did I ever tell you how she came to me and told me where one of those men was? I destroyed him, stopped all his plans. She gave me the tools."

UNKNOWN PARTY 3: "Yes, my brother. You mentioned that to me a long time ago. That is good, but he was just one of them. There are many more."

KHATTAB: "Is your faith wavering?"

UNKNOWN PARTY 3: "It is not wavering. I am faithful to her. I am just worried."

[end excerpt]

April 14, 2004
Stare Kiejkuty, Poland
CIA Site LAPIS

Mark Romero Diary

I DON'T WANT to be one of those people who keep a "dream journal." I swear I don't. It's silly and pathetic. But I had a really FUCKING [all caps and underlined three times in original] disturbing dream—no, a true fucking NIGHTMARE [all caps in original]—last night. It hasn't even gone away after waking up. Here it is three or four hours after I got up and I can't stop thinking about it, so this is my attempt to get it out of my head by putting it down on paper.

Here goes:

Well, first, I should note that I've been having trouble sleeping. Not surprising; this always happens to me when I'm under stress. Hard time falling asleep and then the slightest noise wakes me up during the night and then I can't fall back to sleep. So I went to see good ol' Doc Richards a couple days ago. Told him I've been having trouble with sleep. He says no problem, hands me a bottle of melatonin, says take one, or two if I don't have to wake up at zero dark thirty. I told him I didn't want to get hooked on sleeping pills and he said don't worry about it, it's a chemical your body produces when you sleep anyway, this is just more of it, then waves me out of his office. So I've been taking one of those every night. Not sure that they help much, but you never know. So I took one of those, then drifted off to sleep. It was surprisingly easy last night. Should have known that was too good to be true.

But I'm also not someone who gets nightmares a lot. I mean, sure, every now and then I have a bad dream, but not often, and I don't get shook by them. You have a bad dream, it wakes you up, it feels shitty for a couple minutes, then it literally fades from your mind and doesn't bother you after that. Right?

Not this one.

Anyway, so in the dream everything starts off in blackness. Just total darkness. I can't see anything. So I'm just standing there or floating there or whatever I'm doing there in blackness for a while, then I start feeling and hearing things all around me. I realize that it feels really hot and humid, like when you're in a jungle or Florida in August or something and it's just so hot and humid that you instantly break out in a sweat and water just keeps pouring out of you. The air all around you is just so muggy and filled with water that it feels like you're swimming through soup. There's a little breeze, but it doesn't cool me off, it's just hot, wet wind blowing on me. Then I start hearing things. Again, kind of like being in a jungle or someplace tropical. Not only do I hear the wind, and what sounds maybe like tree branches being blown by the wind, but animals and all the other shit that lives in a place like that. Not people noises, not cars and civilization, just weird animal noises. I'm not sure what kind of animals. Pretty close by. Not like right on top of me or in touching distance, but all around me, close by and then off in the distance too.

Then it starts to get a little lighter out. Not bright, but bright enough that I can start to make out shapes around me. That didn't make me feel any better. Quite the opposite, actually. I was kind of floating or suspended above a jungle or forest that was spread out before me. Really, really dense trees and plants, vegetation everywhere. It was almost a kind of swamp or swampy jungle, it was so wet. I realized that the whole place stank. Rotting vegetation, but also just plain rot and corruption. It made me gag, and I remember starting to kind of retch or dry-heave, but I stopped it before that could happen. I was just kind of gazing out across this landscape when I realized that there was this huge, dark shape ahead, a good ways off across this jungle area. I thought it was a mountain at first—it was hard to tell in the gloom—but it wasn't. It was shaped too regularly for that. It was like a black pyramid sort of thing. Definitely something man-made, well, artificially constructed anyway. I couldn't make out any specifics about it because it was so dark and too far off.

Then I started moving toward the pyramid. I don't know how. I couldn't see behind me or to my sides really, but it didn't feel like anyone was pushing me forward, I was just moving. I tried to exert force against it, but I couldn't. There was no traction, no way to stop the momentum. I was just totally powerless and being forced closer to this thing. I kind of swooped lower—again, not my choice—and crashed through the trees and got much closer to the ground. I could feel the leaves of the trees brushing against me, leaving wet, sticky trails on my skin as I touched them. I started picking up speed. It was hard to see anything in the forest, but I could feel things all around me. Presences. Things watching me. Just standing there in the shadows, focused on me. Not doing anything, just staring as I flew past them toward that goddamn pyramid.

I could feel myself starting to sweat and shake as I approached the pyramid. I tried to cry out and shout and scream but I couldn't. I couldn't even open my mouth. My entire body felt like it was in a vice, like I was strapped down or being gripped by something tight that was pressing on my entire body, every muscle, and just freezing me in place. I started to slow down as I neared the pyramid. I could see that I was approaching an entrance to the pyramid. It was this kind of vast, open, cavernous entrance in the black stone of the pyramid. I could also see as I got closer that I had had the scale of the pyramid way off—it was vast, far larger than I had initially thought. This thing would have dwarfed the pyramids in Egypt or South America. I tried to look up when I was near it, and while I still couldn't move my head, I could shift my eyes and the pyramid seemed to just continue upward forever once I was close.

Then I stopped, just kind of hovering there for a minute. I heard some massive creaking or shifting sound coming from inside the pyramid. It sounded like stone blocks or timbers and metal shifting, being pushed aside, falling over. Then silence for a moment, then a loud, slow, ponderous kind of thumping and dragging sounds. Like something incredibly large and heavy was being dragged a little, then pausing, dragging then pausing. It was getting louder and louder, closer and closer, though I still couldn't see anything inside the pyramid. It was utterly pitch-black inside there, and there was still no movement or any sense of what was going on. That made me want to get out of there even more than before, and I could feel myself straining, but still nothing, no way to move.

Then I felt something tighten around me, on my arms and across my chest, and I looked down to see what it was. I still couldn't move my head. I could only see a little bit because of the angle, but I could see some kind of black, scaly arm or tentacle thing gripping me. I couldn't see what the tentacle belonged to—it must have been behind me or enough to the side that I couldn't get a larger frame of reference—but I could feel an impossibly tight grip tightening and squeezing me, and I could feel some sliminess on my skin as it closed around my arms. That made me close my eyes and I could feel myself straining and struggling. I tried to tell myself it was only a dream, that it wasn't real and I could just wake up, wake up, wake up, and I was straining until I could feel myself starting to black out, all the blood rushing to my head, then I opened my eyes and I was laying in bed. I sat bolt upright and looked around, but everything was normal. It took me a few seconds to assure myself that the jungle and the pyramid, and whatever was gripping me, was all gone. My heart was racing and my blood pressure was probably sky high, but I was back in my bed.

So that's where we're at. Pretty fucking horrible, right? Though it doesn't look that bad now that I see it written down like that. It just looks mundane. Scary but mundane. Some kind of hidden menace and creepiness, but still. Just a dream. It was all just a dream. A simple work-stress dream, that's all. If I told a psychoanalyst about it, not that I ever would, I'm sure they would say that I've just been under a lot of work stress lately and it's been getting to me, so relax, take some time off, stop worrying about it, and get on with things. And then probably ask me when I started wanting to fuck my mother and kill my father or something.

April 16, 2004
Stare Kiejkuty, Poland
CIA Site LAPIS

Mark Romero Diary

WEIRD, WEIRD DAY. Every fucking day in this place is strange, of course, but today takes the cake. I don't know what fucking happened.

So I woke up this morning, got into my workout gear, and was going to head out to do some PT. Quick five-mile run outside because the weather was nice and then some lifting downstairs in the exercise room. After that, I come back, take a shower, get dressed, etc. Well, that was the plan. I stopped off to take a leak in the bathroom down the hall (there are a couple on this floor, and I use the one a couple doors down from my quarters). Maybe I was still a little sleepy and not quite as alert as I should have been because it was only while I was taking a leak that I realized that there was shit everywhere. Not actual shit, exactly, but mold and fungus and mushrooms growing and all kinds of stuff like that. The whole bathroom had been overtaken by black mold and various fungal growths. Dingy smears of mold and black spots everywhere. You're saying, well sure, it's a communal bathroom in Poland, of course there was mold everywhere. No. This place has been spic-and-span. Say what you will about LAPIS, but we've been keeping this place spotless. Cleaned every day, lots of bleach and antiseptic everywhere. Hell, the place smells like a hospital half the time.

And here's the weirdest part: none of it was there eight hours previously when I brushed my teeth right before going to bed.

This wasn't even normal fungus: there were obscene growths that I swear to God looked like human organs and body parts and, yes...lots and lots of phallic symbols. Everything was green and purple and all kinds of bizarre colors. You just looked at those things and you knew they were poisonous or psychedelic or both. I started freaking out and left the bathroom and started seeing it everywhere in the hallway. In the corners, on the floor, on the walls, everywhere.

So I started walking down the hall and found a couple of the security guys, and they were starting to notice this stuff and they told me that it was everywhere. "What do you mean 'everywhere'?" All over the fucking place, they said. So I walked downstairs and they weren't kidding. I started yelling for the others, and people started popping out of their rooms. It took a little bit, but we raided the janitorial closet and organized some cleaning parties and started scrubbing and cleaning up. Mops, brooms, brushes, vacuum cleaners, and lots and lots of soap and water and bleach.

Eventually we even woke fucking Dave up and he stumbled out of his bedroom. The guy was so visibly still drunk from the night before that it wasn't even funny. He started yelling at people for waking him up then went back inside his room and slammed the door. Christ. What a pathetic fucker.

Every time we'd think we had cleaned it all up, it would come back. I'm not shitting you about this. I was on my hands and knees scrubbing with a brush and soapy water and bleach and would clean up an area, then walk away and come back an hour later and it was like I had never even cleaned any of it up.

Eventually—and I do mean eventually, because this took the better part of the day—we had gotten everything cleaned up and the mold and weird fungus shit was pretty much all gone.

I talked with Michal later in the day. I think I've mentioned him before. Good guy. He's the local Polish intel geek who's been assigned to be our liaison here at LAPIS. He's always running around trying to make sure everything is running smoothly. Seems pretty good at his job because he's a people pleaser. Clearly his bosses have told him that he's got to keep the CIA happy.

Anyway, so I saw Michal downstairs in the afternoon and asked him what the fuck was going on. He started off really apologetic because he thought I was going to bitch him out the way a bunch of other people already had. It wasn't his fault that any of this happened, though that didn't stop Dave from screaming at him for 15 minutes after he finally dragged his sorry hungover ass out of bed. The Polish guards on-site had called Michal in as soon as they realized what was going on and he arrived a little while later. As he told me, and tried to tell Dave, none of this shit was here last night. When Michal left for home in the evening, the place was spic-and-span. I can vouch for that. Of course, Dave told him that was bullshit and there was no way the place could get this moldy and filthy in one day. While I would normally agree with that, well, apparently that's what happened.

No fucking clue. Here's hoping the place doesn't get infested with mold again any time soon.

No real progress with the Engineer. Fuck that fucking guy. We've been steadily interrogating him every day, subjecting him to EITs, etc. etc. Today was mostly a waste though because of the clean-up on Aisle 7 needed. He gave us a couple additional names after a waterboarding session yesterday, but it's unclear if those will pan out. It's probably not that he's outright lying—I think he really does know guys by the names he gave us—but I don't think those names are going to lead to us magically catching those guys and wrapping up his whole network. It's a fine art. You have the name of a guy who's affiliated with Al Qaeda. Okay, what do you do next? How do you translate that name into catching the asshole? It might be his real name, it might just be an alias. There might be a thousand guys by that name. Even if you have his real name, he might not be using it anymore. So what do you do next? Fortunately, we have a million and one analysts working on all this shit and running these leads to ground, but still.

Not to be on the Engineer's side, but let's face it: by this point, he doesn't know where any of these assholes are. He's been out of the loop for weeks, and they're all moving around constantly in different countries. They've got dense social networks and friendly governments for the most part, and they blend in, stay a while, don't cause a ruckus, grease the right palms, then move on to some other unobtrusive location. How's Khattab going to know where any of those guys are right now? But I know, I know, that's the wrong way to think about it. These are all pieces of the puzzle and we're slowly assembling it. One guy's name might mean nothing now, but in a year when someone else mentions the same guy, or we find someone else's phone, we'll be able to start connecting the dots. It's all baby steps.

I hate baby steps.

April 18, 2004
Stare Kiejkuty, Poland
CIA Site LAPIS

Mark Romero Diary

WEIRD EXPERIENCE LAST night. Strike that. Not weird [underlined in original]. Awkward, uncomfortable, embarrassing. I'm used to the merely weird here in LAPIS, this is something altogether different. Yet another dream strange enough that it's worth writing down. Christ, I hope no one ever finds this journal and reads it. Anyway, here goes:

First, let me just say that it's been a while since I've had sex, okay? Months. I've been deployed and stressed out and tired and working like crazy and in some extremely non-sexy situations and not even interacting with many women at all, much less women I would or could have sex with. My wife is very far away and I've never cheated on her. It's hard to imagine myself doing that—I mean, sex is great and all, but I can just jerk off and be done with it, I don't have to destroy my marriage and become a divorced dad and never get to see my daughter again just because I'm momentarily horny, okay?

All right, enough throat clearing.

It didn't even take me long to fall asleep, which was nice. I was asleep pretty much as soon as my head hit the pillow. Next thing I knew, I was inside of what looked like the honeymoon suite at some kind of cheap roadside motel. Massive California king-sized bed. Mirrors everywhere, including the ceiling. Heart-shaped Jacuzzi right there in the room. A bucketful of champagne chilling on the table. And me, naked and in bed with my wife Jessica...and Deb. Yes, that Deb. The one I see every day here at LAPIS while my wife is who knows how many thousands of miles away. And yes, they were naked as well and already crawling all over me. Everyone looked oiled-up and sweaty and we all looked really damn sexy, if I do say so myself.

By this point they were already making out with each other and I, of course, started joining in. They both seemed super into it and things got very...energetic. No idea what Deb is normally like, but Jessica was way more rambunctious than normal. Sex with Jessica is good, but she's a pretty reserved person and that carries over into the bedroom. Of course, we've never had a threesome and Jessica has never suggested that she's also into women, so...

Anyway, we did all the usual things. Sucking and fucking and well, it was a pretty amazing experience. It seemed to go on and on, really vividly, like far more vividly and memorable than most dreams I've had. I'll typically just recall a detail or two and then it's gone after I wake up, but this one was very linear and coherent. So it was weird in that way too.

Eventually I started cumming—this part gets a little hazy (well, it was a dream, what do you expect?) because it was like I was fucking both of them simultaneously. I mean, it felt like I was inside each of them at the same time and right as I started cumming, it started to hurt, like sharp pains, like it was catching on a piece of metal or thorns or something, which is not what you want to feel when you're right at the cusp of orgasm. So I looked down and it looked like I was sliding in and out of something black and shiny, kind of like a beetle's carapace. I remember thinking, *What the fuck is that?* and started pushing and shoving Jessica and Deb away and they started scratching and shoving me. But all the while I was still pumping away and then I came, despite all that, and then kind of blacked out or something. Like I think I actually passed out for a second (is that even possible when you're already asleep?), and then I woke up.

It took me a second to recover, then I kind of put my hand down there and realized that I was covered in semen. I brought my hand up and realized what it was. My eyes were kind of bleary—just woken up and all that—but there was a LOT [all caps in original] of it and it looked kind of weird. Like, kind of a dark grey and clumpy. Not normal. It was super, super sticky too; again, not the normal consistency, which I realized when I started trying to clean myself up in a hurry. Very weird and disgusting and clean-up took forever. Got all over the sheets, but they're all dry now (it's almost bedtime). I would swear that it smells weird in here now. Kind of like something's rotting, like decaying, wet leaves. I'm either imagining that because I got grossed out this morning or it's left over from the fungal plague the other day (thank God that crap has not returned). You use enough bleach, you can kill anything.

Oddly enough I woke up feeling pretty refreshed this morning for once. I was pleasantly surprised at that. Maybe sex dreams, even weird ones, help with that?

So yes, this was probably my first wet dream in almost twenty years. I can't say that I ever had very many. I think my first one was probably when I was thirteen, maybe fourteen, then I probably had a couple a year for the next few years, then not really any more (that I recall) after I started having sex. Lost my virginity my senior year of high school with my girlfriend at the time, then it was off to the races. Man, once you realize girls want to have sex as much as you do, it's a real eye-opener, you know?

I don't want to make too much of this dream. Let's face it, I'm away from my wife, haven't seen her in months, don't have contact with very many women at all; it's like being a Ranger all over again. I work with Deb every day and see a couple Polish women around LAPIS, but they are all pretty old and...not what I'm looking for. We've been politely discouraged from spending much of our off-hours time in the village nearby, so there's just not even a visual outlet when it comes to seeing attractive women.

I don't want to make too much of it because things are pretty stressful right now and I've been away from home (and Jessica) for a long time. I don't love that I was apparently (subconsciously?) fantasizing about Deb, but let's face it, she's the only decent-looking woman I've seen in a very long time. Also, why did the spunk look so nasty? That's definitely not something I'm comfortable talking with the doc about, so let's just hope I was imagining that.

But it is weird that this didn't happen in the Army. I was likewise without access to women, either for fucking or just to look at, most the time, and I was never much of a fan of jerking off hastily in my bunk or in the toilet. But you've got to do what you've got to do, and I guess I always had enough of an outlet with Rosie Palm and her five sisters that this just never happened.

April 20, 2004
Stare Kiejkuty, Poland
CIA Site LAPIS

Mark Romero Diary

OKAY, THIS IS becoming weird and annoying. And by weird, I really mean awful. More bad dreams. Nightmares, sort of, kind of, but not exactly. Really unsettling [underlined in original] dreams. The kind that leave you shook when you wake up and then you return to all day. It probably doesn't help matters that they're so strange that I'm now starting to dread falling asleep. I mean, what kind of fucked up dreams am I going to have when I am finally able to fall asleep? Yeah, that's not exactly conducive to a good night's sleep.

Is it possible to annoy even myself with my whining? Probably. Anyway, got to get these thoughts down.

This one was less a full dream, or at least not a full dream that I can remember like it was a movie I was watching/experiencing. This was more like a series of impressions, feelings, visual flashes that I woke up with and that then came back to me over the course of the day as I went through my day-to-day.

I'm fucking seriously fed up with this. Here's what I can remember:

I was sleeping in my quarters right here in LAPIS, and I woke up. (No, I didn't actually wake up, I don't think, maybe I did, I don't know. Anyway.) I was still in bed, just kind of laying there with my eyes half-open and not quite ready to get up when I heard footsteps in the room with me. The floors here are hardwood floors and it sounded like someone was clomping around in shoes right here. I tried to turn my head to see who the hell it was, but for some reason I just couldn't. It was like my whole body was paralyzed. The room was dark, and while I could move my eyes a little, or use my peripheral vision, I couldn't see much. Whoever it was was out of my line of sight.

So not only was it terrifying because it felt like I was paralyzed, but there was somebody walking around my room. Which there definitely shouldn't have been because I keep my door locked and no one else is authorized to be in here. Then the footsteps stopped next to me on my lefthand side, just out of my field of vision, but I could feel that there was someone standing there, just watching me. The feel of this presence [underlined in original] was overwhelming. And terrifying. Who does that? Who just stands there and watches you sleep, or watches a paralyzed person in bed? Then I could gradually see this black figure moving closer and starting to touch me. I couldn't see what this person looked like; it was too dark, and it was just black on black on black. I don't know why, but I had the distinct impression it was a female figure.

This whole time I was desperately struggling to move, to raise my arms or jump out of bed or something, anything. But I just couldn't move at all. I was paralyzed. I could feel my chest start to tighten and my lungs not fully inflating as this figure kind of crawled on top of me. I could feel more and more weight on me and it got harder and harder to breathe. I was literally suffocating to death in that dream or whatever the fuck it was.

I knew if I could only move a little or make a sound or something that it would be okay, and the spell would be broken, so I was pouring all my willpower, all my effort into moving or screaming. I had closed my eyes when this thing crawled on top of me, so I couldn't see it anymore but I could feel myself trembling inside my chest this whole time. Everything started to go dark, then I was finally able to let out this pathetic-sounding little squeaky yell. Then I was able to do it again, louder that time, and then maybe a third time. I opened my eyes and was able to move my arms and get up out of bed.

Christ, that was terrifying. I've never had something like that happen before and I hope to God I don't ever again. Seriously one of the very worst experiences of my life. Was I asleep the whole time and just dreaming about waking up, then I actually woke up?

You've got to be a little careful in a place like LAPIS, or at the CIA or the military for that matter. There are lots of things you just don't say to people, or ask people about. A bunch of taboo topics, sure, and you've also got to watch out for your reputation. It would be the end if you went around talking about your weird dreams and asking other people about their dreams and all that. You'd be the dream guy forever. Every interaction would involve someone asking you what dreams you had last night. But if you can be subtle about it and work it naturally into conversations, you can try to suss stuff like that out.

Long preamble, but I've kinda sounded out Pete and Deb and a couple other folks here at LAPIS on the whole dream situation over the last couple days and most of them—also very subtly—mentioned that they've also been having bad dreams. Now, I couldn't get into specifics with any of them, but that was my impression. No one wants to be reported as a loony, so no one would say much, and Pete blew me off completely, as expected, but it does sound like I'm not alone in this. Everyone I talked to cited stress, and we all agreed that LAPIS and our work here is very weird, etc. As Deb said, "We're in a pressure cooker here. We need to produce results, and that takes time." That's probably all it is, of course.

But I did pop into Dr. Richards' office this afternoon between sessions with the Engineer to ask him about sleep aids and all that again. He told me to take an extra melatonin, said it won't hurt, just might make me a little groggier first thing in the morning. So that's what I did. We'll see if that helps tonight.

I don't know what the fuck happened to me last night, but I am kind of dreading falling asleep tonight.

April 22, 2004
Stare Kiejkuty, Poland
CIA Site LAPIS

Mark Romero Diary

HAD A NICE walk with Michal, the Polish liaison dude, today. Well, pretty nice, but also a little weird. Okay, maybe even more than a little weird. I don't know—maybe he's just trying too hard to be friendly. That can come off kind of weird, but it wasn't really Michal who was weird, so much as the woods being weird. Creepy. I'm not a huge let's-go-hiking-in-the-woods guy. Don't get me wrong, I did plenty of that in the Army, I've probably spent waaay more time in forests than I'd ever have thought possible, but it's just not my go-to first choice for a place to hang out. So maybe it's just me.

Anyway, I've talked to Michal a few times in the past and he's always seemed like a good guy, so when I saw him downstairs this afternoon, he suggested we grab some coffee and then go for a little walk in the woods. He seemed a little jittery—too much coffee maybe?—but I was mostly done for the day, so I said sure. Besides, he's been here longer than anyone else at LAPIS because he was the guy the Poles sent over to outfit the building and grounds as a black site. He worked with a team from the CIA to get it all up to spec, then they went home (lucky bastards) and Dave and the rest arrived. I had some questions for Michal because even though I've been here for three weeks, I'm still very much trying to get the place figured out, and since he's sort of an outsider, I thought he might have some interesting things to say.

So Michal led us out through the main gate and then around the fence line to the woods outside LAPIS. This area I knew: I take this same route every morning for my run, but I have always stuck to the road; I've never veered off into the woods. He described the area as beautiful, peaceful, joyful, all that good stuff. The guy was beaming as we entered the woods. I've never been quite so enthusiastic about hiking in the woods, but okay, whatever floats your boat.

He started telling me about his wife, Magdalena, and his two little boys. It sounds like they've been married six or seven years and the boys are a few years older than Katie. He showed me pictures of the boys (not Magdalena), but I wasn't able to return the favor because, well, carrying around pictures of your loved ones is terrible fucking OPSEC, but whatever. I forget the sons' names, I always kind of zone out a little when people are telling me about their kids. I mean, it's not like I don't care about other people's kids, but... Aw hell, this is my journal and no one else is ever going to read it, so, no, I guess I don't really care about other people's kids.

Michal described his wife as having turned sour, fat, and unhappy since they got married and she'd had the two boys. Yikes. Not a happy camper. He wanted to talk about girls. I always kind of think it's weird when some guys want to talk to other guys about the women they're fucking, or cheating on their wives or whatever. It's fine, you do whatever you want, but leave me out of it. Anyway, he was in the Polish Army for a while, then he moved into their intelligence service, so I can definitely relate. Seems like he's pretty ambitious, and from what he said, his career has been off to a great start. Definitely seems like being the Polish liaison to LAPIS/CIA is a feather in his cap.

The woods themselves were pretty dense. Lots of old-growth trees; it doesn't look like these woods have been chopped down and harvested for a very long time, if ever. No real paths or anything to speak of, and lots of very thick tree-cover overhead. Just the occasional patch of sunlight, but otherwise it was pretty shady. Dark, even, in spots, like very shadowy, and you can't see very far once you get about a hundred yards in. Just too many trees and leaves and not much sun. Quiet—not many animals and no people at all, which only makes sense because there aren't many locals to begin with and there's no way the Poles are going to let random hikers get anywhere close to LAPIS. Kind of desolate, and maybe just a little creepy, though I can't put my finger on why it comes across that way. It's actually beautiful and probably a good place to just hang out and think. Kind of alluring in some ways. I think I'm going to have to come back to the woods and go for a walk again here.

There was one point when we started hearing something big, and I mean really fucking BIG [all capitals and underlined in original], crashing through the trees and underbrush in the forest. It sounded like it was pretty far away, and Michal blew me off when I asked him what the hell it was. He said it was probably just a deer or something. Yeah. Probably.

By that point I was getting the feeling of being watched. I don't know why, but sometimes you just have that feeling. While Michal was chatting away, I started looking around to see if I saw anyone, but I didn't see a soul. The feeling didn't really go away either, which I didn't love.

Also, I'll note that I'm not a squeamish guy. I'll eat pretty much anything, including snakes and bugs (Hooah!), but toward the end of the walk, Michal pointed at my arm. I looked down and there was this kind of stick insect on my forearm. I don't know what you call those things, but their body looks like it's a stick and they have these long spindly legs. I tried to brush it off but it started crawling up my arm really fast so I grabbed it. It had some kind of pincers or hooks that got stuck on the fabric of my jacket, so I had to tug a little to get it off me, then I threw it somewhere. Then I realized that my hand where I had grabbed the bug was all sliced up. What the fuck?

At that point I suggested we get the hell out of there and told him I needed to get back to LAPIS. Just a bunch of little razor cuts on my fingers and palm, each maybe half an inch to an inch long. Poured some alcohol on them and got them bandaged no problem when I got back.

What a creepy fucking place.

April 23, 2004
Stare Kiejkuty, Poland
CIA Site LAPIS

Mark Romero Diary

I'VE TALKED ABOUT how weird the Engineer is. (He's super weird.) Very disturbing guy, always grinning, showing way too many teeth, leering at Deb, or me, or someone else totally inappropriately. I mean, there's something wrong with this guy. We knew that—see psychological assessment of the guy—but yeah. Today was an especially weird one. So weird, in fact, that I don't actually know what to make of it.

Today was just Deb and me in the interrogation room. Pete wasn't there, he was sick. Shitting his guts out all day, from what I heard. Which itself is strange because I think he's been eating the same stuff that the rest of us have, but for whatever reason, he's had a bad case of food poisoning. So just us plus the Engineer in the interrogation room.

This was more of an unstructured session where we were trying to get him to open up more generally rather than having a very specific line of questioning we were trying to get answers on. Those kinds of sessions can produce long-term benefits even if they don't immediately provide a key detail you can pounce on. So we were letting the Engineer talk, and he starts asking us about ourselves. Now a little bit of that is okay, because ultimately you do want to build up a rapport with detainees, but of course you don't want to reveal anything too personal or damaging or whatever because, well, they're fucking terrorists. So he started asking me about my girlfriends and shit like that.

Then he told me how as a teenager I used to masturbate incessantly in high school and college thinking about big, soft, pillowy breasts and women in low-cut tops and stiletto heels and short skirts showing off lots of legs. And how I lost my virginity to a girl who was desperate to get laid in the back of a car when I was in high school. Which was disturbing for several reasons, not the least of which is because that more or less describes what actually happened with Denise Caroti in senior year. And yes, those are the kinds of things I used to think a lot about in high school.

Then he very slyly says, "Mr. Mark, I bet you really like it when it's a girl with nice big breasts and she's completely naked except that she's wearing high heels and she kneels down in front of you and sucks on your cock and takes the whole thing in her mouth at one time. Right, Mr. Mark? *Debbie Does Dallas!* That's your favorite, right?" Then he just sat there grinning at me.

Then he started in on Deb:

"And you, Miss Deborah, I know all about you too. You lost your virginity at fifteen, tsk tsk, to a much older boy who took advantage of you, but that's not surprising because you gave lots and lots of blowjobs, always on your knees, in cars, in school, college, the Air Force, everywhere, right? Always giving it away because you wanted boys and men to like you. Then you got pregnant in college and had an abortion. That is grave sin, Miss Deborah. Very grave sin. Life is sacred, living things should flourish and spread across the Earth. That is the natural order of things."

I was stunned. I mean, what the fuck? Who says shit like that? I mean, okay, even if there are some cultural differences, or it's just locker room talk, or whatever, okay, but that wasn't why it really bugged me. It bugged me because he was exactly right. He described my thing. Everybody's got a "thing," and that was mine. That's one of my favorite fantasies that he just described, I mean one that's guaranteed to get me off every time. I don't know about the stuff with Deb, but based on the fact that she looked like she wanted to puke or cry or both, I suspect he hit way too close to the mark on her too.

Lucky guesses?

Of course, we told him he was full of shit and asked him how he knew all this stuff, or thought he knew all these things about us. He smiled—Christ, I hate it when he smiles—and he said he was just a lucky guesser, or maybe a little bird told him.

I think Deb and I were both stunned by all this and both of us moved him along to more structured questions because we didn't want him to know how badly he had gotten to us. We ended the session fairly early after that. How do you pretend like that shit didn't just happen and start asking him about what he was doing at some point in some Pakistani city?

So Deb and I wrapped things up not too long after that and had a long talk about what the hell that was all about. The two theories are (1) he's obviously just fucking with us and did a classic cold reading of us and came up with generic sounding stuff that would seem to fit the truth and (2) there's a breach and someone has been leaking personnel files, or he's been able to overhear conversations he shouldn't have, or something like that. The second is obviously serious, but unlikely, and would warrant immediate action if we thought that was the case. If the first is true, then we just need to reorient our interrogations with him and ensure he understands we're not going to tolerate that kind of bullshit anymore.

So I took one for the team and went and talked with Dave about it. I tried to be a little coy because I didn't want to have to tell Dave exactly what was said, so I told him it seemed like he referenced some personal information from our backgrounds, etc. Dave had the audacity, the fucking audacity, to say, "You're a fucking amateur. This asshole is playing you and playing you hard. There's no fucking breach. No one handed this guy a copy of your personnel files and he studied them in that little box we keep him in before using that information against you. Are you fucking kidding me? You guys need some adult supervision over there. Get your head in the game, Romero."

You know what I hate most about that? Well, there are a lot of things I hate about that. His tone, his demeanor when he deigns to speak to me, the fact that if he was doing his job right, we would actually have some "adult supervision." All of that and a lot more. But I also hate that he's right. Sometimes it takes an asshole to point out the obvious to you. Of course the whole thing was just bullshit and the Engineer knows how to play people and get under their skins. I mean, we know that AQ trains its people for counter-interrogation, and obviously the Engineer is using that training against us. It's nothing more than that.

Dave's right, almost certainly right, and that's why it's so infuriating. It's uncomfortable when the Engineer pulls this shit on us, and that's why he does it. It's just that he was so on the nose. I mean, if it's all based on guesswork and reading people and bullshitting, well, he got really close to the truth. I mean, I didn't go into exhaustive detail with Deb when we talked afterward, but she felt the same way. I know that he got very close on my history, and it sounded like the same for her. Christ.

April 24, 2004
Stare Kiejkuty, Poland
CIA Site LAPIS

Mark Romero Diary

I DID NOT like how today's session with the Engineer went. At all. Yesterday he was talking all kinds of shit about Deb's and my past histories with sex and guessing all kinds of things exactly on the nose. Okay, that was weird and uncomfortable, but also entirely possible to have done through a bunch of guesswork, studying us at the same time we've been studying him—which he undoubtedly has been—and the use of classic cold reading techniques the way a lot of con artists do along with those assholes that pretend they can commune with your dead relatives and all that.

Today's session though...not so much.

The Engineer started telling us about this dream he had, a "very special dream." One from the Black Mother. Whatever. Anyway, he tells us that she knows all of us and knows all about our lives and secrets in our hearts and all this kind of nonsense. So I asked him for an example.

Without missing a beat, he said, "Your boss, Dave Andrews, is an alcoholic who is barely able to keep it together, he's going through a really nasty divorce, his wife has been cheating on him for years, and he's impotent." I looked over at Deb and we were both just aghast. I don't know the full story, but I know he's right about the drinking. But as far as I know, he's never even interacted with Dave. Then it occurred to me that he used Dave's last name. There's no way he could have known that, so I asked him about it and he said that it was in his dream.

He said that one of the security guys likes little girls in frilly dresses. He said that Dr. Richards likes to be spanked by his girlfriend who he calls "Mommy." He said that one of the other CIA guys here is so bad with women that he now obsesses about women laughing at him and turning him down for dates when he masturbates. He said that one of the other security guys forced himself on dozens of women in college and afterward and was way more of a monster than anyone we think we're fighting against. I mean, what the actual fuck???

Then he said, "You guys think that the USA and the CIA are the heroes of the world, but you're all just sad and pathetic and contemptible. I am telling you about what your heroes are like when they're behind closed doors. These are your stalwarts of America. They are dogs. Pigs. Dog shit." Then he just sat there like he dared us to do something about it.

I assume this stuff is a product of his insanely fertile imagination and he's saying this shit to fuck with us, but it was really bizarre and uncomfortable.

At that point the whole thing was just too weird and Deb went to get security to take him back to his cell and put him in a stress position for the rest of the day. We had a long talk about what the hell just happened after he left. I mean, on the face of it, it's almost certainly all bullshit. Almost none of what he said can be verified or corroborated in any way, so it's probably just him shit talking. There's a tiny piece of me that wonders if we've got a leak or something inside LAPIS and someone is telling him things he's not supposed to know about, or maybe he just overheard people talking and has patched that together with lies. I don't know.

So we decided on an impromptu waterboarding session. Deb and I went to his cell with a couple of the security guys and I told him that he was going to be waterboarded. He just laughed and laughed and laughed. He was still wheezing with laughter as the security guys dragged him to the other room we usually use for waterboarding and got him strapped in. Once the water started flowing, the laughter stopped, but even so, I'm not going to lie, I was pretty freaked out by the whole thing. After we finished up with him and the Engineer was taken back to his cell, I asked Deb, "Who the fuck is running this thing? Us or him?"

She did not have a good answer to that. The EITs are not having much of an effect on him. What the hell is left?

April 25, 2004
Stare Kiejkuty, Poland
CIA Site LAPIS

Surveillance Camera NV401-17 (LAPIS Staff Breakroom) Recording Transcript
Attendees: Mark ROMERO (CTC/RDG liaison, CIA), Deborah SULLIVAN (interrogator, contractor)

[ROMERO and SULLIVAN enter room at 8:43 PM (local), sit down, and start eating and drinking.]

[begin excerpt]

ROMERO: "How did we end up here? I mean here at LAPIS, interrogating this freak and trying to pry the truth out of him and...well, not torturing him, but something close to that. What are we doing here?"

SULLIVAN: "Jesus, Mark. That's a deep question. Are you having second thoughts or something?"

ROMERO: "No, that's not what I mean... It's just that... Oh, I don't know. It seems pointless sometimes."

SULLIVAN: "You're in a weird mood tonight."

ROMERO: "Probably. Is it worth it, what we're doing here?"

SULLIVAN: "Yeah, of course it's worth it."

ROMERO: "In what way? What have we learned that's meaningful yet? What's the point of it all?"

SULLIVAN: "Well...we haven't had a major breakthrough yet. That's your frustration. You're hoping he's going to spill his guts and volunteer to tell us everything we want to know at some point. That might happen someday. Hell, it could happen tomorrow. But it might never happen. And that's okay. We're still picking up little pieces, here and there, and assembling them. We've learned about his movements and some of his contacts. We know some phone numbers that he's contacted, and we might get a hit on one of those at some point. We're waiting for them to make a mistake, and then we're going to pounce. They're going to use one of those phones someday and we'll get a location for them, and we'll send some knuckle-draggers like you in there and they'll vacuum up a bunch of those guys hiding out in a safehouse somewhere. It's only a matter of time."

ROMERO: "That's the ideal scenario. The best case we can probably hope for."

SULLIVAN: "Possibly. That may have to be enough. It's not like we don't find new things to talk to him about. We go back and get him to fill in the blanks all the time, get him to revisit things we've talked about before, cross-check that against his previous statements and stuff that other assholes like him tell us at other places like LAPIS, or stuff we intercept, or whatever. It's all grist for the mill."

ROMERO: "Grist for the mill. Jesus. And we're just grinding it up, day after day, hoping we can bake some bread one day."

SULLIVAN: [agitated] "Look, do you want another 9/11? You know what this guy worked on. I mean, I don't know if he was head of their biological weapons program or not, but he was involved, okay? We know that. He's admitted it. If we hadn't snatched this guy, they could have kept developing new weapons, and eventually something would get through. You want an entire city hosed down with anthrax or something worse?"

ROMERO: "No, no, of course not."

SULLIVAN: "They still haven't caught whoever was sending those anthrax letters, remember? I mean, that was some domestic terrorist or lunatic probably, not AQ, but think about what that would do in a subway system or a mall or something. Just keep reminding yourself what we're trying to stop here."

ROMERO: "Yeah, I get it…"

SULLIVAN: "You know what I think?"

ROMERO: "What? And don't tell me I'm full of shit."

SULLIVAN: "No. I think that the Engineer is really starting to get to you. I think all the freaky shit he says, the really personal stuff he says about you, and me, and the other people at LAPIS is starting to get to you. He's been trying to get under our skin and it's working on you. It's working. And you know what else I think?"

ROMERO: "No, but I'm sure you're going to tell me."

SULLIVAN: "I think you should take a couple days off. Switch places with Pete. We'll get him to come back and help with the Engineer, and you start talking to the other detainees. It'll be a fresh start, they won't be needling you the way the Engineer is, and when you're ready in a week or whatever, you can come back to the Engineer with a new perspective."

ROMERO: [heated] "No way, no fucking way. This is my baby and I'm not stepping away from it. Nope."

SULLIVAN: "Okay, okay, have it your way. I'm just trying to help."

ROMERO: "Okay. No dice though."

SULLIVAN: "All right."

[end excerpt]

May 1, 2004
Stare Kiejkuty, Poland
CIA Site LAPIS

Mark Romero Diary

I THINK I made a major mistake. Like, one of the worst things I could have possibly done.

Here's what happened last night:

It started out like a normal Friday night. We were all ready to blow off some steam and were set to drink some beers and maybe watch a movie in the breakroom or something. I showed up with some beers and Pete and a couple other guys were there and we had a low-key kind of evening. I was there an hour or two and we were watching Stallone in *Cobra* because who doesn't like watching Stallone gunning down murder cultists?

At some point in the middle of the movie, Deb came in and joined us. Okay, that was fine. Then after the movie, Pete and the other guys started talking about going out to a bar in town. Pete was already starting to get shit-faced and I did NOT [all capitals in original] want to deal with that, so I turned them down and so did Deb for whatever reason. They took off.

Deb said she had a bottle of the good stuff squirreled away in her quarters. She asked me if I wanted some, so she went to get it. She brought it back, and yes, it was good Scotch, though I'm no connoisseur. We were listening to music and just hanging out on the couch in the breakroom and it just happened. She scooted over right next to me and signaled very clearly that she wanted to kiss and I just did it without even thinking very much. That's how it happens. You just do something without thinking through the implications very much, or at all, and you've just changed your whole fucking life.

So then we started making out on the couch because it was quiet and no one else was around by that point and then she said, "Let's go to your room." Of course I knew what that meant, but at the time, right at that very second, that sounded like the perfect and obvious thing to do. So I went back to my room, left the door unlocked, and she joined me there a couple minutes later. Just slipped right in, locked the door behind her, and started taking her shirt off.

Then, well, we were on the bed fucking, me on top. It was not even all that great to be honest. Just very mechanical. Unfeeling. I assume she came. I think she did. It was hard to tell because by that point we had both been drinking a lot. I really kind of zoned out in the middle of it all. I remember thinking that everything felt really out of control and I didn't want to be there. I remember thinking, *I don't want to do this anymore*, and then, well, I'm not exactly sure what happened next. It felt like I was slipping out of my body and floating up and out of my back. I was just kind of floating in the air above my body, watching it fuck Deb. I couldn't control my body, or what it was doing anymore, and so I just kind of floated there for a while as I (my body) finished up. It seemed like it took forever, way longer than I wanted. Then I just kind of snapped back into my body. Honestly, it was kind of terrifying because (1) nothing like that had ever happened to me before, so what the fuck was going on? and (2) it felt really out of control. Like, if you're not in control of your own body, then who (what) is?

When we were done, we talked a little, but not much. Deb fell asleep almost immediately. Before she did, she was really slurring her words, which makes me think that she probably had more to drink than I realized. She was pretty out of it.

So then when I woke up—late for me, and I felt like ass and kind of hungover, though not exactly, if you know what I mean—she was already gone. I never heard her leave. That was a good thing. It definitely saved an awkward conversation and her having to do the walk of shame out of my quarters first thing in the morning. I skipped my run this morning.

In hindsight, of course, there's no way I should have agreed to start drinking with her, and once I decided to do that, the rest was pretty much inevitable. I have lots and lots of regrets about the whole thing. I am really disgusted with myself on this one. What would my daughter think of me if she knew I had done this? The thought of it makes me want to puke. I have literally gone through the day with my stomach acid churning and making me feel like I'm going to hurl at any moment.

But you know, there was something that just came over me when Deb came into my room, and as she was taking her shirt off, the lust factor was just dialed up to 11 for me. It was all I could do to hold back and not tear the rest of her clothes off and just throw her on the bed and fuck her brains out in that moment. You want to know the absolute worst part of it all? As disgusted with myself as I am right now, and as much I wish I had made a different choice, there's some part of me that just wants to fuck her again.

May 2, 2004
Stare Kiejkuty, Poland
CIA Site LAPIS

Mark Romero Diary

SO I HAD the biggest fucking fight of my marriage with Jessica today. It is probably not a coincidence that Deb and I fucked two days ago.

It didn't start off that way. I wanted to tell her how stressful everything has been for me lately. I'm not a whiner. Well, maybe I whine in this stupid journal, but not to her, or anyone else for that matter. But I just wanted her to listen to me whine for a minute. I didn't need her to fix anything for me, not that she could anyway, I just wanted her to listen and tell me that sucked and that she was sorry to hear about all the crap I have been dealing with or whatever. Just the basics. The bare fucking basics you should be able to expect from your wife.

But she interrupted me with a litany of how shitty her life is and how many things are going wrong with the house, the car, her job, the kids, and then she blows up that she didn't sign up to be a single mother and get stuck dealing with all the shit on her own without me there pulling my weight. She was talking faster and faster and kind of scream-crying in a way that I have literally never heard her do before the entire time I've known her. She said, to top it all off, that she and Katie have both been having sleep problems and weird dreams and nightmares and that she's been operating on two hours of sleep a night for the last week.

That set me over the edge. I was going to tell her how fucked up my own sleep has been lately, but never mind about that now. I just fucking blew up at her. I told her to shut the fuck up and that I had some things to unload on her just like she unloaded on me. I couldn't help myself. I gave her the long laundry list of all (okay, most) of the stuff that has been stressing me out and what my life is like and why I just needed her to listen and support me and be there for me without adding to all my shit right now.

She was quiet, and after a minute or two I told her I needed to go and that we'd pick this up another time and hung up.

Jessica has always criticized me for being too willing to give up on people, either cut them out of my life completely once there's a problem in the relationship, or just mentally set them aside when I'm doing other things and don't have time to maintain the relationship. Maybe I come back to it, maybe not. She's said that it makes people feel like shit when I do that, which I get, and that it means I'm focused on myself and what's going on in my life rather than on friends and family. Out of sight means out of mind to me, she says. I can't say that she's wrong. I've always been really focused on my achievements and my goals rather than other people. In school it was sports and keeping my grades up, then it was the Army and becoming a Ranger, and focusing on the mission when I was an officer, and now it's the work I'm doing at the CIA. That's not to say that I don't love her, or my daughter, or my family, or my friends, but...I think about them when I'm with them, and not much, if I'm being really honest here—and why not be honest in your own journal (please let's not call this a diary, I'm not a 12-year-old girl)—when I'm focused on other things and they're not around. And right now, my work and what we're trying to do here at LAPIS is what I'm focused on.

The Engineer might very well hold the key to the entire AQ biological weapons program. He knows exactly what their capabilities are—he helped assemble those capabilities, after all—and he knows everyone involved. He also knows what they're planning to do with them. And most importantly, he knows if planning is already underway for a BW attack on the homeland. For all we know, there's one or more operational cells already activated inside the United States, ready to hose down a city or an airport or something else. Right now. As we speak. That seems pretty fucking important to me right now, Jessica. Really fucking important. So I'm sorry if I can't be drawn into the drama about the tax bill or car problems or you having to deal with daycare and all of that bullshit. I am literally trying to save American lives, Jessica. Whole fucking cities. Bitch.

The problem is that I can't discuss the 800-pound gorilla in the room with her, or anyone else, of course. That's really [underlined three times in original] been bothering me. I've got to keep that to myself. Got to give it some time to settle down. I am never getting together with Deb again. NEVER (all capitals and underlined three times in original]. It's weird because Deb hasn't made things strange at all since then. Hasn't even mentioned it or alluded to it in any way. Still. It's awkward as hell for me. Looking forward to being done here at LAPIS, not that the end is in sight or anything.

May 4, 2004
Stare Kiejkuty, Poland
CIA Site LAPIS

Mark Romero Diary

I KNEW TODAY'S interrogation session with the Engineer was going to be bad when he began with, "I had another dream last night."

One problem is that, as of a couple days ago, we have a new guest at LAPIS: some low-level AQ schmuck. I can't imagine that we'll get much out of this guy, from what I've seen. But the issue is that Pete is taking the lead on interrogating the new guy, which means that it's just Deb and me with the Engineer for almost all of our sessions these days. That is a little uncomfortable, given...things.

Anyway, so today it was going along normally with us really just wanting to zero in on some of the Engineer's movements around Pakistan and Afghanistan in 2002 and 2003. He fucking sidetracked us by talking about his stupid dream and how in his dream Deb and I were having sex. The whole time he had his patented shit-eating grin, which is creepy as hell if I haven't mentioned that previously. He talked about how in his dream we were hanging out together and were just overcome by heat and lust and had to enjoy each other's bodies and give each other pleasure and I needed to spread my seed and be fertile. He said that his mother of darkness was very pleased and that we were following her wishes by fucking and making a baby.

We both promptly denied all of it and said that he was full of shit and was going to just shut up and answer our questions. Deb was pretty upset and slapped him pretty fucking hard a couple times, and he did shut up about it, though he was still smiling. He must have cut the inside of his mouth when she slapped him because a string of blood started trickling out of his mouth and he just left it there on his chin during the rest of the interrogation session.

After we wrapped things up, we talked about it a little and agreed that once again he was just trying to fuck with us. I messed up at one point and said something about a "lucky guess." It was one of those moments where as soon as you say something, you know you fucked up and it was the wrong thing to say. Deb just shook her head and said something like, "Yeah, he thought he was making a lucky guess, but he got it wrong and did it just to fuck with our heads." And her finger was pointing up just a little so only I could notice it, toward the fucking camera in the upper corner of the room.

Fuck fuck fuck fuck fuck

May 6, 2004
Stare Kiejkuty, Poland
CIA Site LAPIS

Mark Romero Diary

AFTER ANOTHER NOT-very-useful interrogation session today, I decided to go for a walk in the woods at the end of the day and clear my head. It seemed like a good idea at the time. Quiet, peaceful, a place I could be alone and try to figure things out. We can all use a little time to ourselves to try to figure it the fuck out, right? Ah, LAPIS, you never disappoint.

It was probably around 1700 when I headed out, but I wasn't worried because sunset wasn't until 2000 or so (it's not even summer, but with the northerly latitude, it comes pretty late here). Plenty of time. I wasn't in the mood for an extra run, I just wanted to go for a walk/hike. Someplace quiet. So naturally I headed out into the woods, planning to do something similar to what Michal and I did, so I just started walking, making sure I had a clear sense of where I was in relation to LAPIS. No interest in going too far and getting lost in the woods.

So while I was walking, everything was going fine, then I thought I saw something kind of "off" on my left in the distance, like movement. Maybe a person, maybe an animal. I kept my eye on it but thought I saw it going behind a tree and then not reemerging. It had looked like maybe either a person wearing dark clothes or maybe a small-ish brown or black bear. (What color are bears in Poland?) But then I didn't see it again. I stopped for a second and called out, but no one said anything and I didn't see it again, so I kept walking, occasionally looking back in that direction. Nothing.

Kept walking for a ways, then thought I saw something again over on my right. Same thing? A second person? Bear? Then nothing. Just disappeared. Nothing. Kept walking. Then I heard something crashing through the trees/undergrowth behind me, but I didn't see anything.

At that point I was regretting not being armed, but I mean, I just went for a walk in the woods. There are a couple dozen security dudes with guns not very far away guarding a black site. I'm a big tough guy. Why the fuck would I need a gun around here? The Poles picked this area because it's remote and the locals know not to fuck with us.

So I kept walking but keeping my head on a swivel because let's face it—this all could have been strictly my imagination. For all I knew, there was maybe a deer or a young bear or just some fucking squirrels in the woods with me and that was what I was reacting too. Not good when a Ranger gets spooked by some wildlife, right? That's how badly stressed I am these days. I wasn't about to go back to LAPIS and report that Bambi had scared the big bad Ranger and CIA paramilitary officer so I ran home to mommy to hide behind some guys with guns.

Anyway, I kept going and didn't see anything further for a while, so I thought that everything was fine and I had just gotten spooked for no reason at all. Then, on a small rise of maybe 4 or 5 feet in height, maybe thirty yards ahead, I saw what looked like some kind of black things scuttling in the underbrush and behind the trees, things refusing to crawl into the light, never giving me a chance to see them fully before they hid or disappeared again. I don't know what they were. They looked like maybe black cats or dogs or something, but they didn't exactly move like cats or dogs, if you know what I mean. So I stopped abruptly—no interest in tangling with some weird animals if I don't have to—then I heard some big branches cracking behind me, along with the sounds of footsteps in the leaves right behind me, like a few feet away. I spun around and for a split second I could have sworn—literally, I swear to God—I saw some kind of huge all-black figures, not human, but vaguely humanoid, all around me in a semi-circle and starting to close in on me. My head started to swim, like it felt really fuzzy, like a sudden onset worst-hangover-of-your-life kind of thing. My adrenaline should have been pumping and I should have been in full-on fight-or-flight mode, but I just felt really lethargic and sleepy and like I couldn't even bring my hands and arms up, much less engage my legs to start backing me off.

Then I just blacked out. One minute I thought that there were people or things or black shadows or something closing in all around me, whatever they were, and then *bam*, the world just disappeared. One minute I was terrified out of my mind and the adrenaline was starting to pump, and then the next minute I was just lying on the ground of the forest and night had fallen. No memory in between those two points. I just woke up. I wasn't groggy at all, wasn't in pain, didn't feel anything weird. I stood up quickly, my head maybe starting to spin a little, and I checked myself out. No injuries, didn't feel sore or weird. Perfectly fine.

It was weird; my watch had stopped working at some point today, so I don't know exactly how long I was out there. When I stumbled back to LAPIS it was about 2200, so I guess I was outside for the better part of five hours. I guess the battery died or something. It said it was 11:11 when the hands stopped moving, but I know it was working this afternoon after that, so no idea. It wasn't an expensive watch, so no big deal there, but I guess I'll have to pick up a new one the next time I go into town.

What the fuck was that? Am I hallucinating? Was it some kind of waking dream, or sleep-walking? Do I have some kind of medical problem? It would have to be serious, like a fucking brain tumor pressing on my skull, for something like this, right? I mean, if there's some kind of brain problem, it's got to be serious. I don't know. I should get checked out, but it's not like I can do that at LAPIS. If I report it, then just to be on the safe side they'll want to fly me home, and then I'm completely out of the game. They'd never send me back here. I'd never see the Engineer again. The whole case would be assigned to someone else and they'd have the fucking breakthrough the next day and be a world hero. I'd be back home in the 'burbs getting MRIs.

Fuck that.

I was talking with Bill, one of the security guys, when I finally got back to LAPIS. (Which turned out to be a quick 10-minute walk back from where I woke up, which makes me think I had also gotten twisted around and lost and was walking in a circle.) Bill's a good guy, seems like he's pretty high-speed low-drag, and friendlier than most of the assholes around here. I didn't mention that I had just been lost in the woods and had...blacked out or something. How would that sound? I'd look like a fucking dipshit. It would become a whole thing. I'd have to get checked out by the doctor and maybe get some kind of medical issue or seizure or something listed in my medical records. God only knows what that would look like. No interest in a desk job forever.

So I asked Bill if he ever goes out into the forest outside the grounds, for a hike or just to see what's around or whatever. Bill gave me the weirdest look, one of those looks you give the homeless guy pulling his pants down to take a shit on the bus. "Are you fucking kidding me? No way would I go into those woods. I walked around there once when I first got here and had a really intense feeling like I was being watched the whole time. I didn't see anybody back there, but that whole place creeped me the fuck out."

I kind of mumbled something to the effect of, "I know what you mean," and wandered off. I will admit that I feel kind of weird and gross right now about the whole place. LAPIS, the woods, I don't know. Kind of faintly nauseous and...I don't know. Kind of violated.

I don't know what I mean by that exactly. Like, not physically violated, like I've been raped or something, but I don't know. Just kind of strange. Off. Unsettled. Maybe even a little scared, for no particular reason at all, like my adrenaline is pumping at a low level and my fight-or-flight impulse is being triggered. I'm definitely a "fight" guy rather than a "flight" guy, but it's almost like there's this little voice in the back of my head saying, "Get the fuck out of here, go home, run." Just spooked a little today, I guess.

Probably nothing a good night's sleep wouldn't fix.

May 7, 2004
Stare Kiejkuty, Poland
CIA Site LAPIS

Mark Romero Diary

YOU KNOW, IF you had told me that I'd be writing about my dreams in this journal when I started, I would have laughed at how insane that sounded. But now, after my dream last night, I think I need to stop apologizing for including stuff like this. This is my life now, I have to express this, and it's not like there's anyone else to talk with. The doctor is worthless, and I'm now avoiding Deb outside of the interrogation sessions because of, well, you know. Pete's an okay guy, but this is definitely NOT [all caps in original] the kind of thing guys talk about with other guys.

I didn't have a wet dream for probably twenty years and now I have two in a three-week span? What is going on with me?

In this one, I was here in my room at LAPIS. Because of course I was. Where else would I be? I was sitting on my bed, then I felt...some kind of presence in the room nearby, so I stood up. There she was, right in front of me. I say "she" because I have no idea who this was, or who it represented in the dream or whatever. Some woman dressed in sort of long black raggedy robes with long black curly hair hanging down over her face. I couldn't even see her face, though the whole room was also pretty dim. There was like a really dim, kind of diffuse lighting in the room. For whatever reason, the overhead light and lamps that I have were not on.

Anyway, as soon as I saw this woman I became incredibly aroused. Like, mindlessly, animalistically aroused, and walked a couple steps over to her and stood in front of her. I stood there for I don't know how long, her with her head kind of bowed. I still couldn't see her face or much of anything about her, but then she kind of raised her arms out and to the sides, like for a big embrace, and I felt myself rushing toward her, getting swept up by her arms or wings or ropy tentacles or whatever her limbs were, and being pressed into her, really hard. Like inescapably hard. There's no way I could have freed myself had I even wanted to, not that I did of course.

At some point in all this I started thrusting into her with my...groin. I don't even know if I had any clothes on, or if she was naked or what. Dreams don't have to make a lot of sense, right? I remember the very distinct feeling of fucking her. It felt warm and soft and very, very wet and slippery. Kind of like what I imagine fucking a warm...pool of molasses would feel like. It felt incredible. I remember feeling like, at the same time that I was fucking her and thrusting into whatever it was that I was thrusting into, she was also thrusting into me. It didn't hurt, and I don't even know what she was thrusting into—was it my ass? My abdomen? I don't know. It just felt like there was this rhythmic thrusting into me, filling me up. I felt the pressure from it—it definitely felt like something was inside me—but it didn't hurt, it was actually kind of a pleasant sensation of being filled up and feeling kind of contented at that. Now don't get me wrong, that's not my thing. Never been with a dude, never fantasized about it, never wanted to try it, and obviously I still don't. So this was completely outside of my experience and comfort zone and I'm probably not even explaining the sensation especially well. If I had to explain it somehow, it was kind of like what I would imagine a woman being fucked and impregnated would feel like.

But if so, what was this woman fucking me with?

At some point in all of this, I became aware of smells. Like, powerful scents, not just a faint whiff of something. It took me a while because it felt so good and obviously my mind was on other things. It...she didn't smell terrible, but kind of like damp, wet leaves, or decaying vegetation in a soggy forest. The longer I was in it, the more I could sort of discern some rot underneath all that, like rot being masked by something sweet. I was kind of blissed out, and I guess continuing to pump away, but at some point I opened my eyes and tried to focus on what was right in front of me. It was still dark, and I could tell she, or whatever was covering her, was black, but then as I looked closer it was like I could see that she had flesh or skin poking through some tears in her robes or whatever was covering her. It was like seeing inside the rotting crevices of her flesh, seeing *life* [underlined in original]. Red, wet, teeming life, ready to burst forth from under the soft black of her decayed outer layers of meat.

At that point she started raking me across the shoulders and back and down my sides, and it felt like I was in the grip of something like a gigantic octopus with long tentacles or tendrils of seaweed draped over my back, but also not letting me go. I mean, it's not like I wanted her to, I was still thrusting and I could hear myself making grunting animal noises the whole time, but I also knew there was no way I could pull free. Then she pulled me closer to her, like pulled me right into her bosom, pressed up against her, and I could feel the pressure from whatever she was thrusting or burrowing inside me increasing. It wasn't painful exactly, but it felt like I was a balloon getting blown up, being stretched tighter and tauter.

This whole time she was completely silent. I was making plenty of sounds, but I didn't hear her say anything or even make any kind of noise. That was a little unnerving; it was like a cone of silence had descended on us, completely blocking out the outside world and every other sound except for whatever noises I was making.

I could feel the tension building up inside me and knew that I was close to cumming, and I could feel her also starting to almost tremble and it felt like her thrusting inside me was building up as well, then I just came. It burst out of me, basically no warning at all, and it felt like a gushing fire hose. At the same time, it felt like my entire dick was filled with fire, and I remember throwing back my head and just howling like a banshee. It went on and on forever and I think I blacked out. I can't say that the actual orgasm was even pleasurable. It was painful and terrifying, if anything, though while I was fucking her—or whatever it was we were doing—it felt good. But the actual culmination? Christ.

So then I woke up on my bed, naked, wet, gross. No one else in the room with me, of course. I'm not even fully sure if I actually awoke, or just dreamed I had awoken. I only stayed awake for a minute, then fell back to sleep, then woke back up again when my alarm clock went off at the usual time this morning.

It was weird because when I took a shower this morning I realized that either when I was washing up or while I was asleep I must have cut myself a little with my fingernails or something because there was some blood washing down the drain. Never what you want to see when you're taking a shower. Then I realized that my shoulders were both kind of tender to the touch. When I checked it out in the mirror, sure enough, there were some scratch marks.

Why am I scratching myself in the night? What does all this mean? I don't know; I mean, I have a lot of bizarre shit that's been happening to me lately. Things here at LAPIS have been weird, and obviously I'm pretty isolated here, and under a lot of stress to produce results, and then there's the giant elephant in the room—I fucked Deb and am having marital problems. I guess it's all that shit poured into a big kettle and then put on boil.

Having said that...well...I'm pretty fucking worried. Am I going to crack up? I've seen other guys break before in the military and it's fucking ugly. Leads to washing out, and I don't want that to happen. I've worked too hard to get where I am, sacrificed too much (my family? a normal life?), and the work itself is too important. I am uniquely qualified for this work, this is where I need to be. But these dreams aren't normal. What happened to me in the forest, whatever the fuck that was, that's not normal. The Engineer and LAPIS and this whole fucked up situation, none of this is normal.

I've got to say, I am more and more disgusted with myself these days. Given the content of my dreams lately, what exactly is rolling around in my subconscious? Do I have a guilty conscience? It can't be all stress. I can't just chalk it up to weird stress dreams, right? I mean, is this the stuff that gets me off these days?

Gross.

May 9, 2004
Stare Kiejkuty, Poland
CIA Site LAPIS

Interrogation Transcript: Omar Abu KHATTAB
Interrogation Session 09MAY04-1
Attendees: Omar Abu KHATTAB (detainee), Peter DABROWSKY (lead interrogator, contractor), Deborah SULLIVAN (interrogator, contractor), Mark ROMERO (CTC/RDG liaison, CIA)

[excerpt]

KHATTAB is secured and seated across the table from DABROWSKY, SULLIVAN, and ROMERO in Interrogation Room 3.

ROMERO: "You're not looking so hot today, KHATTAB."

KHATTAB: "Being tortured and waterboarded and abused the way that you do to me, I am not surprised."

DABROWSKY: "All you have to do is be cooperative. Answer our questions, volunteer information, give us what we want to know, and we will treat you very differently."

KHATTAB: "Okay. I will do that. I must also tell you about my dream from last night because it contains a very important message for you all."

SULLIVAN: "If you must, then we're moving on to other topics."

KHATTAB: "I want to tell you all about my dream last night, a very powerful dream. They are all powerful when they come from omm Al shayateen, but this is one that I understood very clearly from her. She communicated her message to me loud and clear and I will obey, as I strive to obey her in all things."

ROMERO: [sigh] "Okay, go ahead, you might as well tell us. Briefly."

KHATTAB: "Okay, I tell you. She appeared to me beautiful, very beautiful as she always is, and took me into her arms and showed me how much she loves me."

SULLIVAN: "Right, yes, and then?"

KHATTAB: "Then she tell me, 'Omar, my beloved, I have something very important to tell you. Something you must understand very clearly. I want you to reveal me to the Americans. Everything about me. They need to know all about me. They cannot harm me, or you, for you are my loyal servant, and nothing they do matters. Nothing they do can stop my plans from happening. They will see all my revealed glory and beauty, and they will live long enough to see all my plans happen. My will is going to be done. Everything I and you and my other servants have been working so hard to achieve will take place. The Earth will be transformed according to my will. Each person, each animal, each plant on Earth will be transformed, will take on new forms and be enlisted in my service. Everyone and everything will be born anew and the world will be remade in my image. The world will become mine, and part of me. I and the world will be one. Forever and ever. No one can stop this from happening. So. You understand?"

SULLIVAN: "Um, sure, I guess so."

KHATTAB: "It is very important that you understand. I want you to know all about her. *She* wants you to know all about her. She does not want to be your enemy, she wants you to know and love her, just like I do. She doesn't want to be your enemy. *I* don't want to be your enemy. It's not too late for you to come to love her like I do. All she wants is to create life. Create beautiful life everywhere, make the whole world become part of her. To make the whole world part of her kingdom."

ROMERO: "KHATTAB, it sounds like you want to tell us a lot about omm Al shayateen or omm Al thalma or whatever. You've told us about her before. That's great that you want to tell us about her and her plans and all that, but that's not what we're interested in hearing about. We want to know about Al Qaeda and BIN LADIN and ZAWAHIRI. *That's* what we want to know about. You know that. You know that's what we care about. We want to know about the biological weapons work that you did for Al Qaeda."

KHATTAB: "You don't understand, Mr. Mark. I am trying to tell you about the important stuff. The stuff that you need to know about. You're asking about the unimportant stuff. The Al Qaeda stuff doesn't matter."

DABROWSKY: "Well, see, Omar, that's where we've got to differ with you. I mean, sure, it's great that you want to talk with us about your religious beliefs and all that, and we'll listen. We'll hear you out as much as you want. You can tell us all about that stuff. But later. What we need to know is about what you were working on with Al Qaeda. What you guys were planning to do with the biological agents you were working on. Understand? We know you guys were planning a bunch of attacks using biological weapons and, you're going to have to pardon me, but [angry, almost screaming] THAT'S REALLY FUCKING IMPORTANT BECAUSE ENTIRE CITIES FULL OF PEOPLE COULD DIE! [calmer] So that's why we're going to give you some time to tell us about the fucking Mother and all that, but that's right after you tell us about the fucking biological weapons. Understand?"

SULLIVAN: "Let's take a little break. Okay?"

ROMERO nods then exits the room briefly and returns with two security personnel, Earl FOSTER and Nelson WERTHER. FOSTER and WERTHER exit the room with KHATTAB. ROMERO, DABROWSKY, and SULLIVAN remain seated and begin speaking shortly after the door closes.

SULLIVAN: "You're a little worked up there, Pete. You okay, buddy?"

DABROWSKY: "Sure. Sure I am. You know, I just get pretty tired of the bullshit, you know what I mean? We've been working with the Engineer and these other assholes for fucking months, years in some cases, and it's all one layer of bullshit on top of another. Bullshit, bullshit, bullshit. All these guys are the same. They want to find some topic that's safe to talk about so they can fill the time, waste our time, with something that's immaterial so they can avoid answering the tough questions and tell us what we really want to know. Religious stuff is always a good topic. They can spend hours and hours talking in circles about that stuff. There's a limitless well of religious crap they can feed us and none of it means *anything*."

ROMERO: "Well, and this guy is kookier than most. I mean, the religious stuff he's spewing is not exactly standard Islamic doctrine. I don't even know where he gets this stuff."

DABROWSKY: "Exactly. He could be making it all up as he goes along, for all I know. I've never heard of any of this stuff. This is beyond the counter-interrogation training they give these guys. He's either crazier than a shithouse rat or he's a master bullshit artist."

SULLIVAN: "Or both."

DABROWSKY: [nodding] "Or both. Exactly."

ROMERO: "So, about all the weird shit that KHATTAB brings up. All these crazy dreams he wants to tell us about and whatnot. I mean, sure, he's undoubtedly a liar, and he's probably crazy. I mean, we've seen the psychological workup on this guy. But is he delusional? Does he believe the stuff he's telling us? Does he think he's telling us the truth? Or is he making it all up, like you said, Pete?"

DABROWSKY: "Well, I guess we really need to start drilling down into that stuff. We can start trying to assess the consistency of this stuff, come at it from different angles, see if he repeats the same things, what new details he adds over time, and all that."

SULLIVAN: "We should probably do that, but...I don't want us to get derailed spending too much time figuring out the depths of his religious delusions when what we really need is to keep hammering away at the important stuff."

DABROWSKY: "I hear you, but... I don't know. [sighs] It feels like we've only just scratched the surface with this guy in all these weeks. It doesn't feel like we've gotten fully inside his head yet. It feels like we need to go deeper to really understand him so we can make him crack."

SULLIVAN: "Yeah..."

ROMERO: "Pete, I remember you were the one who was talking about sleep deprivation when I first got here. You said it was your secret weapon. So, what do you think? Is that all part of what's going on here?"

DABROWSKY: "So...there's a state of consciousness between when you're asleep and when you're awake. Dreams obviously take place while you're asleep. But there's this other state called hypnogogia. I think that's technically right between being awake and falling asleep, and the one between being asleep and waking up has a slightly different name, but whatever, it's basically the same thing. You can have really bizarre, powerful hallucinations during hypnogogia, and being chronically sleep-deprived—the way that our guest is—can make that even more likely."

ROMERO: "So you think that's what's happening here? He's hallucinating?"

DABROWSKY: "Maybe. He could be in a state of prolonged hynogogia. He might be imagining that all kinds of bizarre shit is happening to him, crazy-ass dreams from some goddess and all that, but it's really just that chronically sleep-deprived brain of his doing it."

SULLIVAN: "Well how do we tell? Wouldn't we need to bring in a sleep expert or something to study him?"

DABROWSKY: "That could work. I mean, we could talk with Richards, but...."

ROMERO: "Richards sucks."

SULLIVAN: "Yeah, he's not going to tell us shit about the Engineer that we don't already know. He's Mr. Bad Ideas."

ROMERO: "All right, well, let's break for lunch, come back and start this with a fresh perspective."

DABROWSKY, ROMERO, and SULLIVAN exit the room.

May 10, 2004
Stare Kiejkuty, Poland
CIA Site LAPIS

Mark Romero Diary

I CALLED JESSICA back today. Took me a while to cool off after our last call, and I wanted to wait until I was at a place where I could try to come back together with her before reaching back out.

I tried to patch things up with her, I really did. Things were awkward and stiff from the get-go, as I expected, and Jessica would never really loosen up long enough to meet me halfway. I needed some kind of sign from her that she was really willing to let things go and come back together with me, and I just didn't get that from her.

Then she wouldn't put Katie on the phone, said she was sleeping and had taken forever to put down so she didn't want to wake her up so I could talk with her and she could hear daddy's voice. Fuck. What a bitch. I mean, for Christ's sake, I'm in the middle of nowhere and missing seeing my daughter grow up. The kid has no idea who I am. The last time I saw her, she was just a teeny baby. She's not going to have any memory of me at all. When I get home, whenever that finally is, she's not going to remember ever having seen me or heard my voice. But obviously Jessica just wanted to punish me today.

The whole thing just feels shitty. Shit piled on top of shit piled on top of more shit. It's a raw open wound.

Fuck her. Fuck them. I'll see them when I see them, whenever that turns out to be. Could be months, I don't give a fuck.

May 11, 2004
Stare Kiejkuty, Poland
CIA Site LAPIS

Mark Romero Diary

I'M NORMALLY ONE of the first people awake in LAPIS—comes with the territory in the Army—and usually I go for a run and work out, then take a shower and get going with my day. Not many people are up and around at that time of day. I normally see one or two of the security guys roaming around inside and that's about it before I head out.

But this morning, for some reason, I woke up sitting on the toilet in the bathroom down the hall from my room. I was naked. Clothes strewn about on the floor. I remember looking down at my junk and seeing...something. I don't know what. All I remember is that I thought there was stuff all over my belly and groin, like black and red viscous goo or blood or spunk or all of that mixed together, and under all of that, well, for a split second I thought that my dick looked really different. Like, it was something completely different, like some other kind of organ or something on an insect or one of those nature videos where they zoom in on some freakish creature and it looks like it's from out of this world but it's really what a mosquito or skin mite looks like under an electron microscope. I put my hand down there, slid it across my stomach and felt this thick mucousy slime, and ran my hands through it even though it was disgusting. I distinctly remember a long string of it dangling from my right hand to my stomach. Was it coming out of me? Did something get on me? Had I been wallowing in something? Had someone put this slime and filth all over me?

Did it come out of my dick?

Whatever it was, whatever I was seeing, or thought I was seeing, it freaked me out immediately. Obviously. My adrenaline started pumping, I jumped up and ran over to the sink where there was a mirror and started trying to see what was going on. By the time I got there, it all looked normal. Like, whatever I had seen, or thought I had seen, on my abdomen and groin was gone. No trace.

I remembered thinking, *What's happened to me? What have I done?* Ugh. Christ, what's wrong with me?

Then I vaguely remembered that when I had woken up earlier this morning, before I blacked out or whatever in the bathroom, I had thought that I was covered in awful shit, or even been transformed into some kind of monster or something, which obviously freaked me out, so I ran down the hall to the bathroom to check it out. I remember looking into that mirror over the sink and seeing it, really seeing my whole body there in front of the mirror, and it seemed true, like I really had been changed.

Exactly what I saw in the mirror is kind of hazy now, thank God. It was all black and wet and slimy and not even remotely human anymore. It was the smells that I really remember though. Those have stuck with me. I remember smelling myself and realizing that I was smelling rot and shit and raw meat and then thinking that it was me [underlined three times in original] that was reeking. Then, I don't know what happened. I think I kind of slumped down, or tried to sit down on the toilet, or just kind of passed out, I don't know.

All this is kind of hazy now. It stuck with me earlier in the day, but by now (2147 as I sit here getting ready to go to bed), the details are starting to fuzz out a little. I'm grateful for that.

At some point after that, I kind of came to and realized that I had been hearing someone banging on the door to the bathroom for a while. I kind of mumbled something finally and heard, "You okay in there? Everything all right?" Took me a second, but I said something of, "Yep, be out in a minute." I got my shit together, unlocked the door, and stumbled out. I'm sure that Vasquez must have thought I was hungover and puking my guts out or something, but he didn't say anything as I pushed past him.

I don't really know what happened in there. I mean, the simplest explanation has got to be the right one: I had a bad dream. No, strike that, too mild. I had a FUCKING NIGHTMARE [all caps in original]. I mean, it was probably, almost certainly, just that. Stress, fatigue, weird stuff going on here at LAPIS, psycho discussions with the Engineer, etc. etc. If that's not a recipe for a bad dream, I don't know what is. But what if I hallucinated it? What if I'm hallucinating shit now? What does that mean? Am I sick? Brain tumor? Something else equally terrible?

What if I really did see myself transformed and it wasn't a dream or hallucination?

I mean, I know that's not true, but...

Also, and maybe more importantly, did I lose some time in there? How long was I in there? I don't know—that's the problem. I'm not sure exactly when I went into the bathroom, because let's face it, when I rushed in there I was pretty freaked out and not really paying attention. Christ. What the fuck is going on with me? I've never blacked out before. Well, maybe once or twice in college when I had WAY [all caps in original] too much to drink a couple times, but I was stone cold sober last night. I had zero booze, so that couldn't possibly be it.

Get your shit together, Mark. Get your shit together!!!!!

May 12, 2004
Stare Kiejkuty, Poland
CIA Site LAPIS

Interrogation Transcript: Omar Abu KHATTAB
Interrogation Session 12MAY04-1
Attendees: Omar Abu KHATTAB (detainee), Peter DABROWSKY (lead interrogator, contractor), Deborah SULLIVAN (interrogator, contractor), Mark ROMERO (CTC/RDG liaison, CIA)

[excerpt]

KHATTAB is secured and seated across the table from DABROWSKY, SULLIVAN, and ROMERO in Interrogation Room 3.

ROMERO: "Okay, okay, I can tell you're dying to talk about it, so I'll bite: How did you meet the Mother? I assume you're talking about meeting her in the flesh, and not metaphorically, or talking about dreams, right? You met her in person? Where did you meet her?"

KHATTAB: "I met her in Iram, the city of pillars. It is a place mentioned in the Holy Quran, in Surah al-Fajr. Do you know it?"

ROMERO: "No, my Quran memorization is a little rusty."

KHATTAB: "You joke, Mr. Mark. The Quran says, 'Have you not considered how your Lord dealt with 'Aad – / With Iram – who had lofty pillars, / The likes of whom had never been created in the lands.' It was once a place of glory and majesty, great glory, never before seen anywhere in the world, and nowhere is as beautiful today as it once was. It is ruined now, it is from long ago. The pillars have been torn down mostly, but some of them still stand. It is not all part of the desert, but the sands have covered most of it. But it is really what is under the city of Iram that is most important."

ROMERO: "You met her under the ruins of the city?"

KHATTAB: "Yes, but I am getting ahead of myself."

ROMERO: "Okay. Tell it however you want to."

KHATTAB: "Very well. [pauses] There came a point when I could not avoid her any longer. She had been coming to me in dreams for a very long time. Quietly. Showing herself to me little by little. Never quite showing me her face but demonstrating to me how much she loved me. Treating me with great kindness and tenderness and love. Eventually she was more and more insistent, telling me that I must come to her, for she had need of me, that it was my destiny to come and be hers, to dedicate myself fully to her. These dreams, these messages, became more and more persistent. Then she told me that I must leave Jeddah and go to her. So one morning when I woke up, I knew that my time had come. I decided to leave everything behind and go to her."

ROMERO: "Wow, that must have been quite a change for you. You decided to give up everything and head out into the desert because she had been appearing to you in dreams."

KHATTAB: "Yes. I did not mind giving up everything for her. It was a small sacrifice. My life without her meant nothing. I knew that going to her and serving her would mean that I finally had a true purpose in life, not like everything that had come before. That was meaningless. I knew that she would reveal all the secrets of the universe to me."

ROMERO: "Man. Is that so?"

SULLIVAN: "Who did you tell you were leaving? Who went with you on that trip?"

KHATTAB: "No one. No one at all. I didn't know anyone else who knew of the Mother then."

ROMERO: "Where did you go when you left Jeddah?"

KHATTAB: "I traveled south and east, into Yemen."

ROMERO: "How did you know where to go?"

KHATTAB: "I didn't, then. Not completely. I knew that she could be found in Yemen, in the desert. In an old, old place. A quiet place full of darkness and peace, and even some cool, still waters nestled among the sands."

ROMERO: "So you only had a general plan for where to go? How did you expect you would find her?"

KHATTAB: "I knew that she would tell me more as I approached and got closer to her. It is her way. She tells you a piece of what you need to know. Then you trust her, and do what she says, and then it becomes clearer and she shows you more, until you know it all, whatever you need to know to serve her."

SULLIVAN: "Okay. So you left Jeddah and entered Yemen."

KHATTAB: "Yes. It was a great voyage, it took me many weeks of travel. I went from Jeddah where I was staying at the time. I went to Sanaa at first, then traveled by car to Seiyun because it was as close as I could get by vehicle. Then I hired a man to take me north from there, toward the Rub' al Khali, the Empty Quarter. He tried to desert me after two days and steal my water and food and other possessions. I could not allow that, plus he knew where I was going, so I had to take care of him."

SULLIVAN: "You 'took care of him'? What do you mean? You killed him there in the desert after he tried to rob you?"

KHATTAB: [nodding] "He was trash. So I left him there and continued on my own. By then I realized that I didn't need him anyway. I had the Mother guiding me, she was all I needed. I just needed to have faith in her. I did not need some trash piece guiding me."

SULLIVAN: "Okay."

KHATTAB: "I didn't know exactly where I was going, but I knew the general direction. I knew that she was driving me onward and I knew that it was important to her, so I did it. I just walked and walked and walked. I had some food and water but it was so, so, so hot. The sun was beating down on me but I kept walking until I eventually had to stop because I was exhausted. That night, a sandstorm came and it was very powerful. I was worried it would blow me away or bury me under too much sand to dig away from me. It lasted for hours, but I survived. Then the next morning I came upon the ruins of the city. I didn't even notice at first. There were broken pieces of rock in the mountains and I looked around and realized that there were carvings on some of them. The sandstorm must have uncovered them. If it had not, I would have probably walked past it, never knowing what was there. Then I continued on a little ways more and saw that there were more of these things, and with my imagination I realized that they were pieces of broken pillars and buildings and things like that. I knew it was Iram that I had reached. Then I knew I wouldn't die because I had found her."

SULLIVAN: "So what happened next after you got to the city?"

KHATTAB: "I was overjoyed. I walked around more and then I found a cave, a small little tunnel hidden there in the rocks. I did not have a light, so I had to walk and crawl through the tunnel in darkness. I kept one hand on the wall and could feel carvings and things, but I couldn't see what they were so I didn't know what they meant. I went deep, deep underground and it became very cold. I was shivering, like being out in the desert at night, but eventually I could feel moisture in the air on my skin. Then I could feel presences all around me, brushing past me, surrounding me. Watching me."

SULLIVAN: "Presences? What do you mean?"

KHATTAB: "I do not know. I could tell that there were things there with me in the dark and cold and damp. I could not see them. I did not know what they were. Sometimes they would touch me a little, briefly, but I did not know what they were."

SULLIVAN: "Were they people there, living underground?"

KHATTAB: "No, not people. People had not been where I was for many, many years. Centuries. It was terrifying because I didn't know what they wanted. But I thought of the Mother and kept walking. Then I came to a little room at the end of the tunnel, a small little room so deep in the earth. Then there was a light that glowed a little and there was life and warmth in the room, and I knew that I was in her presence. I fell to my knees and put my forehead to the ground and prayed to her. I could not look upon her. But she took me in her arms and I could feel how much she loved me. I think I fell into a deep sleep and she brought me to her world with her. I saw her beauty and felt her warmth. She gave me a part of her to take back with me to the world when I woke up. Then eventually I woke up and saw the piece of herself she had given me. I wasn't scared anymore. I knew I was on a mission for her."

SULLIVAN: "So what did you do then?"

KHATTAB: "I took the piece of her and brought it into myself, made it a part of me. I would have only done that with her permission, of course. Otherwise, that would have been a great violation. But she wanted me to. So I swallowed this tiny piece of her and it began to transform me. It almost killed me. For days and days it almost consumed me, she was so hungry. I had to give her some of my essence so that she could live and grow. I thought I might die. But I did not, and eventually after a couple days I was able to leave Iram and travel back through the desert to the world. The piece of her grew inside me over time, and that was where the black seeds came from."

ROMERO: "The black seeds? You have mentioned those before. What are they? Explain them to us."

KHATTAB: "Yes. They are parts of her that grow and then they can blossom and grow themselves. They can change the world."

ROMERO: "That's pretty vague. How can they change the world?"

KHATTAB: "They can make this world, the world we live in, more like her world, where she comes from, what she wants our world to be like."

ROMERO: "How, specifically, though? Have you seen this happen?"

KHATTAB: "No. She has not yet allowed me to see the growth and transformation. But one day...one day soon she will."

ROMERO: "So you're just taking this on faith?"

KHATTAB: "Of course! She would never deceive me. The Mother is always truthful in everything she says and does."

DABROWSKY: "How many black seeds were there that grew inside you?"

KHATTAB: "There were six or eight, maybe ten or so of them over time. I don't know. I gave them all away as she instructed me."

DABROWSKY: "What do you mean you gave them away? Who did you give them away to?"

KHATTAB: "Her servants. The other people who love and worship her as I do."

DABROWSKY: "Who were these people?"

KHATTAB: "I did not know them. I had never met any of them before. They were from all over. When I would meet them, I gave them the seeds. I did not talk with them much. They are good servants of hers, I am sure."

DABROWSKY: "How did you know who to give them to? How did you meet these people?"

KHATTAB: "She told me. She came to me in a dream as she always does and told me to give them to so-and-so, a man I would meet the next day at a particular time in a particular place. She told them to meet me there in the same way. Then I would give them a seed or two and they would depart. I would go on my way."

ROMERO: "So...why did you have to go to Iram? If the Mother is all about life and growing things and all that, why was she in the middle of the desert? That seems pretty...inhospitable. Why didn't she just give you...whatever she gave you when you were in Jeddah? Why did she make you go through all that?"

KHATTAB: "She told me that a long time ago, a terrible group of men—I don't know who they were—managed to break off a piece of her being and take it from her. They traveled to the desert, in the middle of the wasteland, and hid it away from her in a sealed tomb under the ruined city. It was as far away from life as they could get. They were very cruel, these men, they did it to hurt her. It was a terrible, terrible thing they did. I had to fix it."

ROMERO: "Wow."

DABROWSKY: "That is quite a tale, Omar. Quite a tale. I've got a question for you."

KHATTAB: "Yes, Mr. Pete?"

DABROWSKY: "Do you really expect us to believe all of that steaming pile of horseshit? Or even *any* of it? Any at all?"

KHATTAB: "Wh—what do you mean?"

DABROWSKY: "Well, I mean it's all such a giant, crazy pack of lies that it must have taken you weeks to come up with all that. I mean, every time we've had you in a stress position or you were being waterboarded, I can only assume you were cooking that bullshit up. Did you really think we were going to fall for any of it?"

KHATTAB: "It is the truth, Mr. Pete. The Mother came to me and told me that I could reveal it all to you. I don't have to hold anything back from you anymore. She wants you to know all about her and her plans for the world."

ROMERO: "Okay, KHATTAB. We'll have to take your word for that. All right, well, let's move on to some other topics for now. We can come back to this later."

[end excerpt]

May 14, 2004
Stare Kiejkuty, Poland
CIA Site LAPIS

Secure Telephone STU-3/67088 Recording Transcript
Call Participants: Mark ROMERO (CTC/RDG liaison, CIA), Deborah SULLIVAN (interrogator, contractor), Peter DABROWSKY (interrogator, contractor), Gerrold SCHULMAN (NE, senior analyst)

[Call begins at 2:01 PM (local)]

ROMERO: "Okay, hello, this is Mark calling, I've got you."

SCHULMAN: "Um, yes, it looks like the phone says we're classified at the Top Secret level. Right? Right. Yes, that's what it's showing on the little screen. Gosh, that's tiny print, but it says 'top secret' on it so I guess we're good. Right?"

ROMERO: "Here too. Thanks for taking the time to talk with us today. Must be pretty early in the morning for you. I'm Mark, I set up the call with you, Gerrold. My colleagues Deb and Pete are here on the call with us. We've got you on speaker phone."

SCHULMAN: "Um, okay, this is Gerrold, call me Gerry. Good to talk with you all."

ROMERO: "Same, Gerry. So I guess we all know why we're talking today: We need to talk about the Engineer and what he's been telling us. You've got access to all the cables we've been sending, right, Gerry?"

SCHULMAN: "Uh, yes, that's right."

ROMERO: "And you've seen the tapes or read the transcripts or whatever of at least the most recent set of interrogation sessions we've sent over, right?"

SCHULMAN: "Um...yes, I think so. If we're talking about the same ones."

ROMERO: "Well, I'm talking about his trip to Yemen. What he told us about that. Right? You've seen that one?"

SCHULMAN: "Yes."

ROMERO: "Well... What do you make of it?"

SCHULMAN: "You want my totally unscientific and unofficial opinion?"

ROMERO: "Sure."

SCHULMAN: "He's crazy. Utterly looney tunes. He's making the whole thing up. I mean, he probably believes all this stuff himself. Maybe he's just created the whole thing to screw with you guys, but I suspect he probably believes it all. You saw his psych eval. He's delusional. That's all there is to it. Nothing more than that."

SULLIVAN: "Yeah, you could very well be right. That's definitely a likely scenario, and it's one we've spent a lot of time discussing ourselves."

ROMERO: "Sure. I don't think that's necessarily wrong, but I think we need to dig into it a little more, some of the specifics, okay?"

SCHULMAN: "Sure. Happy to."

ROMERO: "So, what's the chance that he traveled from Saudi Arabia to Yemen, and at some site in the deep desert he either found or was given some kind of biological weapon? Maybe some old Soviet bioweapons."

SCHULMAN: "Um...it's possible. I don't think it's likely, but of course anything is possible."

ROMERO: "That's not exactly a ringing endorsement, Gerry."

SCHULMAN: "Well, no...um...because I don't think it's likely. And if that *is* what happened, then we still need a lot more information about the specifics. Also, keep in mind, everything he's given you so far is information that is, one, currently unverifiable using other sources, and two, couched in language that is...more religious or fantastical than factual. You know what I mean?"

ROMERO: "Okay, well, let's delve into the religious stuff a little. You're an expert on Islam, right, Gerry?"

SCHULMAN: "Well, no one really likes to consider themselves an 'expert' on some topic, but yes, I got my PhD in Islamic Studies at Yale and I've been at the Agency for the last twelve years, so I'm pretty conversant in Islam and the Islamic world."

ROMERO: "Great. Sounds like an expert to me. So tell us about the 'Mother' or female figure he always refers to. I'm not going to attempt to pronounce it. You know what I'm talking about."

SCHULMAN: "Okay, yeah, sure. So, at various points, either in his conversations with you guys or in his journals that were captured, he refers to this being—and I do think he's always referring to a singular entity and not several with slightly variant names—as 'omm Al shayateen' or 'omm Al thalma' or even 'omm sherreera' once or twice, though that one's less common. Those are some pretty spooky names. I would translate them as 'mother of demons'—'shayateen' are demons—or 'mother of darkness'—here, keep in mind that the word darkness there doesn't necessarily have a negative connotation the way it does in English or European cultures—or 'evil mother.' He doesn't really think of her as evil most of the time, it seems to me, just a couple times in his notes when he's frustrated or annoyed with her because he wants her to do something or give him a sign or something like that and she hasn't done that. He also calls her by a bunch of names or titles that you would use to, um, describe a lover, that sort of thing. Like 'beloved' or 'love of my heart,' stuff like that. Things that suggest he loves her and so forth. Kind of romantic sounding titles, almost."

ROMERO: "So what do you make of it? Had you ever seen these titles or phrases used before? Do you know who he's talking about?"

SCHULMAN: "No, not really. Not at all, actually. I mean, the romantic references, sure, those are common terms, common idiomatic expressions of love, but not the mother stuff. We couldn't find any other references to those titles."

ROMERO: "*Any* other?"

SCHULMAN: "Yeah, like no one else uses these phrases to describe anyone that we have ever seen. We checked all the databases, the Internet, religious books. None of them talk about this kind of thing."

DABROWSKY: "So that's weird, right?"

SCHULMAN: "Yeah, it's weird. I mean, it's certainly peculiar to the Engineer. No one else is talking about this person but him."

DABROWSKY: "So that could suggest that it's his personal delusion."

SCHULMAN: "That's certainly possible. It's kind of suggestive in that direction. If these ideas were shared by other people, well, you'd almost certainly expect to see other references to them, either in classified or open sources, and there's just none of that."

ROMERO: "What's your theory on who this person is? Or what she is? Is this some kind of demigoddess or something? I mean, I thought they worshipped Allah?"

SCHULMAN: "Um, yes, that's right. There's no way that a devout Muslim, or even a not-very-devout Muslim, would say the things that the Engineer has said about this being. I mean, he's talking about her as a kind of goddess, a replacement for God, I think, based on what he's said. The dogma surrounding this entity is unclear—he's been pretty vague so far—it's just not consistent with anything authentically Islamic though, I can tell you that much."

ROMERO: "So what are we talking about here? Is the Engineer not actually Muslim? I mean, he's a member of Al Qaeda, for Christ's sake."

SCHULMAN: "Sure. I think what we're seeing here is a case of syncretism."

ROMERO: "Say that again."

SCHULMAN: "Syncretism, you know what I mean?"

ROMERO: "No. Remember, Gerry, we're at the tip of the spear here."

SCHULMAN: "Okay, um, it's a kind of blending of two different religious belief systems, where ideas from one are blended into a dominant one and then you've got this kind of weird amalgamation or mishmash that comes out the other end."

ROMERO: "Okay..."

SCHULMAN: "So I'm not an expert on this by any means, but I think one example you might be familiar with would be the kind of Voudou that's found in Haiti. That blends some African traditional religious beliefs with the more dominant Roman Catholicism of the French colonizers to create something entirely new, something that looks Catholic, sort of, in some ways, but that also has a lot of the traditional religious ideas still in there, and some entirely new elements besides. I think that's what we're maybe talking about here. I think the Engineer is still using the Islamic framework and mental model—how could he not, he grew up in a Muslim country with a fairly devout family and friends—but he's somehow mixed in these new ideas that he's been telling you guys about. I just don't have any idea where he got this new set of ideas from. Maybe Yemen? Maybe some kind of weird unorthodox tribal beliefs, something local to some out-of-the-way area, maybe something pre-Islamic? I have no idea."

ROMERO: "Hmmm. That's kind of interesting. I can see some directions we could go in to try to get more at that. What do you think?"

SULLIVAN: "Yeah, I can see that. It's definitely an angle we can take to ask him about, drill down into that more."

SCHULMAN: "Everything you've given me is really intriguing. I don't mean to be dismissive about any of the information you've shared. We clearly need to keep digging. I've been talking with a lot of the other analysts here, including several Yemen subject-matter experts. I've called in everybody who might have an idea. We just don't know exactly what you're dealing with here. There are just too many open questions and not enough answers. We've been having some heated debates about what it might mean, what you guys have stumbled on, but we need more if we're to reach any kind of definitive conclusions."

DABROWSKY: "Oh yeah, I'm picturing you guys having a fun ol' time back at HQ debating about this shit while we're out here in [inaudible]."

SCHULMAN: "Yep, exactly! But look, guys, the truth of the matter is that you're going to have to get me more information here. I've done what I can with what you've given me so far. It's all intriguing stuff, but...you know how it goes: garbage in, garbage out."

ROMERO: [sighing] "Yeah, I hear you. I get it. You're doing what you can. We'll try to get you more information. More pieces of the puzzle."

SCHULMAN: "That would be great. You've got my contact info, so just send me whatever you get and I'll take a look. Who knows, it may jog something loose."

ROMERO: "Okay, great, thanks, Gerry."

SCHULMAN: "Okay, yeah, sounds great. Have a fabuloso day."

ROMERO: "Sure. You too."

[Call ends at 2:24 PM (local)]

May 16, 2004
Stare Kiejkuty, Poland
CIA Site LAPIS

Mark Romero Diary

I DON'T KNOW what the fuck happened to me last night. This has never happened before.

I woke up at dawn out in the woods. I was in my t-shirt and shorts, just like I normally wear to bed, but I was sitting on the ground propped up against a tree and had been sleeping there apparently. No idea for how long.

When I woke up, I had no idea where I was, and it took me a while to figure anything out. Kind of disoriented actually. I started wandering off in a random direction and fortunately, thank God, after a few minutes I could see the rear chain-link fence at LAPIS. Can't tell you what a relief that was.

I walked around to the front gate and the security guys were surprised to see me. They said that whoever was manning the booth over night had never logged me out. They assumed I had been out for an especially early long run or something. They didn't ask about why I wasn't wearing shoes, or why I looked like hell. Thank God.

I didn't say much, just waved and went inside for a long hot shower to think things over.

My legs and arms are kind of scratched up, not too bad, just a bunch of surface scratches from branches and things like that. The soles of my feet have a couple deeper cuts on them, but nothing I couldn't patch up and put some Band-Aids on. Walking on them is going to suck for a couple days though. I am all-over sore and exhausted.

What if this happens again? What the fuck do I do?

May 18, 2004
Stare Kiejkuty, Poland
CIA Site LAPIS

Interrogation Transcript: Omar Abu KHATTAB
Interrogation Session 18MAY04-1
Attendees: Omar Abu KHATTAB (detainee), Deborah SULLIVAN (interrogator, contractor), Mark ROMERO (CTC/RDG liaison, CIA)

[excerpt]

KHATTAB is secured and seated across the table from SULLIVAN and ROMERO in Interrogation Room 1.

KHATTAB: "Haven't you ever wanted to see what I am talking about when I have told you about the Black Mother's vision for the world? Her beauty? Don't you want to see her and what she has planned? I have told you so much about it. Don't you want to see it for yourself?"

ROMERO: "Uh...sure. I'm curious."

KHATTAB: "Then behold."

[Note: Audio feed of camera in Interrogation Room 1 detected a change in tone and timbre of KHATTAB's voice that had not been previously heard. Beginning with the sentence "Haven't you ever..." KHATTAB's voice became deeper here and more resonant, though his voice remained well within the normal human register. As he was making this statement, both ROMERO and SULLIVAN remained silent and unmoving in their seats, with no gestures or movement detected in the video feed. The camera's angle was poorly positioned for providing facial expressions of either ROMERO or SULLIVAN, but their postures suggest they were staring straight ahead at KHATTAB during this time. They remained silent during this period. Because the camera was in black and white only, and relatively low-resolution, no color change in KHATTAB's eyes could be noted.]

[Silence, no movement for twelve seconds.]

ROMERO: "Wh—what the fuck just happened?"

[SULLIVAN retches, bends over while seated, then gets up and leaves the room quickly.]

KHATTAB: "She allowed me to show you her world, her vision for this world. How it needs to be transformed in her image."

[Note: KHATTAB's voice returned to its previous register with this statement.]

ROMERO: [holding his forehead] "Christ. Christ. I feel like I was just hit by a ton of bricks."

KHATTAB: "You have seen her majesty and her glory. Wasn't it beautiful?"

ROMERO: "I don't know what I just saw, but that wasn't beautiful."

[end excerpt]

May 18, 2004
Stare Kiejkuty, Poland
CIA Site LAPIS

Mark Romero Diary

TODAY WAS A weird one and I'm not sure what to say about it. Very [underlined in original] weird session with the Engineer. Something happened to me and Deb and I don't know how to describe it.

Afterward, she and I talked about it because it was so strange, and we even reviewed the tape of the session to try to figure out what happened, but we couldn't come up with any real answers, or at least none that make any sense.

I thought the Engineer's eyes were getting huge and dark and then my head or the room started spinning and things went black for a second. When I opened my eyes, I was standing in front of LAPIS— right in front of the main building here, with my back to it, but I could recognize the front lawn and see the security gate and the main road coming up to it through the trees. I could sense some people behind me, though for whatever reason I didn't or couldn't turn my head to see who they were. Deb was on my right and she and I were holding hands for some reason. I could feel her hand, which was very warm, gripping mine tightly. My attention was fixed on...I don't know what it was. It was some kind of, I don't know. Some kind of shallow crater in the ground and a kind of garden planted inside, lots and lots of plants. It looked very tropical, very jungle-y, lots of unknown plant species there. Not exactly normal plants either, stuff that seemed to kind of move on its own, even though there was no wind. It was a clear, sunny day, no breeze, but these things were kind of waving on their own. Then all of a sudden the garden started growing in size, with all the plants getting bigger and spreading out, and I could see animals emerging from the garden, some birdlike things that kind of popped up, and some animals that crept forward from the jungle area and came toward me. I don't know what those things were. Nothing of this Earth, that's for sure. Hideous. Absolutely hideous. Some were small, some bigger, almost as big as a man, then as the garden kept growing and growing, I could hear loud crashes in the jungle and strange animal cries and screams, then the boom of really big things—bigger than my sight could encompass actually—starting to emerge from the rear of the jungle. It started growing more and more, like at a visible rate, sweeping toward us. I could hear the overlapping cries and struggles of the weird animal things, plus a lot more in that jungle that I couldn't see yet. Then the smell hit me, lots of festering rot and kind of a swamp stink, like filth and watery shit to an overpowering degree.

Then I could feel the Black Mother put her hand on my shoulder. I don't know how I knew it was her because I still couldn't turn my head to look at her, but I knew it was her all the same. I could just see her black fingertips on my right shoulder, and I could feel it clamping down hard and squeezing my shoulder until that was a lightning bolt of pain. Then right before the jungle swept over us—I wanted to move, I wanted that so bad, but I just couldn't make my feet move, or any other muscle even twitch—I heard her starting to laugh. It was a crazy, deep, cackling sound, hideous, like no other laugh I'd ever heard, but I knew that's what it was. Then I blinked and it was all gone and I was sitting back in my chair in the interrogation room staring at the Engineer.

So what does it all mean? I have no idea. It's unsettling as hell, and I don't like any of the implications of this. I mean, what happened is impossible, unexplainable, and suggests that there might be something more than strictly natural going on here. I don't even want to think about the possibility that the Engineer has been telling us the truth of the matter all along, even if it's just the truth as he sees it. Think about it: even if he somehow managed to slip us a drug that made us hallucinate (How would he do that? He gets body cavity searches routinely, his cell is bare walls and floor, no way to hide anything, no one here at LAPIS is helping him fuck with us, etc. etc.), how would he have made us hallucinate the same thing? Deb and I talked about it and we both literally saw the same things. No way that could have happened normally even if he managed to give us some kind of hallucinogen or party drug or something. No way.

But, of course, there's no proof of any of this. Nothing we can hang our hats on. We watched the surveillance video from the interrogation room backward and forward, over and over, frame by frame. His voice changed at one point, but anyone can change their voice, so there's nothing freaky about that. Then Deb and I just kind of zone out and stare straight ahead, right at him for a few seconds, so that's weird, but you can't even see what our facial expressions are really because of the angle. Then it looks like we kind of snap out of it and are freaked out by something. But it's not even clear what we're reacting to in the video. We were just sitting there quietly one second, then we're freaked out the next. It doesn't make any sense. Certainly nothing you could show anyone else and they'd go, oh yes, something supernatural just happened, or he hypnotized them, or he slipped drugs in their drinks or something. Nothing at all.

I could have sworn that right as we were slipping under, or whatever, and being shown the vision, there was some kind of movement under the Engineer's jumpsuit over his chest, just something subtle. Deb said she doesn't remember that, and I couldn't see it on the video, but it's also not exactly zoomed in and it's black-and-white, so it's impossible to say if I just imagined that or what. It doesn't appear in the video if it happened. I'm also pretty sure that his eyes turned all black at the same time (Deb agreed with me), but again, if that happened, you can't tell it on the video. And we checked the timestamp on the video. There's no missing time at all. Or, at least, if there was, he had the help of expert technicians who had access to the footage and helped him edit it, so I think we can rule that out.

Things were so weird and left unanswered that I went to see Dave to kind of fill him in and see what he had to say about it. I knocked and then barged in. Who knows what that guy's doing all day. One day I'm sure I'm going to catch him drinking at his desk. Anyway, I told him what happened, generally speaking, and what we saw when we reviewed the tape (not much) and asked for his advice. Big mistake. Here's what he told me, and this is pretty much a verbatim transcript: "Don't get spooked here, Romero. You and your little girlfriend there need to pull your shit together and keep it professional. Stop imagining things. Nothing fucking happened. You're tired. You're stressed. Maybe you were drinking or using drugs? Who knows? The bottom line is that you don't want some kind of psych eval write-up on your record. If you get that, your career's over. So just shut up. Go take a walk, or workout, or watch TV, or jack off. Nothing. Happened. Do whatever you need to do to relax. Now get the fuck out of my office."

So I got the fuck out of his office. What a fucking joke. I tried to warn him. Mark my words, I tried to fucking warn him.

May 19, 2004
Stare Kiejkuty, Poland
CIA Site LAPIS

CABLE #RX396117-04

SUBJECT: Initial Analysis on Omar Abu KHATTAB Trip to Yemen in Spring 2000

DATE OF CABLE: 19 MAY 2004

1.   Recent interrogations of Omar Abu KHATTAB at Site LAPIS have revealed a possible account of his travels in Yemen in spring 2000 that suggests he may have come into possession of some quantity of unknown biological weapons materials at an unknown site in Yemen.

2.   KHATTAB's account is framed in quasi-religious terms, and a previous psychological evaluation of him based on a set of his past writings suggests ongoing mental health dysfunction, making analysis difficult (see CABLE #RX348201-04). Note that KHATTAB has not been subjected to a more rigorous psychological evaluation by experts while in detention at LAPIS.

3.   The following is as close to an accurate account, stripped of religious/potentially delusional language, from what can be pieced together:

● KHATTAB seems to have received a tip (from parties unknown) telling him that he could secure biological weapons materials (precursor agents or complete biological agents) of an unknown type and quantity at an unknown site in Yemen.

• At the time of this tip, he was living in Jeddah, Saudi Arabia, and traveled to Sanaa, Yemen, by unknown means. He then traveled by car to Seiyun, Yemen, and then set out with a guide to a site he described as "Iram, city of pillars."

• Before he reached Iram in the Rub' al Khali (the Empty Quarter, a desert area), KHATTAB claims to have killed his guide.

• KHATTAB then describes locating the city of Iram (through either happenstance or unknown means) and entering the city. There, he located an underground area that contained what he described as "black seeds."

• KHATTAB then left Iram with some quantity of the black seeds, returning to Seiyun and Sanaa with them.

• Over time he gave away six to ten black seeds (presumed to be his entire supply) to various unknown parties.

4.   Details of this trip and KHATTAB's activities during it are sketchy and need further development.

5.   Information gaps (not an exhaustive list):

• Did the KHATTAB trip from Jeddah to Iram actually take place? (remainder of questions assume the trip did take place in some form)

• How did KHATTAB learn that he needed to travel to Iram?

• What did KHATTAB believe his purpose for traveling to Iram was?

• How did KHATTAB locate Iram? What is the exact location of Iram?

• Who did KHATTAB meet in Iram, if anyone?

• What did KHATTAB find in Iram? What is the nature of the black seeds? Are there other materials related to the black seeds still in Iram?

- How many black seeds did KHATTAB leave Iram with?
- Who did KHATTAB give the black seeds to? For what purpose?

6.   Speculation: Obviously the most significant concern about this trip is that KHATTAB may have found or been given access to a stockpile of biological weapons or materials that could be used to manufacture biological weapons. This could have been some sort of abandoned Soviet or Yemeni biological weapons facility hidden deep in the Yemeni desert, perhaps in a deep underground structure. The black seeds could be a codephrase for these biological weapons, and the individuals to whom KHATTAB gave the seeds could have been disbursing them for either storage/later use, or they could have been facilitators/couriers who provided the seeds to operational/attack cells for use in biological weapons attacks either in the homeland or against U.S./allied interests abroad.

AUTHOR: Mark R., CTC

May 21, 2004
McLean, Virginia
CIA HQ

CABLE # RX397729-04

SUBJECT: Response to Speculation on Omar Abu KHATTAB Trip to Yemen (CABLE #RX396117-04)

DATE OF CABLE: 21 MAY 2004

1.   The speculation that was laid out in Cable # RX397729-04 is possible, though highly unlikely, and is inconsistent with other known data. This theory cannot be corroborated with other sources at the present time.

2.   The bulk of the former Soviet biological weapons program was housed at various facilities in what would become Kazakhstan (see Report # 501233-98, "Soviet Biological Weapons Program: Overview and Retrospective"), though some additional facilities were located in [redacted] and [redacted]. While South Yemen was an ally of the Soviet Union during the Cold War, that friendly relationship ended in 1990 with the reunification of North and South Yemen. There were no known transfers of Soviet biological weapons technologies, materials, agent stockpiles, or scientists to Yemen during the Cold War, nor is there any record of such materials or personnel acquired by the present-day Republic of Yemen. Yemen is not known to possess biological weapons, and there is no evidence that either the Marxist South Yemen or the current Republic of Yemen have ever pursued them. Yemen is a party to the Biological and Toxin Weapons

Conventions (BTWC), with no known violations of these Conventions.

3.   It is remotely possible that some Soviet biological weapons materials could have been transferred to Yemen clandestinely. That is highly unlikely, however, and there is no known evidence to support that conclusion.

4.   The likeliest possibility is that Omar Abu KHATTAB is attempting to deceive by providing details of an elaborate hoax and "wild goose chase" to absorb time and resources and prevent the uncovering of more information about the Al Qaeda biological weapons program.

5.   Advise additional collection from KHATTAB, focusing on the current status, locations, and key personnel associated with the Al Qaeda biological program, to ascertain new data that can be corroborated by other sources.

REPORTS OFFICER: Brian H., CTC

May 23, 2004
Stare Kiejkuty, Poland
CIA Site LAPIS

Mark Romero Diary

YOU'RE NEVER GOING to believe what happened to me in the shower this morning, *Penthouse...*

I was taking my morning shower and had shampoo and soap in my eyes so I couldn't see anything while I was washing up. I put my hand on my stomach, or maybe actually a little below my belly button, and I felt something weird, something that shouldn't have been there. It felt soft and a little mushy.

Obviously I opened my eyes immediately, promptly got soap and shampoo in them, had to wash them out, etc. Comedy of errors. Fucking hilarious. Ha ha. But I'm sure I saw something that looked like a dirty white/grey/brownish cluster of mushrooms or fungi or something growing on my lower belly, or at least just sitting there. Absolutely disgusting!!! So while I was trying to make my eyes stop burning, I was clawing at my stomach area with my other hand to get whatever it was off me.

In a few seconds I was able to open my eyes again, and I could have sworn I saw something—maybe whatever I felt/saw very briefly—being washed down the drain. I don't know. Was that my imagination? It looked like kind of a dark or black lump, but I admit that I only saw it for a split second. I looked really closely at my body, believe me, and there was nothing there. Maybe that area was a little red, but then again I was clawing and scraping at it with my fingers to ensure I had gotten all of it off, whatever it was.

Assuming I saw/felt anything there to begin with.

I felt around on the rest of my body, looked at my back in the mirror when I was done with my shower, etc., and there was nothing else there that I could find.

It feels like it's been hard to get clean all day. I keep thinking I smell the faint whiff of something rotten all day. Maybe something like curdled milk. Is it me? No one said anything all day, not even Deb or Pete, and we were working together in the same small space all day, but you can't really ask someone, "Hey, do I smell like rotting flesh?" You know what I mean?

This afternoon I couldn't take it anymore, so I consulted with Dr. Richards. That guy is never busy. Poked my head into the infirmary and asked him if he had a minute. I'm one of his favorite people (kidding, of course; I'm assuming a guy like him has [underlining in original] no "favorite people.") Without telling him what I saw, or thought I saw exactly, I told him I was worried I might have picked up a fungal infection or something. He was skeptical, I could tell, but he examined the area, said he didn't see anything unusual. He gave me some kind of topical cream for fungal infections or dermatitis or whatever and told me to "apply it as needed." So I told him a little more about what happened, or what I thought happened. He started asking me about stress and told me I was imagining things. Said, "You don't want to start seeing things that aren't there, Mark. Trust me. Just rub some of this cream on it and forget whatever it is you think you saw."

Richards probably thinks I'm a hypochondriac by this point.

I could have sworn there were some light grey spots on my stomach tonight when I looked after dinner, but I couldn't be sure, the lighting wasn't great. Put some of the stupid cream on it then looked again just before I started writing this tonight and everything looked normal to me. It doesn't itch or anything, but I'm going to keep a close eye on things to see if anything pops up, literally or figuratively.

May 25, 2004
Stare Kiejkuty, Poland
CIA Site LAPIS

Mark Romero Diary

SOMETIMES FUNNY STUFF happens here at LAPIS. Not every day, but much like the Army, stress and the intensity of the mission causes otherwise normal(ish) people to do the craziest, funniest shit. The stuff I saw in the Army... Well, there are no words. Anyway, I was going about my day this morning, kind of mid-morning for me, I needed to take a leak. I was on the first floor and went into the bathroom. It's been retrofitted as a standard kind of public restroom with a bunch of stalls and a couple urinals and a couple sinks. It's got some fancy tilework and some of the fixtures look pretty antique, but the bottom line is that it's a public restroom.

Anyway, so I go to the bathroom and head to the urinals because I had to piss like a racehorse. Standing at the leftmost urinal with his back to the door was one of the security guys. I think his name is William, or Will, or Bill... I forget. Someone pointed him out to me and told me his name a few weeks ago but I forget exactly what it was. Doesn't matter. His pants and underwear are down around his ankles, so he's bareass. And I can see that based on the rhythmic hand/arm motions, he's jerking off. Just going to town, pumping away as hard and fast as he can.

So I think I said something to the effect of, "What the fuck, dude?" and kind of laughed. It took him a second, like maybe more like ten or fifteen seconds, but he slowly turned his head around, not otherwise moving or taking his hand off his dick, and just looked at me bleary-eyed. Totally out of it. Eyes open but nothing going on inside. I just needed to take a leak, so I picked the urinal farthest away from him on the right, did my business, washed up, and got the hell out of there as fast as I could. When I left, he was still standing there, working his dick.

Good Lord. I mean, what the fuck, right? What are some people thinking when they do the crazy shit they do? I mean, in this case I guess good ol' Will, or Bill, or whatever was just drunk, but Jesus.

So later this afternoon/early evening when I stopped off to take another leak before knocking off for the day and heading off to dinner, I go to the same bathroom and holy shit, there was mold everywhere in there, mostly by the urinals but also spreading out on the left-hand side of the room toward the toilet stalls. It was toward the end of the day, and I doubted Michal was still around, so I called him on his cell phone and told him he needed to get some cleaners in there fast before the mold and fungus overtakes us again. I didn't want to have another one of those "mold everywhere, must clean everything" freakouts at LAPIS. I took a walk later and could see Michal's guys finishing up. I could smell the bleach way down the hall. That stuff will kill anything. Should be fine now.

May 27, 2004
Stare Kiejkuty, Poland
CIA Site LAPIS

Mark Romero Diary

TALKED WITH ONE of my security buds, Robert, this morning. He's ex-Army, all-around good guy. Also not the kind of person to get freaked out over nothing. He told me that they've started finding animal carcasses along the fence line here at LAPIS, mostly outside, but some inside too, near the main building. Dead squirrels, dead rabbits, a dead fox, a bunch of stuff that was all ripped up and they have no idea what it was. Yesterday morning they even found three dead headless things lined up all in a row right near the back door of the kitchen. They don't know what's killing them or leaving them around here because most of the sensors are set to be triggered by people-sized things, and if it's a fairly small animal, like, say, a medium-sized dog or something, the sensors wouldn't alert on them. Cameras have picked up some dark furry things, and some of them are probably getting in by digging under the fence, but it's hard to say in the dark with dark-colored, fast-moving things. This is probably bullshit, but Robert said not only are these little critters they just found all ripped up and covered in blood, but they even thought some of them looked kind of twisted and unnatural, like they're mutated or something. "Decidedly abnormal," he said. Great. Not sure what that means or if it's all just utter bullshit. I will definitely have to keep my eyes peeled when I go out for runs, not that I want to run into some rabid dog that's killing bunnies around here.

But I did start asking around a little, and several people confirmed. The weird sensor readings have been happening for the better part of a month. Apparently they even called some technicians out from HQ to check it out to see what's going on. The dead animal carcasses seem to be newer, with them showing up for the last week or so.

I saw Michal in passing this afternoon and asked him what he thought about the whole thing. He looked pretty jumpy to me when I asked him. Skittish. I'm not going to say he looked "scared" when I asked him about the dead animals, but...yeah. He looked scared. He has no idea, that much was clear. He said he suspects a local farmer may have set some poison out in the area to kill some predators getting to his chickens, said his buddies were going to look into it. Then he tried to really unconvincingly laugh it off (for a career intel guy, Michal is a really lousy liar). He stopped chuckling when I asked him how close the nearest farm was to LAPIS. He said about six or eight kilometers away. Okay. So how could the farmer's poison get into the woods all the way over here then? And how could some kind of barnyard poison have mutated the animals? I mean, what kind of poison are Polish farmers using to kill foxes or whatever? Agent Orange? Something special shipped straight from Chernobyl? The security dudes are starting to get freaked out about this.

So, no idea what all this is about or what's going on. Probably just standard weird shit that happens in Polish farm country.

I was kind of tossing and turning last night and didn't get a good night's sleep, so I ended up waking up kinda late today (not like me) and didn't do my usual run this morning. Not a big deal, I knew I'd have some time at the end of the day to do a run after the workday was done and the sessions with the Engineer were over. Plus, given how far north we are, nightfall comes super late. So late this afternoon I changed into my running gear and went outside and was getting ready to go when I looked out at the forest that surrounds LAPIS and just stood there for a little while. I was just staring out at that black wall of trees and remember thinking that God only know what's inside that tree line. I spooked myself. No reason for it, but just looking at it sent a shiver down my spine and made the hair on the back of my neck stand up. I went back inside and gave up on the run. Maybe tomorrow. I've been keeping up with my PT lately, so no need to go today anyway.

May 29, 2004
Stare Kiejkuty, Poland
CIA Site LAPIS

Mark Romero Diary

NO MOLD LATELY, thank God; the cleaning efforts seem to have paid off there, but LAPIS has become infested with these nasty, stinging black flies lately. Always buzzing around you, landing on you while you're trying to eat, sleep, talk, just sit in a chair and do some work. They're fucking everywhere. Well, almost everywhere. There were a couple buzzing around the room today when we were interrogating the Engineer and it was bugging (ha! No pun intended) me and Pete and Deb but seemed to be leaving the Engineer alone.

In fact, when that fucker saw us ineffectually trying to swat the flies, he gave me a humongous maniacal grin. It took everything I had not to haul off and just beat him unconscious right then and there. Technically, I could have grabbed him and slapped him "to get his attention," but I didn't dare because I knew if I started doing that I wouldn't be able to stop. An image of me beating the shit out of him, with him on the floor and me just kicking him over and over again in the face, absolutely destroying his face and wiping that smile off it, with Deb and Pete trying to pull me off of him, flashed through my mind. I didn't want to destroy my career over this asshole though. He's just not worth it. I've worked too hard to get where I am and I'm not going to let some asshole like him, or me losing my temper over nothing, end it all. That fucker Dave would love to can my ass and put me on a plane home. He'd fucking love it. No way. That's not how this is going to go.

It took me a little bit to calm down, then I told Deb and Pete to give him some waterboarding today. We haven't done that with him for a while, but it's time to knock some sense into him and show him we're serious. I told Deb and Pete (privately) that I was getting a little worked up and Pete told me to get out of there and take a walk while I cooled off. I think he could tell it wasn't a good idea for me to stick around right then. I'm not normally prone to fits of rage but, Jesus, I was in a mood today. Not like me. I'm not that kind of guy. It worries me a little, I have to admit, but after an hour or so of running I calmed down.

Later when I saw Michal, I asked him if these gigantic black horse flies are normal for Poland around here this time of year and he kind of shrugged noncommittally about them. Didn't seem too bothered by it, but then again, he probably hasn't been bit by one of these fuckers yet either. They fucking hurt!

I was talking to one of the security guys yesterday and he was telling me that one of the guys—he didn't say who—got freaked out the night before because he had a cut on his forearm, I don't know, some kind of gash, and he freaked himself out because he thought he saw maggots crawling around inside the wound and under his skin. Like skin rippling from worms crawling around and all that. So the guy went to see Dr. Richards and he took one look at it and told the guy that his arm was fine, it wasn't infected or contaminated or anything.

But you know, I get it. We're being overrun. I've started seeing these big black cockroaches everywhere too, just scuttling around and crawling all over things lately. Christ, they're probably all getting in the food too. The chow here is not bad, and there's always plenty of it, but the local Polish women who make it don't exactly strike me as the types who are super into cleanliness. There's no way you could pay me to venture back into the kitchen here at LAPIS. I don't want to see what goes on back there. I'm sure I'd never eat here again.

Dave even issued a very terse little internal memo this afternoon that I would boil down to "Everyone shut the fuck up and calm down." We're getting some fumigators in to take care of the problem, it's just taking the Poles some time to get some guys cleared who can do the work because, well, this is still a fucking black site and we don't want everyone and his brother crawling all over the place and asking questions. Loose lips sink ships and all that. Not that I want them to close down LAPIS, but let's face it, that wouldn't be the end of the world, would it?

Flies, maggots, roaches, worms, God knows what else. This place is going to hell.

June 1, 2004
Stare Kiejkuty, Poland
CIA Site LAPIS

Mark Romero Diary

I'M STARTING TO get a little worried about my pal Michal, our Polish liaison. Okay, more than a little.

He couldn't stop talking about the Black Madonna of Czestochowa (yes, I did have to look that up on the Internet), which is a famous (infamous) icon of the Virgin Mary and Baby Jesus that is housed at some monastery south of here, and it's got a really long and convoluted history. I would write that down here, but I was mostly zoned out as he was telling me about it today. Why was he telling me about this?

Well, I guess I unknowingly made a mistake telling Michal a week or so ago about all the crazy shit that the Engineer has been telling us. Well, not everything of course, but Michal is our liaison officer with the Poles, and we're allowed and even encouraged to keep them somewhat in the loop on what we're uncovering here at LAPIS as a sign of goodwill and interagency cooperation and all that crap. So I guess that Michal has been connecting the dots between the Black Mother that the Engineer is involved with and this famous Polish icon.

Anyway, it's supposed to have been painted by St. Luke (the gospel guy) on wood from the table that Jesus, Mary, and Joseph had in their house. Yeah right. No one knows exactly how it ended up in Poland, but it's been associated with Poland for centuries. It's essentially a national treasure (maybe THE [all caps in original] national treasure). Lots of stories about various medieval bigwigs trading this thing around and moving it here and there, taking it on military campaigns with them to bring divine favor to the cause and all that. Then there was some story about it saving the monastery where it was stored from a siege, which they successfully held off and won the war, and some kind of fake copy of the icon made as a ruse (I didn't quite follow that part), and then after the war was won the entire country of Poland was placed under the protection of Our Lady and her being made honorary queen of Poland. Along the way were a bunch of attempts by thieves to steal the painting, and damaging it but never being able to destroy it, and the thieves always met terrible fates (of course). Lots of miracles associated with the icon too, miraculous healings and all that. There was a lot more to it, but essentially, it's a really magical/miraculous icon of this really important representation of Mary, who has a deep and abiding connection to Poland. Personally, when you look at Poland's history of invasions and being wiped off the map completely several times...it's hard to see how she's intervened on their behalf, but whatever floats your boat. If you're a Pole, according to Michal, this thing is a BIG [all caps in original] deal.

As with the spelling of the name of where it's housed/on display, I had to look up what this thing looks like after he talked my ear off about it for a half hour. It's suitably creepy, as you would expect for a medieval icon, and the reason for the name is pretty clear: for some reason the skin of both Mary and Jesus is really dark, like mahogany, as though they're, well, black, as in of African descent or something. No idea why, though let's face it, if they were real, they probably were not exactly fair-skinned and blue-eyed the way they're usually depicted.

So that's all weird stuff to me, but it's a normal level of weirdness I can handle. Don't get me wrong: I was raised Catholic. Went to Catholic school for eight years, we always went to mass growing up, I was married in the church, etc. etc. Work in the Army and now the CIA has not exactly lent itself to being strictly observant, but it's not like I'm a religious skeptic, okay?

But the shit that Michal was telling me today and connecting it all up with what the Engineer has been telling us about the Black Mother is batshit crazy insane.

I'll make a confession here (an unofficial one): I have always thought that religious zealots are pretty nutty. Religious zealots of all stripes, including Catholic ones. I mean, sure, go to Mass a few times a year, get baptized, maybe don't eat meat on Fridays during Lent and stuff like that is fine. But the stuff where it drives you to kill, or die, or believe all kinds of crazy shit? No way. Overtly religious talk and conspiracy theories and the end of the world and all that, it's always made me uncomfortable. And Michal was definitely making me uncomfortable (and kind of worried about him, to be honest).

Essentially, he made a lot of the kinds of tenuous connections that only conspiracy theorists and fanatics can about both the Black Mother that the Engineer believes in—which I foolishly, in hindsight, mentioned to Michal—and the Black Madonna of Poland. He's at the point where he thinks they're the same person, and that it was destiny, fate, her will, divine law, what have you, that brought the Engineer to Poland carrying her name and will. He thinks that the Engineer brought word of her to LAPIS because it's here in Poland that she's going to usher in a new world, transform the Earth into heaven and all that kind of thing. Honestly, it was disturbingly close to some of what I've heard the Engineer say, not that I was going to let Michal know that.

I cut him off when he started talking about wanting to talk to the Engineer about all this. No idea how he would respond if we brought Michal in, but no way that HQ (or Dave) would ever sign off on this, even if I thought it was a good idea, which I don't for the record. The answer to interrogating one nutjob is not to bring in a second nutjob to fuel his fantasies and delusions and give the Engineer more crazy talk ammo that he could feed us. Christ, that could set us back weeks, months.

Anyway, Michal is now on my official Crazy People List, a list that grows by the day here at LAPIS. He's not getting anywhere close to the Engineer if I have anything to say about it.

June 3, 2004
Stare Kiejkuty, Poland
CIA Site LAPIS

Mark Romero Diary

TALKED WITH MICHAL again today—he said he had some important stuff to update Dave on, and I saw him in the hallway after that meeting, so I pigeonholed him to ask him what was going on because he looked like he was about ready to cry. Fortunately I was able to avoid having to talk about the Black Madonna today and kept him on task.

Michal told me that there have now been at least four deaths or disappearances in the area near LAPIS over the last month or so. They don't know if there are any more people unaccounted for/bodies that might be found at some point. That was unclear, but four of them for sure. A couple of them were local teenagers and the others were hikers or people passing through. They know that the two teenage boys are just gone. No bodies, but there were no indications they were running away from home, etc. Who knows where they went, but those are being treated as "suspicious." They did find two bodies of adults out in the woods within five or ten miles of LAPIS and they were, according to Michal, "shredded." Just torn apart. So bad that they're thinking it was maybe a bear or pack of wild dogs or wolves or maybe a boar or something. Kind of freaky. Michal's people are keeping the local cops and search parties away from LAPIS—the Poles are good for stuff like that so we don't have any nosy nellies—and he said we should keep our eyes peeled. He said it's been all over the local news, but hey, not speaking Polish and all, I don't exactly tune in for the news at 11 every night.

Michal said that he went to Dave to update him on the situation and, per Michal's bosses, suggest that we consider moving the "guests" out of LAPIS temporarily out of an abundance of caution. Unsurprisingly Dave got upset at that suggestion and told him it's all bullshit and to go back to his superiors and tell them to go fuck themselves, we're not moving LAPIS. Michal acquiesced and said he would convey the message. Can't say I'm shocked that that was Dave's reaction because that's how he mostly reacts whenever I go to him to update him or tell him we need to take some kind of action.

So I guess LAPIS is staying put.

But fuck, what the hell is killing these people? Is it all a coincidence? How many people have to die in a forest before you admit that maybe, just maybe, there's something weird going on? On the other hand, I think I've mostly been spooking myself out there. I mean, sure, I thought some weird shit had happened, but it's not like I've actually seen any dangerous animals or people in the woods. Honestly, it could all be disconnected. You know how people get. A couple kids run away from home, and then something else weird happens, and it all becomes some grand conspiracy theory when in reality, it's just standard routine stuff going on.

Nothing to see here, folks, go back to sleep, I guess.

June 4, 2004
Stare Kiejkuty, Poland
CIA Site LAPIS

Mark Romero Diary

AMONG OTHER THINGS today, the Engineer told us that the Mother gave him a gift by implanting a black seed within him. He didn't just receive the ones in Yemen that he claimed he gave away; she also came to him later and gave him one that she either put into his body or that he somehow took into himself. (Swallowed it? Shoved it up his ass? Who knows. He's hopelessly vague about stuff like that and we can never pin him down on it.) It's been there for many months or a couple years—again, unclear—and it's been slowly growing inside him, germinating like an actual seed, and it is somehow transforming him. He is "becoming." Becoming what, I obviously asked. The tap dancing began: becoming something like a more perfect version of himself, he is somehow becoming more like she wants him to, she is transforming him into her vision, etc. etc. All bullshit of course.

I mean, if we take what he's saying at face value, it's a mix of lunacy (how could this have happened/be happening?) plus alarming (he's got something inside him that is changing him physically/biologically). Freaky, and if true, we should do something about that. But it's also so completely outlandish that it's impossible to believe. I mean, it's so crazy that it casts doubt on the whole "black seed = bioagents" theory, and probably means that we shouldn't read too much into any of that and certainly shouldn't think about the black seeds as anything real.

But we've got to do our due diligence, of course. Got to check out the claim and see if it holds any validity. Plus, I mean, we don't really know what to make of any of this. Occam's razor says the Engineer is just a crazy person. A delusional nutcase who is either kidding himself/fantasizing/imagining the whole outlandish story or he's just screwing with us and has finally taken it a step too far. Just to be on the safe side, out of a complete abundance of caution, we took him to the infirmary and let Dr. Richards work his magic.

So the Engineer got his full body cavity search. Maybe that was what he wanted all along, I don't know. I was treated to seeing his...well, everything, way more than I wanted to today, and afterward, when we put him back in his cell, the consensus was that he's crazy, or just fucking with us, or both. I mean, he fed us yet another crazy story, got us to check it out, and made fools of us for believing it (even a little). Or maybe he does believe his own story, which makes him even loonier.

It didn't help that he had a hard-on and was grinning the whole time that Dr. Richards had his hand up Khattab's ass.

Scumbag.

Richards didn't find anything, of course, not that we actually expected he would.

June 6, 2004
Stare Kiejkuty, Poland
CIA Site LAPIS

Mark Romero Diary

TODAY WAS ONE of those really fucked up days you never expect to have.

Look, I can't claim that I knew Michal well. I've only worked with him for the last two months, and it's not like we were great buds. But we did work out together a few times, and had some beers a couple times, and went for at least one long, weird walk in the woods. Besides, I have always considered myself a good judge of character. It's kind of my job in some ways. Yeah, I'm probably just a glorified knuckle-dragger, but I have been in some situations where my life literally depended on me rapidly figuring out who I could trust and who I couldn't. And I had thought that Michal was a guy I could trust. Maybe a little squirrely at times, but who isn't in the intel business? It comes with the territory. And sure, he seemed to have gotten a little too into the whole Black Madonna thing recently, but that's just a Polish religious/superstition thing. There are lots of little old Polish ladies who believe in all that stuff and a hell of a lot more and never end up killing their whole family.

Fuck. Fuck. Fuck.

I knew something was up when I saw a bunch of the Polish intel guys drive up and go to speak with Dave. They came out of his office a while later and Dave called a meeting and told us that the Poles needed to talk with us individually and that we weren't to talk amongst ourselves until everyone had been interviewed.

That's not suspicious at all. Of course, the gossip mill began operating full speed. We were speculating that someone had fucked up big time while off-duty. I figured that some of the security guys must have gotten wasted and got in a bar fight or something in town. I saw it a million times when I was in the Army, and eventually that kind of shit catches up with you. A little while later they came to get me and started asking me about Michal. (How the tables have turned, the interrogators got interrogated.) What's he been like lately, did he talk much about his family, when was the last time I saw him, what his mood was like during that last conversation, etc. My stomach sank when I could see the direction this was all going. I was pretty honest with them. I told them I considered him a friendly acquaintance and that we talked or hung out a couple times a week but that he had seemed kind of weird lately. I mentioned that he had seemed especially conspiratorial-minded with the religious stuff and that I had been avoiding talking with him about that because I didn't want to start it up again.

The guys I was talking to seemed decent enough, so I asked them what had happened. That's when they told me that Michal seemed to have gone nuts and killed his wife and two sons and then himself. Shot them all. Left some crazy shit scrawled in blood on the walls about Mary and the Black Madonna and all that sort of thing.

Jesus fucking Christ. Why? Why would he do that?

Needless to say, I have been feeling pretty fucking awful about it. Clearly the guy started going nuts because of...well, I have no idea why, or what would have driven him to that, but I guess I should have said something to someone about him.

But what? What could I have said that would have led to him getting some mental health treatment and not just get fired or institutionalized in some Polish asylum for the rest of his life? What were the warning signs I should have been on the lookout for?

The Poles were actually pretty good about the whole thing and said there was nothing I could have done. They asked me more specifically about the religious stuff he had been saying and I told them what I could recall, without referencing anything that the Engineer told us that I shared with him, because I think that stuff might have been the final trigger for sending Michal over the edge. These guys didn't need to know any of that. It's not like they're cleared for it, and in hindsight obviously I shouldn't have mentioned it to him. But Jesus, how could I have known that it would send him off the deep end?

This evening before dinner they sent over the new FIA liaison officer to replace Michal here at LAPIS. He's a guy named Jan, older than Michal, this kind of skinny, bald, chain-smoking dude I had seen around once or twice shortly after I first got here. Dave introduced him to us briefly and said that he's been read into what we're doing here and anything we would have needed from Michal we should now go to Jan for. That's fine, but he seems to be running around angrily yelling in Polish all the time on his cell phone. Great first impression, dude, though I can imagine he's got a mess to clean up, what with a crazy ass murder-suicide to hush up.

Christ. LAPIS, man.

June 8, 2004
Stare Kiejkuty, Poland
CIA Site LAPIS

Interrogation Transcript: Omar Abu KHATTAB
Interrogation Session 08JUN04-1
Attendees: Omar Abu KHATTAB (detainee), Peter DABROWSKY (lead interrogator, contractor), Deborah SULLIVAN (interrogator, contractor), Mark ROMERO (CTC/RDG liaison, CIA)

[excerpt]

KHATTAB is secured and seated across the table from DABROWSKY, SULLIVAN, and ROMERO in Interrogation Room 2.

ROMERO: "So what are the black seeds that you've talked about previously? I need you to be very specific on this."

KHATTAB: "I have told you before, Mr. Mark, but I am happy to help you understand better. The black seeds are the way that the Mother will transform the world that we live in and make it more pleasing to her. The black seeds will be planted in her gardens and then they will blossom and grow and spread and expand. Together the black seeds will change the face of the earth and everything in it, everyone, and then when it is done she will be pleased."

ROMERO: "Okay, so how do they do that? What's the exact mechanism for how the seeds 'transform the world'?"

KHATTAB: "The black seeds are just how the Mother works her will on the Earth, or one of the ways, she is very powerful. But she transforms the Earth by having the black seeds grow and produce wonders and multitudes. They transform the land and the sky and the waters and birds and animals and people. All of it."

ROMERO: "So the seeds have to grow somewhere for a while?"

KHATTAB: "Yes."

ROMERO: "Where do they grow? In the ground? They have to be planted?"

KHATTAB: "Yes, they have to be planted. But not in dirt. Dirt is too filthy for them, it is not good enough for her holy seeds."

ROMERO: "So where are the seeds planted then?"

KHATTAB: "In people, of course. People who become her holy vessels. It is a sacred gift to be made the vessel where one of her seeds is planted."

ROMERO: "Do you have one of the black seeds planted inside you?"

KHATTAB: "Yes, she has blessed me by making me one of her holy vessels for the seeds."

ROMERO: "So you have one inside you, growing, right now, right here, physically in this room?"

KHATTAB: "Yes."

ROMERO: "Should we be worried about that?"

KHATTAB: [laughs] "No, of course not. It is still growing."

DABROWSKY: "I'm not trying to be insulting, KHATTAB, but reading between the lines here, it kind of sounds like you don't know much about what the black seeds will actually do when they grow or germinate or whatever. It seems like you have this vague sense that they'll do great things and the Mother will be pleased and all that, but you don't seem to know exactly what they'll do."

[KHATTAB is silent.]

DABROWSKY: "Well, is that true? Do we have that right—you don't know anything more on that than what you've shared with us?"

KHATTAB: "The Mother will reveal herself and her plans to all of us, her faithful and infidels alike, when it is the time and place of her choosing. Then she will reveal herself and her plans to the whole world, and all will be transformed. The good and faithful to her will be richly rewarded, and the wicked and unfaithful will be punished in her wrath."

DABROWSKY: "Okay, that's what I thought."

[excerpt]

KHATTAB has been removed from the room and ROMERO, DABROWSKY, and SULLIVAN are seated.

ROMERO: "So what do you guys think about all this? I know that we go 'round and 'round about this, but is he just crazy or are we onto something here? Is this black seed shit just a metaphor for biological weapons?"

DABROWSKY: "Ah yes...the old ravings of a madman question."

SULLIVAN: "Here's a crazy idea: what if the Al Qaeda bioweapons program is headed by some woman whose name we don't even know, and she's the one who KHATTAB is calling the Mother and all that? What if he's just working for this mystery woman and *she's* really the one behind all this?"

DABROWSKY: "I don't know, that sounds pretty far-fetched. These guys are hardcore jihadis, they don't even like women, they wouldn't actually put a woman in charge of anything, would they? I don't think we know of any women involved in a serious way with Al Qaeda, do we? Just a few wives who sometimes courier things and stuff like that."

SULLIVAN: "Maybe. Hear me out though. Do you guys remember 'Dr. Germ'?"

DABROWSKY: "No, who's that?"

SULLIVAN: "I had to dig up her name: Rihab Taha AL-AZAWI. She's the one who convinced Saddam to invest so heavily in biological weapons. The Iraqis had a bunch of women involved in their programs. Hell, this could even be her, for all we know. Maybe there really is a link between AQ and Iraq, cooperating on a BW program."

ROMERO: "Okay, so why don't we float her name to the Engineer, see if he reacts? We can dive into links with Iraq."

DABROWSKY: "He's never really talked about Iraq, has he?"

SULLIVAN: "Not that I can recall."

ROMERO: "I don't think he's ever mentioned Iraq. I don't remember reading that he's ever been there."

SULLIVAN: "Suspicious much?"

DABROWSKY: "Not really, I just mean we don't have any indications that Al Qaeda and Saddam were ever in bed together, despite that bullshit they tried to trot out before the invasion."

SULLIVAN: "Yeah, okay."

ROMERO: "It's an interesting theory. Let's check it out. What have we got to lose?"

June 9, 2004
Stare Kiejkuty, Poland
CIA Site LAPIS

Mark Romero Diary

DEB HAS BEEN a really moody bitch lately and a generally unpleasant person to be around. Every little interaction with her is more painful than it needs to be. You say something, she contradicts you, or asks if you've thought about X, or whatever. Christ. Who needs that? She's being a really shitty colleague. I don't know what's going on with her.

Maybe she's not feeling well? Stressed out? Coming down with something? I don't know. I'm trying to be charitable here and give her the benefit of the doubt. But ultimately, I have to say, who cares, do your fucking job, Deb, and stop being such a bitch to your co-workers. It's the professional thing to do. We're all under a lot of pressure here, you don't have to add to other people's stresses.

June 10, 2004
Stare Kiejkuty, Poland
CIA Site LAPIS

Mark Romero Diary

BUSY DAY, REALLY fucking busy day, but an awesome day. Had a real breakthrough today.

Obviously we've been pressuring the Engineer for specific, actionable intelligence ever since he got here: names, dates, locations, specific actions he took, phone numbers, things we can check out with other sources and corroborate. It's been a game. It always is with these fuckers. They know the kind of stuff we want, and they hold out for as long as possible on giving it to us. Khattab has been the same. But he does seem to want to actually talk about the Mother and the black seeds. Pete, and I think the guys back at HQ, think it's all bullshit. Just a delaying tactic, or the kind of religious mumbo-jumbo that these guys can spend all day talking about, but that doesn't actually help us. Deb's not been sure, and neither have I, if I'm being honest, but I've been hopeful. So we've tried to zero in on the black seeds and get him to be more specific about those. What are they exactly, who did he give them to, when did he give them away, what was going to be done with them, where exactly were they taken, etc. He's pleaded ignorance on most of that, but of course that's been a smokescreen. If these things are so important to him, how could he have just given them away to strangers he had never seen before because a dream told him to. It's all bullshit.

He's talked about "gardens," the locations where the black seeds would be planted and then blossom into...whatever it is that the seeds grow into. These gardens would be the places that would be most like what the Black Mother wants the world to look like or transform into, and again, he's been pretty vague about what that would look like exactly. I suspect it's because he doesn't actually know or have a firm idea. Whatever. Or, obviously, there's a possibility that they don't do anything because they don't actually exist and are just a lie or a figment of his demented imagination.

So we were talking to him about these gardens and drilling down into it, and pressuring him about them, and this afternoon he finally told us where—he says—one of these gardens is. It's in southern Afghanistan in the Zabul province at a compound in the mountains. Now, keep in mind that these places don't exactly have addresses, so we had him give us directions verbally several times in different ways, then busted out some maps and had him pore over them and show us where this place is. It sounds like he visited this place a couple times before they had actually set it up as a "garden."

But we've checked, and there really is a compound where he told us there would be one, and we've got HQ looking into it and cross-checking that location with other intelligence, combing through satellite and UAV footage of the area, etc.

We'll see, but this is exactly the kind of thing we have been hoping to get out of him. Of course, it could all be nothing, but it could also be a specific geographic site associated with AQ's bioweapons program.

Cross your fingers.

June 11, 2004
Stare Kiejkuty, Poland
CIA Site LAPIS

Mark Romero Diary

OKAY, EVERYTHING IS a go. Wow. This all came together very, very fast, but that's all to the good and exactly what should have happened. The Engineer gave us some truly actionable intelligence, which we dutifully passed along and, surprise, surprise, it checked out with other means, and so it's being added to the target list for a SOF raid tonight.

Woo hoo!!!!!

The place is a significantly large compound in a pretty remote mountainous area that's not all that far away from the border from Pakistan, so perfect AQ terrain and exactly the kind of place where they would set up shop to do things that wouldn't get a lot of interference or notice. My understanding from talking to the targeting analysts is that this place has been getting a fair amount of traffic in and out for a while but is currently pretty quiet. They know that there are people inside the compound though, because they've more or less been able to determine that a lot of people have arrived at the site in recent weeks and not all that many have left.

The plan is to send in a special operations team, which in this case is going to be supported by some number of CIA paramilitary guys. Some of these operations have Afghan special forces involved, but not this one because of the sensitivity of the site. They'll come in fast and hard, mostly via helicopter, with some guys already there at the site surveilling it as the op begins. They'll have a gunship or two orbiting overhead to provide fire support if needed, and they'll probably have a Predator or two there as well. I don't know if those will be armed for fire support, but probably, because this one is high priority. They'll swarm inside the compound, take down anybody who presents a threat, then disarm and gather everybody up. They'll probably end up taking some/all of the dudes there prisoner, and will seize as many documents, laptops, hard drives, etc. etc. as possible.

Could be a real treasure trove. There's been some debate about if they should go in wearing MOPP gear because of the potential for biological weapons on site. I think they'll probably err on the side of caution and go in geared up for that. I would, even though they're insanely hot and sweaty and constrictive, because nobody wants to choke to death of some hideous disease you picked up in some hellhole.

It's a standard kind of nighttime raid, these guys literally do this stuff every night. Often they're even hitting more than one site in a night. I've been on many of these, and it's exciting and important. This shit is why people join special forces units.

I mean, look, the whole thing could end up being a bust, but this is why we've poured so much blood, sweat, and tears into interrogating the Engineer. This is it.

June 12, 2004
Stare Kiejkuty, Poland
CIA Site LAPIS

Interrogation Transcript: Omar Abu KHATTAB
Interrogation Session 12JUN04-1
Attendees: Omar Abu KHATTAB (detainee), Peter DABROWSKY (lead interrogator, contractor), Mark ROMERO (CTC/RDG liaison, CIA)

[excerpt]

KHATTAB is secured and seated across the table from DABROWSKY, SULLIVAN, and ROMERO in Interrogation Room 3.

ROMERO: "We sent men to visit the place you told us about the other day, one of the Black Mother's 'gardens.'"

KHATTAB: "See, Mr. Mark, I gave you good information. I gave you exactly what you have been wanting, a specific location like you always ask."

ROMERO: "Yes. We want to talk with you about what they found there."

KHATTAB: "Okay."

ROMERO: "I want to show you some pictures taken at the location you gave us."

KHATTAB: "Okay."

[ROMERO opens a folder and lays out a series of large photos on the table in front of KHATTAB, who appears to study the photographs, picking them up and examining them closely for several minutes in silence.]

KHATTAB: "Yes, Mr. Mark?"

ROMERO: "What do you make of these photographs at the compound?"

KHATTAB: "What do you mean?"

DABROWSKY: "Tell us what you see. What does it look like to you?"

KHATTAB: "These are not very good photos..."

DABROWSKY: "Those are extremely high-quality photos."

KHATTAB: "It is very hard to tell what is going on in them. To me, everything is black, shadowed, hard to see."

DABROWSKY: "Do you know what that blackness is that's covering everything?"

KHATTAB: "No."

DABROWSKY: "It's not shadows. It's mold. Fungus. Spores."

KHATTAB: "Okay."

DABROWSKY: "Do you know anything about that?"

KHATTAB: "No, I don't know anything about that. It's like mushrooms?"

DABROWSKY: "Not mushrooms. Related to mushrooms. We're having it analyzed. It's not found in Afghanistan. It's not native to the region, whatever it is."

KHATTAB: "Okay."

ROMERO: "Well?"

KHATTAB: "I don't know what you want me to say. There are dead bodies everywhere. It looks like your men killed everyone there."

ROMERO: "No. We didn't kill anyone there."

KHATTAB: "Okay, whatever you say. It looks like there are dead bodies in most of these pictures. Are they sleeping?"

ROMERO: "No. Twenty-three dead people. Twelve men, five women, six children. All dead. They were all dead when we got there."

KHATTAB: "Okay."

ROMERO: "Is that what you expected we would find there at the compound?"

KHATTAB: "No. I have never been to the compound. I had heard it was there and you wanted to know, so I gave you the location. But I didn't know what was inside."

ROMERO: "Do you know how all those people died?"

KHATTAB: "No."

ROMERO: "Me neither. Some of them don't have marks on them. They're just dead. Unknown causes. Most of them, though, it's pretty obvious: they were torn apart. Just shredded. Not even shot or stabbed or anything. It was like wild animals killed them or something."

KHATTAB: "Okay."

ROMERO: "Just 'okay'? That's all you have to say?"

KHATTAB: "Well, I don't know what you want me to say. I didn't know any of these people. I don't know how they died."

ROMERO: "So it doesn't surprise you that they were all dead? All killed by...whatever killed them?"

KHATTAB: "Well, yes, it surprises me. I don't know anything about it."

ROMERO: "Is...this [gestures at pictures] what you expected we'd find at this site?"

KHATTAB: "No. Not exactly. I didn't really know exactly what you would find, but I didn't think there would be dead people there. I thought it would be full of life. Like a beautiful garden, with otherworldly delights. A paradise on Earth."

ROMERO: "'Otherworldly delights'?"

KHATTAB: "Yes."

ROMERO: "Like what, exactly?"

KHATTAB: "Well, like happy people walking in a beautiful garden, playing, eating, drinking, just being happy, like that."

ROMERO: "That's obviously *not* what they found. How can you explain that?"

KHATTAB: "I do not know. It is not for me to explain."

ROMERO: "Try."

KHATTAB: "The people at that place must have been bad people. They must have refused to bring the Mother's message to the world. They must have betrayed her. I don't know why they would have done that. They must have been terrible, terrible people for her to punish them like this. I am thinking they deserved the fate that they received. This is justice. These are pictures of justice you have shown me."

ROMERO: "So how do you think these people died?"

KHATTAB: "I have no idea. I told you, I have never been to this place."

ROMERO: "How do you think the ones with no marks on them died?"

KHATTAB: "I don't know. Did they kill themselves? Pills? Poison?"

ROMERO: "What about the ones with all the wounds?"

KHATTAB: "I don't know that either. Maybe the Mother tore them apart? Maybe she sent her servants to do it for her."

ROMERO: "What kind of servants?"

KHATTAB: "I don't know. I have never seen them."

ROMERO: "Are you talking about people? Humans? Or something else?"

KHATTAB: "I don't know. She has people, like me, who serve her, but I don't know them, and she has other things."

ROMERO: "Like what?"

KHATTAB: "I don't know. They come from her world, I think."

[excerpt]

KHATTAB has been removed from the room and ROMERO, DABROWSKY, and SULLIVAN are seated.

ROMERO: "So how do you guys assess this? What the hell happened at the compound?"

DABROWSKY: "That's a great fucking question, isn't it?"

ROMERO: "I guess the biggest unknown is if this was an accidental BW release. Did it drive some of them insane and make them kill the others? I mean, let's face it, this wasn't animals that did it."

DABROWSKY: "Nope, the place was sealed. We'll know more from the autopsies, but no obvious signs of forced entry before our guys got there."

ROMERO: "Right. So if they were storing the weapon there and it accidentally got loose and killed everyone—horribly—there, then, well, it's certainly proof that Al Qaeda has the capability and that the Engineer isn't totally full of shit. I mean, he did actually tell us exactly where to find this site. We wouldn't have found it otherwise. How long would it have taken us to figure out that this was an AQ facility?"

DABROWSKY: "Could have been forever. We might never have learned of this place."

ROMERO: "Right. And if it *was* a BW release, then it's a novel agent, or at least an unknown one. I know the experts haven't all weighed in yet, but the geeks back at HQ said they have no idea what could have caused what we found there. No idea."

DABROWSKY: "Scary."

ROMERO: "Fucking terrifying. And also, that would mean that there's likely more of it out there. Locations unknown. I mean, assuming this was caused by one of the black seeds, then imagine what more of these things could do."

DABROWSKY: "Right. I mean, this was probably an accidental release in a small, very confined area. There were a couple dozen people there at the compound. What if there was a deliberate release in a mall, or church, or school or whatever. Some place with thousands of people packed in tight."

ROMERO: "Yeah, like a football game or Times Square, some place where *thousands* of people are packed in like sardines, then this thing goes off, then people start choking and dying. Then there's a stampede and the killing *really* starts."

DABROWSKY: "Fuck me."

June 12, 2004
Stare Kiejkuty, Poland
CIA Site LAPIS

Mark Romero Diary

DEB SURE HAS been missing a lot of interrogation sessions lately, she's been late to morning meetings when she's bothered to show up at all, etc. etc. I don't know what the fuck is going on with her. Basically, she's either not doing her job or she's been generally checked out lately, and that's really not acceptable. I've talked with Pete about it, and he hemmed and hawed a little about it, and kind of wanted to give her some slack, but ultimately he agrees with me.

She's not pulling her weight around here and I'm sick about it. I'm going to have a come to Jesus session with her and let her know that this is not fucking acceptable. She's going to have to start shaping up.

I'm not going to bitch about it to Dave or anything, but Jesus Christ, woman: Do your fucking job!!!

June 13, 2004
Stare Kiejkuty, Poland
CIA Site LAPIS

Mark Romero Diary

I'M STARTING TO get a little worried about the Engineer. Okay, more than a little worried. It's not that I want him to have a long and happy life, but we haven't extracted nearly enough intel from this guy. The last thing I would want is for him to drop dead from some medical problem before we can get what he knows out of him.

Here's the issue: He's been complaining about stomach discomfort and abdominal pain. His abdomen is now visibly swollen and it's painful to the touch. His appetite has been off, but his bowel movements are normal. (Yes, I have a terrible job that requires me to be aware of a terrorist's shit. This is my life now.) He's not constipated, or at least not much, so it's not like he's all backed up and literally full of shit (he may be figuratively full of shit, however). He attributes all of this to the black seed that he says is growing within him, of course.

We couldn't ignore the problem since it could be something serious. Richards examined Khattab and says that there's something in there. He wants to do more tests on Khattab at a Polish clinic, which is a big pain in the ass to arrange because of the security requirements to move a detainee from a black site then back again, plus the need to keep it secret/secure on the Polish end of things. Jan is helping out on that end, and he keeps saying, "No problem! No problem!" then goes back to yelling at people in Polish on his cell phone, so all I can do is take him at his word.

Ultimately, Richards says that if he doesn't naturally pass whatever the foreign object is, Khattab will need surgery to remove it. I can't imagine that he's going to shit out whatever is causing the bloating and discomfort, so that seems likely to me.

I asked Richards a hypothetical: What if the Engineer swallowed some capsule containing a biological weapon and that's what he's calling a black seed and it's somehow stuck inside him? Are we in any danger from whatever this thing is? He was blasé and said no, just keep a close eye on him, it'll be fine. Yeah right. He's right that we do actually monitor the detainees' waste—thank Christ that's not typically my job—and they're kept under close surveillance even (especially) when going to the bathroom, so there's actually not much of a chance that he swallowed some capsule before we caught him and every time he shits it out, he immediately re-swallows it. Aside from being generally disgusting, it would actually be close to impossible for him to pull that off without us knowing about it. It's not like we let him take a shit, then root around in it, pull out the object, then quickly swallow it again. I'd believe he could do that maybe once without getting caught if his guards were not paying close enough attention, but no way he's been doing that for two and a half months consistently.

Richards is still a dick though.

Dave has authorized the medical transfer, etc. I let Richards handle that with Dave because he seems to pretty much automatically say no whenever I ask him to approve something.

I talked to Khattab this afternoon and asked him how he's feeling because he's seemed oddly peaceful, serene, stoic about the whole thing. He told me that he's not worried, despite the circumstances and discomfort, because he's doing exactly what the Mother wants him to do. He's exactly where she wants him to be. He's doing her work. I guess that's not really so different of a perspective from those old country bumpkins always talking about "doing the Lord's work." But I was kind of unsettled by his reaction. I don't know. I would just think that if it was happening to me, if I had some weird thing growing in or lodged in my stomach and I was going to have to have surgery to retrieve it, I suspect I wouldn't be quite as stoic. Maybe on some level I wish I had that much faith in a higher power. I've just never been all that religious, and the stuff I've seen since 9/11 has not exactly endeared the idea of God to me.

June 14, 2004
Stare Kiejkuty, Poland
CIA Site LAPIS

Mark Romero Diary

TODAY WAS A dark, fucked-up day. I don't even know what to say about it.

Christ, I had to kill something today and I don't even know what it was.

Okay, let me back up a little as I process this. Try [underlined in original] to process this.

Here's how my day started this morning. We didn't plan to have a session with the Engineer this morning, so I was in my quarters. Fucking around, to be honest. But Pete came running up banging on my door and told me that Deb was sick, something was really wrong with her. He and I ran back down the hall to her room and saw three or four people standing outside the door in the hallway, a couple more inside with her. We pushed our way into the room to see what was going on. I asked if someone had already sent for Dr. Richards, and a couple people said they had, that he was coming right up. Deb was laying in her bed, dressed, but also kind of tangled up in her sheets. She was sweating and kind of moaning and clutching her stomach, writhing around. I could tell she was in a lot of pain and scared.

Pete and I were kind of crouched down by the bedside trying to keep Deb calm. I mean, what the hell else could we do? Eventually Richards got there, Dr. Better-Late-Than-Never, and told us all to back off and give him some space and get back to work and all that. He started checking Deb out, and when he pulled back the sheets I could see that her stomach was really distended. Like pregnant lady belly distended. Like, month eight or nine of the pregnancy distended. I was stunned. Just in total disbelief.

Then her stomach kind of rippled, like something was moving in there and stretching the skin out. I guess Richards was stunned too, because he told Pete and I to help him move Deb down to the infirmary so he could treat her.

Things started happening really fast once we got her down there. I didn't know what was going on, but Deb started grunting and heaving. I thought she was trying to throw up or something. I very distinctly remember Richards turning to us and saying, "She's in labor and about to give birth. Did either of you guys know about this?" I don't remember what either of us said, but we were both clearly totally shocked. I mean, I knew that Deb had been kind of weird and sick lately, but I literally saw her a few days ago and she was not pregnant like that. Like, she could have been a few months along, but ready to pop? No way.

Then she was screaming and pushing. I was behind Richards because...well, seeing my wife give birth once was more than enough for me. It's one thing when it's your wife and child, but I guess I don't have very strong paternal instincts because I was not exactly clamoring to repeat the experience. So I couldn't really see exactly what was going on, I was just hanging back, and Pete and I were kind of looking at each other, like what the fuck is happening?

My vision of...whatever it was she gave birth to, or that crawled out of her, was blocked because Richards was standing in the way, but then I caught a glimpse of something red and lumpy kind of slide down from her crotch and end up on one of her legs.

I don't know what the fuck it was. Something horrible and monstrous and inhuman. Not a baby. Christ, I hope that wasn't a baby.

Deb started screaming, "Get it off me! Get it off me! Oh God!" and trying to push it away, but she wasn't making any headway. Richards and Pete were just standing there stunned and not doing shit to help. I had moved and could see it latched onto Deb's inner thigh and I think it was chewing on her. I could see its mouth parts working and Deb was covered in blood, from her crotch down to her feet. The table she was on, everything. A lot of blood.

So I grabbed the thing and pulled it off her and tried to fling it across the room. I had to kind of collect myself for a second after I touched it because, well, what the fuck? It was some horrible giant bug thing that was all wet and gooey and covered in blood, though I could see that it was black underneath all that red, with a shell or carapace or whatever you call it.

I pulled and it didn't come off Deb right away, it had latched onto her, not with its limbs—did it even have hands?—but with its mouth. It had some sort of horrible pincers or fangs or something awful that was just tearing into her and she was screaming. I pulled harder and it came loose, though I saw that it had dug a deep trench in Deb's inner thigh and blood was starting to just pour out of that hole.

The thing kind of flipped around in mid-air as I was holding it, which I could barely do because it was slippery and wet and not at all like a baby but almost like a softshell crab or something. It bit my hand, and then I immediately shook it and dropped it because I didn't want it doing to me what it had done to Deb; then it latched onto my leg and started trying to climb up my leg.

At that point I heard Richards say something like, "What the fuck is that? It's not a baby. It's some kind of parasite or something."

I didn't want to stick my hand down there to grab it again because I really didn't know what to do with it. So I grabbed something off the counter next to me, I don't even remember what it was to be honest, and used that to kind of scrape it off my leg before it could get a good grip on me.

Richards had been yelling this whole time—but not exactly helping me out—and I distinctly heard him say, "Kill it! I don't know what that thing is. Kill it." So I stomped on it over and over again until it was mostly just pulp and blood on the floor.

Deb had passed out by this point, and Richards sprang into action to stop the bleeding, both internally and from her leg. Jesus, there was a lot of blood everywhere. He got her stabilized though, and things quieted down. He eventually got my hand bandaged up where it had nipped me, but that was trivial compared to everything else.

No one blamed me, thank God; both Richards and Pete said I did the right thing. It must have been some awful parasite or something. It had to have been, right? I mean, what else could it have been? Richards says he'll handle it and send it off for testing. What the fuck kind of testing? Genetic analysis to determine what it was? Then they can try to figure out how it got inside Deb?

How in the hell can we all just go back to work after something like this happened?

What the hell am I supposed to do now? What do I tell Deb? How do I look her in the eyes now?

What the hell just happened?

June 15, 2004
Stare Kiejkuty, Poland
CIA Site LAPIS

Mark Romero Diary

I HAD TO take matters into my own hands today. We'd reached one of those points where if I didn't take charge and force something to happen, nothing was going to happen.

My old bosses in the Army would have been proud of me.

I called a meeting of all the key players at LAPIS today to try to figure out what the FUCK [all caps in original] was going on around here and what we should do about it.

Of course, Dave could not be bothered to show up. Before I went to anyone or set the meeting up, I went to him. I knocked on the door to his quarters because he wasn't in his office, humbly waited to be called in, he mumbled something vague so I went in, laid things out for him. He was, well, charitably, "inebriated." Utterly shit-faced. Dangerously drunk. Like drunk to the point that a normal person would need their stomach pumped and a new liver. No use whatsoever, per usual. So I quietly left and got everybody together downstairs.

I invited about a dozen people to the main conference room and everything went way smoother than I thought it would. There didn't seem to be all that much argument or debate, though we took some time to hash things out. People were supportive of the idea that we need to do SOMETHING [all caps in original] and that Dave wasn't doing "enough" (read: anything) to address all the problems that have been going on here. Honestly, I was just glad that no one threw me under the bus.

I asked Dr. Richards to give us a status update on Deb first thing. He's continuing to treat her in the infirmary here in LAPIS, and she's most mostly just semi-conscious, but responsive. Not in a coma or anything, just sleeping and resting. That's the best thing for her. She's lost a good amount of blood, but he gave her a couple pints and she's doing as okay as could be expected. Richards was actually a little dismissive of the whole thing. He said that the likeliest answer was that somehow Deb contracted a weird parasite he hasn't seen before and, despite its appearance, it was not some kind of weird, fucked-up, freakishly mutated baby that she gave birth to (not his words, I'm reading between the lines here). The remains of the thing will be sent in for genetic tests to determine its exact nature, but he doesn't know how long that will take. Maybe a couple weeks. Pete seems pretty shell-shocked about the whole thing (I talked with him more after the meeting), which is not surprising since he and Deb have worked together for a long time.

So that was the elephant in the room I wanted to deal with, but then I brought up all the other issues we've been wrestling with. We're stuck with the Engineer, and believe he still has important information, but he's also got some unknown health problem that could be serious. Hell, it could be the same thing as Deb had, assuming that Richards is right about a parasite outbreak, which I can't imagine he is. Then there's the flurry of weird shit that's been happening around LAPIS, none of which are important in and of themselves, but put together they're suggestive that something truly fucked up and bizarre is going on here. But we've also got the unexplained events near LAPIS, including multiple deaths and disappearances of the locals. What the fuck is going on there? There haven't exactly been any big announcements that they found missing hikers lost in the woods, or caught a serial killer operating nearby or anything. And let's not forget that Michal went batshit crazy insane and killed himself and his whole family. Are we just going to sweep that under the carpet? People heard me out, but the consensus seemed to be that I'm conflating a lot of things and suggesting a pattern where there is none. For example, Richards said that yes, there have been some medical problems at LAPIS, but that's why he's here onsite. The weird shit that's been happening in/around LAPIS doesn't suggest there's anything broader wrong, this is just normal amounts of weird shit, which happens. I got the distinct vibe that everyone wanted to give me the old "don't worry, be happy" message. Bullshit.

I told them that I want to send a dissent cable to HQ, which doesn't require Dave's approval, but they all cautioned me to not do that. They said I'll look like a crank, it'll derail my career, it's the fastest way home, etc. etc. No one wanted to sign. I think Pete was probably with me, but he's a contractor, so sadly his views don't matter much.

It's all too much. I'm sending the fucking cable anyway. I don't care.

June 16, 2004
Stare Kiejkuty, Poland
CIA Site LAPIS

Mark Romero Diary

SOMETIMES YOU JUST have to do something even though you know it's not exactly going to be "career-enhancing." I did exactly what I said I was going to do at the meeting: I sent a dissent cable back to HQ detailing what I see as the big problems here at LAPIS and the lack of action on the part of Dave or anyone else to actually do anything about them.

So how many friends does dear ol' Dave have back at HQ? I don't know. He's got to still have some, and from what everyone says, he used to be a badass at the start of his career, so maybe some people still think of him that way.

Are there senior guys at HQ who are going to read me sending this as insubordination? Yes, probably. But let's list out what the situation here at LAPIS is right now:

- I laid out how we are currently stuck with the detainees, especially the Engineer, not through lack of trying, but we are stymied and need some support on this. I still believe that he's got some really important intelligence in his head that we need to extract, and that that information could stop the next attack on the homeland, which could be worse than 9/11. I also noted how he's got an unknown medical condition and may need serious medical treatment outside of LAPIS if he's going to live long enough to produce that intelligence for us. Not to throw the trained interrogators or Richards under the bus, but we need some assistance to resolve the current situation. Our boss here is not helpful. That's got to be fixed.
- I tried to detail the flurry of weird events at LAPIS that have been happening here, none of which are important in and of themselves, but put together, they are suggestive that

something is going on. I don't know what, but morale here is poor, not just because of the leadership but also because bizarre shit has been happening here routinely. That's just not acceptable. I had to be kind of delicate on that because my #1 goal in all of this is to not sound like a crank or a conspiracy theorist. If they think I'm nuts, they won't take anything I say seriously, and that's the fastest ticket to being bounced out of here.

- I talked about how the immediate area outside of LAPIS has had a series of unexplained events, including multiple deaths and disappearances of the locals, and no one is taking that seriously. For Christ's sake, there could be a security threat in all of this. Who knows? But it needs to be investigated and not just ignored.

- I detailed how Michal went batshit crazy insane and killed himself and his whole family. Are we just going to sweep that under the carpet? I can't say that LAPIS made him do it or anything like that, but when the chief local intelligence liaison is a homicidal maniac, there's a problem. A deep-seated one.

- I tried to talk about whatever the fuck just happened with Deb. She could still die and probably needs to be medevacked and get physical and psychological treatment. We don't know what caused it or what that thing was, but Jesus. Again, are we just supposed to ignore it?

So what does all that suggest? To me, it says we're in real trouble and we need strong leadership from Dave, or better yet, someone else. We need someone to step in and take charge. I'm not saying that should be me. Hell, I know it shouldn't be me. But I also know it's not Dave. He should be relieved for dereliction of duty. And frankly, this is wartime, and in a very real sense command of LAPIS is a wartime command, so he should probably be taken out back and shot for treason, but we won't go there.

Is anyone at HQ going to actually do anything about this? (Other than fire my ass?) I have no idea, but at least when the shit hits the fan no one can say that they weren't forewarned about all this. I don't have all (or even any) of the solutions to what's going on here, but if we don't at least start admitting that there are some really serious problems, nothing is going to get better and may actually get much,

much worse. That's the bottom line. We're on the express train to Shit Town.

June 16, 2004
Stare Kiejkuty, Poland
CIA Site LAPIS

CABLE # RX401232-04

SUBJECT: Major Problems at Site LAPIS

DATE OF CABLE: 16 JUN 2004

1.   Over the course of the last two months, Site
LAPIS has experienced a significant number of
unexplained events that have hampered progress with
interrogations of Al Qaeda detainees and have begun
to pose major risks to the health and safety of LAPIS
personnel.

2.   David Franklin, chief of base at Site LAPIS, has
failed to exercise good leadership and judgment,
which has begun as;ld ksl kdl; asl;dk asd kasd
lasdlas;dl'a asdlas;dlas"as

3.   Dllfg group[wetp-weotewe=p[Deborah Sullivan
asdjilasdqwv ;qwo yqeyd dasdhbbsdklo'j serious health
problems opwi potentially life-threatggggggening
09weubd

4.   [gl sdkjd jsdfuisf nsf sf ipfv opsdf'gip sv
sdkfhcmc Omar Abu Khattab, alias "The Engineer"
awkldwegaw ;se uwu[Qp u8q[0r uqPq JFFJXCN,ASm

5.   Site LAPIS asdhlsdfhsd lsd sdf oiujsdfy; AQ [qup
JFLJj

6.   Local Polish liaison kjdf efh;L; ;fj'FI
FfjljaKL'JF'qik Michal dfjh ff gsd KHFWo;f fo;FYWh
Fojf fn JN

7.   Sfhefh IA weiofjiov mkvm vm djcfi kdfopw do
pqw dwio padj kdj'djkid iwdj 'dkdopcj'dj'DK'D'Dd'JK
outside audit PQODKWOQDJK'q;kd

8.   Awi udfiq wuika JFCk lajf kfj omm Al thalma
'FfIPFJ'qopq Ako'd folK'Fk'fj'K'fpi FK'FJK'FJIOFJ
'f'opI' QWOPik'Q'FK'OFIK'wff ' investigation.

9.   kaw ujqwiu shayateen qwpj wq upq wdiqPIDFqi'¡q
FIOF'FIFIfuFghh;i90I'QE iwq9QWUIQWERU38fo

10.   asjd hasj kdh ksdh ksad hjasfh dfhsfh asfhasf
has sherreera fu89wu8uq pqw pqweueuu euiooQD ;

June 17, 2004
McLean, Virginia
CIA HQ

CABLE # RX401653-04

SUBJECT: Response to CABLE #RX401232-04

DATE OF CABLE: 17 JUN 2004

Please resend CABLE # RX401232-04. Cable unreadable; appears to have become garbled in transmission.

June 17, 2004
Stare Kiejkuty, Poland
CIA Site LAPIS

Mark Romero Diary

SO THE PLAN is to take the Engineer offsite to a closed ward at a Polish hospital that the FIA has arranged where he'll have exploratory surgery to remove whatever the foreign object is that's growing inside his abdomen/stomach before it kills him.

Pete and I had a conversation with Richards today, and the guy was a dick, as usual. He very snottily informed us that he felt the need to remind us to not forget about the Engineer and his medical problem despite the "distraction" of Deb's medical issue, which she brought about by her own actions. What the fuck, man? Some bedside manner. Yes, of course we're concerned about the Engineer and the fact that he's got something lodged in there and if not treated it could kill him. But Jesus, have a heart, man. Something fucking terrible, like absolutely horrific and terrifying, happened to Deb that we all fucking witnessed and maybe it's okay to be a little concerned about her. The thing tried to tear a hole in my hand, for God's sake, and we're just supposed to ignore all of that and just focus on other shit?

Anyway, Richards has consulted with some Polish doctors and some American guy the embassy sent over (or maybe the CIA sent him as a consultant, it wasn't clear) and they're all agreed that Khattab isn't in any immediate danger, as in, whatever it is isn't going to kill him overnight until we can arrange the transfer and get the hospital set up. But they all say that he really does need some additional tests and the surgery. Richards can feel the object when he probes Khattab's abdomen, and I admit that when he was pressing down I could kind of see the outline of something. The abdominal bulge is pretty prominent now. Whatever it is, it's not metallic, it's something softer than that or maybe organic. They're clueless and just need to do the exploratory surgery and extract it to be sure.

June 17, 2004
Stare Kiejkuty, Poland
CIA Site LAPIS
10:55pm local

DR. RICHARDS WAS relaxing with a Scotch in his quarters, feet up on his desk, when a loud knocking startled him, almost making him spill his drink.

"Goddamnit," he muttered. Loudly: "What is it?"

"Sir, medical problem with one of the detainees."

Richards walked over and opened the door, seeing one of the on-duty security men standing there, a pinched look on his face. "Sir, Khattab seems like he's in pretty severe pain. He's complaining of abdominal pain. Looks pretty swollen. I don't think he's faking it."

"How long has he had this pain? He was stable and not in much discomfort when I examined him earlier." Richards walked back inside and slipped his shoes on. He followed the security guard back out into the hallway and locked the door to his quarters.

"I'm not sure. At least an hour or so probably. He started complaining about it twenty or thirty minutes ago, but we wanted to make sure it was legit before we bothered you."

"He's not faking it?"

"No, no, sir, definitely not."

"Okay, let's head down there and take a look. Bring him to the infirmary and I'll meet you there."

By the time Richards had prepped the infirmary, two security guards brought Khattab into the room. Richards gestured toward the examination table and they brought Khattab over to it, slowly shuffling. Khattab moaned slightly as they secured his hands and feet to the table with thick leather cuffs. He was sweating profusely and looked pale.

Richards pulled Khattab's shirt up with one latex-gloved hand and began pressing on the captive's abdomen. Khattab cried out and said, "Stop! Stop!" though Richards continued his exam. Khattab was moaning continuously now and sweating profusely. Richards relented for a moment and was alarmed to see Khattab's abdomen bulge. Something inside seemed to shift and press outward, distending Khattab's belly for a long moment before receding.

"Oh fuck," Richards said. "I'm going to have to operate on this asshole."

He turned and started assembling surgical instruments. "Go get Peterson. He's got some medical training and can assist in the surgery. He's probably in his quarters."

One of the security men asked, "You guys going to be okay here? I can call for an extra security person before I head out. Protocol—"

Richards waved him off. "Just get Peterson. Hurry."

He left and Richards told the other man, "I'm going to have to open him up. You're going to need to scrub in if you're going to be in the room during the surgery. The surgical scrubs are in that cabinet over there."

Both men were donning surgical scrubs and washing up with their backs to Khattab when they heard him thumping on the table, his heels and head repeatedly striking it loudly. His entire body was juddering, his spine arched, as he strained at the table's restraints. Khattab was starting to make a high-pitched whining sound, almost like a dog, and his head was thrashing from side to side, thick ropes of saliva coating his face, the table, and the floor. He sounded like he was trying to form words, but nothing close to a human-sounding language was emerging from his lips.

"Christ," said Richards. "He's seizing." Richards approached Khattab to ensure he was still breathing and had an unobstructed airway when he realized that Khattab's skin was rippling, bulges appearing and disappearing under the flesh of his face, chest, limbs. Khattab's teeth, now looking like two-inch-long fangs, began to protrude from his mouth, piercing the skin of his cheeks and lips, the blood beginning to flow down onto his chest. Likewise, his arms and chest were expanding, beginning to tear through the flimsy orange jumpsuit he was wearing. His skin was starting to darken, taking on an oily sheen.

"Wh-what is happening?" Richards asked. "This can't be happening." He and the guard stood frozen, not daring to approach or touch Khattab, but too captivated to move.

Khattab looked like he was starting to hyperventilate, his breath coming faster and faster, his chest expanding. Then his chest stopped contracting with each breath, his chest ballooning in size, the chest restraints straining to contain his new bulk.

Khattab threw back his head, mouth open as wide as possible, his jaws almost breaking from the strain. A howl began to emerge from deep within his chest, then grew deeper and deeper. His arms tensed, flexed, straining, then tore through the thick leather bands that confined them, first the right then the left. Khattab threw the tattered remains of the restraints on the floor, then reached down to his legs and tore through those as well, not bothering to unbuckle them. He hopped off the table.

Richards and the security guard remained frozen, aghast at what they were seeing.

Khattab's eyes were wild, his mouth open in a terrifying rictus, his teeth now elongated and protruding through the tears in his lips and cheeks. His whole face was distorted, bestial, only vaguely recognizable as the man he once was. His body had likewise changed, was continuing to change. His skin glistened with oily droplets of sweat and other fluids. His muscles continued to spasm and bulge, growing larger as they watched. His hands were bulky claws tipped with torn nails emerging from fingers that were bloated and twisted.

They smelled his fetid breath as he howled, then pounced on them, tearing them apart before the stunned security officer could even draw his sidearm. Richards squealed and cried out in agony as Khattab, or what was once Khattab, began to chew through his face.

***

Peterson and the other security officer arrived at the infirmary a few minutes later.

The place was a shambles when they arrived—the main examination table was shattered and debris was scattered everywhere. Blood streaked the walls and ceiling and was pooled on the floor.

"What the fuck happened?" asked the security man, starting to draw his handgun.

Then they heard something—something big—slithering around, knocking into cabinets in the rear of the infirmary.

"Oh fuck," Peterson said when they saw what was making the noise.

June 17, 2004
Stare Kiejkuty, Poland
CIA Site LAPIS
11:10pm local

THE WIND BEGAN to pick up. Night had fallen and the skies were overcast and growing cloudier by the minute. The moon was nowhere to be seen. The woods surrounding LAPIS were shrouded in shadow. Things moved within those shadows: trees and tree-like things, and beasts both natural and unnatural. The children of the Mother stirred.

Lightning cracked and thunder boomed overhead. Rain began to fall, big droplets pattering down that rapidly became a curtain of rain falling on LAPIS. There was the smell of copper and ozone in the air. The temperature dropped precipitously as the storm increased. Thunder was more frequent now.

The security teams keeping watch over LAPIS, inside and out, were unhappy. They alternated posts every two hours. The best post, of course, was the security control room inside the main building. There, the men had access to air conditioning and heat, food and beverages, nearby bathrooms, and comfortable seats. Their primary function was to monitor the various surveillance cameras and other sensors scattered along the facility's perimeter and on the buildings and grounds, plus coordinate the roving teams on the grounds.

Tonight, there was a single two-man team roaming the grounds, always the least favorite position for security. These men were armed and patrolled the grounds for several hours before rotating into one of the other assignments. Patrolling the grounds was a good way to stay awake, and more stimulating than staring at a bank of monitors inside, but on nights like this when the sky had opened up, they were quickly drenched and knew they'd be miserable until they could get inside, dry off, and warm up.

Two more security men manned the security shack at the entrance to LAPIS. No one was scheduled to arrive at or depart from LAPIS tonight, especially in this weather, so they tried to stay alert while they dreaded having to patrol the grounds in two hours. Maybe the storm will have passed by then, they thought. For all its importance as a black site—all the security personnel were well aware of what went on at LAPIS—this was a routine, mostly boring posting.

"Rover-1, Rover-1, this is Main Security, over," came the latest call over the main security frequency.

"Go ahead, Main Security, this is Rover-1, over."

"We're getting some sensor pings on movement to the rear of Site L outside the perimeter about 50 meters inside the tree line, over."

"Going to check it out, over."

"Roger."

A minute passed.

"Main Security, no movement seen. Night vision's not picking anything up. Just lots and lots of trees. It was probably just branches moving in the wind. We've been seeing small trees and things whipping around out here. Wind's really picking up, over."

"Roger. Alert us if you see any movement. Over and out."

***

The two men monitoring site security from the LAPIS security center in the main building were getting increasingly spooked. The booms from the thunder outside sounded like they were right overhead, and the facility's sensors—*all* of them—were getting tripped on a non-stop basis now. What had started a couple hours ago with contacts and movement being reported in the forest could no longer be easily dismissed as animals, or the storm, or sensor faults.

"We'd better alert the boss," one said to the other.

"Are you shitting me? He's drunk off his ass by now. He's going to be pissed if we bother him."

"He'll be pissed if we don't." He radioed the chief of base, was almost surprised when Franklin responded with a curt, "What do you want?"

The man told Franklin about all the anomalous sensor readings they'd been getting tonight.

"This is bullshit, guys. All bullshit. Just some sensor problem. The storm."

"Respectfully, sir, that's impossible. We're getting too many sensors being tripped. The sensors in the woods are indicating movement, the fence is being tripped, it's happening all over the place at different points. One of the roving teams reported some movement sighted in the woods behind the building earlier. Should we call for back-up, sir? The Poles can scramble a security team and have them here in ten or fifteen minutes max. That's what their rapid response force is for."

"Edwards, are you listening to me?"

"Yes, sir."

"Under no circumstances are you to call for back-up. Do you hear me? The sensors are fucked up or there's a short in the system somewhere. Understand me? We're not going to be a laughingstock because you're getting freaked out by a faulty sensor and a storm. You hear me?"

"Yes, sir. I've logged it, sir. All the anomalies and your order not to call for back-up."

"Good for you, asshole. Don't call me again unless Usama Bin Ladin himself shows up demanding the prisoners be released. Understand?"

"Yes, sir."

The men in the security center looked at each other after Dave clicked off. "Tony," Edwards said, "we're fucked."

June 17, 2004
Stare Kiejkuty, Poland
CIA Site LAPIS
11:25pm local

THE POWER WENT out at LAPIS. Though the building had originally been built as a country estate by an eighteenth-century Polish nobleman, then had been used as a Nazi headquarters during World War II, then was later repurposed as a summer home for high-ranking Communist party officials during the Cold War, it had an updated electrical system throughout; a complete power failure had never happened since the CIA had taken it over. Even in the unlikely event of a massive power failure like this one, LAPIS had two backup generators and two diesel tanks in a barn-like outbuilding on the property that should have kicked on automatically within fifteen seconds of a power failure.

They did not.

At that point, the staff at LAPIS—those still awake, anyway—began to worry. The building got very dark very fast. With no power, there were no interior lights at all, and because a major storm hovered overhead on a night of a new moon, there was no outside light at all. Not even a single star was visible over LAPIS. It might have been deep underground or at the bottom of the ocean for all the light that penetrated inside LAPIS.

The only people who could see anything were the two soaking-wet security guards patrolling the grounds, because they wore night vision equipment that still had plenty of battery life remaining. They called in.

"Main Security, Main Security, this is Rover-1, over."

"Go ahead, Rover-1, this is Main Security, over."

"Looks like we've had a total power failure over the whole facility, Main Security. Aren't the generators supposed to have kicked on by now? Over."

"Roger that, Rover-1, better check out the generators, see if there's a fault. We're not going to be much help to you, Rover-1. Without power, most of our systems are down. We're sitting here in the dark, over."

"Roger, Main Security, we'll check out the backups and call in with a SITREP, over and out."

***

Mark Romero was lying on his bed propped against his pillows and writing in his journal when the room was plunged into darkness. "God damn it," he muttered quietly. "What now?"

After waiting what seemed like a reasonable amount of time for the backup generators to bring the electricity back on, Mark asked, "What the fuck is this happy horseshit?" and began to fumble for the flashlight he kept on his nightstand. It sent a powerful beam across the room and he picked up a handgun, also kept on his nightstand.

Checking that it was loaded and a round chambered, he said, "Better safe than sorry," and prepared to walk downstairs to see what was going on.

***

Grimes and Wallace, the two security officers assigned to Rover-1, the unit that patrolled the grounds and perimeter of Site LAPIS, were cold, wet, and miserable. They had another hour to go in their rotation and couldn't wait to get back inside, dry off, and hit the sack.

Still, they were awake and alert, which was sometimes a challenge when they were at the guard shack at the front of the property or inside in the main security room, watching camera feeds on TV screens and waiting for something to happen, which it never did. Despite the occasional bit of weirdness or unexplained events here, this was a cushy post where nothing much ever happened. They didn't think much about what LAPIS' purpose was, or the work that went on inside the interrogation rooms. They had a job to do—keep the facility secure—and they did it. It wasn't a bad job at all, and better than most.

Except for nights like tonight. The storm would have been miserable enough, but the constant false alarms of movement and intrusions were enough to wear anyone down. They headed over to the former stables that had been converted to a storage building that also housed the backup generators for LAPIS.

There were no lights anywhere, no smell of diesel exhaust, and no roaring generator noise, so they knew that something had gone wrong and the generators had failed to kick on after the power failure. As the men approached, they saw that a door to the building had been wrenched off the hinges and lay on the ground nearby. Nothing but darkness inside the building, though their night vision goggles were picking up no one in the area. They drew their weapons and approached cautiously, Grimes in the lead.

Grimes entered quickly, sweeping the main room, Wallace following closely behind. Empty, save for the large industrial generators that were supposed to be providing power. There was a foul odor about the place, like rot and dung. Wallace approached the generators, immediately noticing that they had been damaged by some large, heavy object, their sides and control panels staved in. *No wonder they never kicked on*, Wallace thought, as he caught just a quick flash of movement from overhead before something large plunged into his face, tearing into his head and face and knocking him to the ground.

Hearing Wallace's startled yelp and then wet, tearing noises, Grimes spun around to see Wallace on the ground, flat on his back, being torn apart by some giant bird or bat that was perched on his throat. No time to say or do anything else before several more of the things swooped down from the rafters of the building.

Grimes managed to get off four rounds, possibly hitting one or two of the things before they were on him, tearing him apart.

***

"Rover-1, Rover-1, come in, over."

Roger Olcott, head of the LAPIS security detachment, was worried. Beyond worried—while the previous false alarms of the last couple hours could easily be attributed to sensor glitches or some other innocuous problem, the gunfire from the grounds was alarming. Olcott was nominally off-duty, but had rushed downstairs to the main security room as soon as the building's power failed.

Still no response from Rover-1, though everyone at LAPIS had to have heard the gunfire outside on the grounds. Couldn't have been a simple accidental weapons discharge, he knew. Though they still hoped that one of the guys had gotten spooked by an animal that had somehow strayed onto the grounds, the power failure plus the gunfire meant that LAPIS was now on lockdown and all security personnel onsite were to be deployed to defend the place.

There were a score of security personnel onsite at all times at LAPIS, and as they called in or reported for duty, they were immediately directed to the armory to don protective vests and grab rifles and ammunition. The security personnel quickly formed fire teams and moved to protect the facility, stationing themselves at all entrances to the building. In addition, Olcott dispatched a fire team to the grounds to check on Rover-1 and otherwise engage whatever enemy force Rover-1 must have encountered. All had been trained and prepared for just such an assault on LAPIS, even though they knew that the chance of such an attack ever occurring was vanishingly small. Yet here they were. The thinking behind these preparations had been that they mostly needed to secure the main facility, ensure that the detainees and classified materials at the site were secure, then hold out until rapid reaction forces from the Polish military, intelligence agency, and law enforcement could arrive onsite and reinforce them. Such a plan did assume that the Poles could be notified and put on the alert quickly. That proved to be a bad assumption in this case.

Despite the best efforts of the communications staff at LAPIS, they had not been able to reach anyone offsite, either by local landlines, cellular networks, satellite phone, or email. Some unknown kind of interference or jamming was preventing each of those means of communications from reaching the emergency numbers. For now, at least, the security team at LAPIS was gradually realizing that they were on their own.

The first group of four security personnel sent to discover what had happened to Rover-1 poured out the rear doors at LAPIS, intent on heading to the generator building where, presumably, Rover-1 had encountered enemy forces. They were tense, and not surprised to see movement in the distance. They slowed their approach and began to move cautiously. The men could see movement, but the heat signatures their night vision equipment were off—these were not the typical heat signatures that would be showing if human or animal intruders had invaded LAPIS. One of the men shouted for the intruders—who or whatever they were—to stop and get on the ground. The forms, more dark shadows and shapeless masses than, say, an Al Qaeda hit team, began to move, to *surge* toward the men.

The security officers opened fire, placing dozens of shots into the center of the moving forms, now maybe only twenty yards away. Roars and bellows followed, and some of the black forms went down, unmoving. Others continued to advance. More forms emerged from the darkness, some as tall as ten or twenty feet. The men began to retch as smells of rot and filth overwhelmed their senses, nauseating them and making it difficult to think of anything except for escape.

"What the fuck *are* these things? Fall back! Fall back!"

One man, slower than the others—or more willing to continue shooting rather than retreat—was snatched by the darkness. His rifle went flying, and before disappearing into the shadows, he was torn limb from limb, his screams stopping abruptly.

After that, the security men began to run.

***

The flying things that had killed Grimes and Wallace in the old stables were now on the roof of the main LAPIS building. The storm didn't seem to bother them. A handful tore at the satellite dishes and uplink systems that had been installed on the roof. They ranged in size from large ravens to massive turkey vultures, though these creatures were hairless and had bat-like wings, unlike true birds. Their skin gleamed with an oily sheen in the rain. They made quick work of the delicate equipment. No satellite-based communications were going into or out of LAPIS tonight.

They took to the skies, wings pumping furiously as they began dive-bombing into the windows of the upper floor, shattering the glass and landing inside.

***

Before venturing too much farther down the hall, Mark realized that he needed to relieve his bladder, and decided to take care of that distraction before heading downstairs. As he was finishing up, he heard the sounds of gunfire—small arms fire, probably handguns from the security personnel—somewhere on the grounds, as well as the distinctive sound of breaking glass from somewhere in the building.

Oh shit, Mark thought. Plans began to flash through his head. He still had no idea what was going on at LAPIS, but he resolved to do whatever he could to prevent the release of the Engineer and the other detainees. The security center and the communications vault were natural strongpoints at LAPIS and he knew that he could link up with other staff, most of whom had some military training, and defend the place if necessary.

No way I'm letting anyone free Khattab. I'd rather kill him than see him set free, Mark thought as he headed out of the bathroom.

***

The Mother's children had been gathering in the woods behind LAPIS for hours, slowly moving closer to the fence line, drawn there by Her call, a powerful drive that they couldn't help but answer. The urge to obey Her, to please Her, was so powerful it was almost sexual in nature. Their very beings, all that they were, were tied inextricably to Her service. None of these things would have existed absent Her will and desire; some, the strongest and most powerful of Her servants, had been brought over into this world from Hers. Others, mostly the smaller, more numerous and animalistic, had been twisted, warped, *transformed* from what they had been in this new world where She sought a foothold.

They had followed Her will to LAPIS, their minds and bodies mere vessels of Hers. She willed them to crash through, or fly over, or dig under the fence line at LAPIS, and so they had.

Her children now owned the grounds of LAPIS. More were streaming onto the grounds through the forest, striding or crashing through the breaches in the fence line. Some, the lucky ones, had already killed for Her. The rest were anticipating more opportunities once they entered the humans' nest.

Then the bloodbath would truly begin.

June 17, 2004
Stare Kiejkuty, Poland
CIA Site LAPIS
11:40pm local

WALT TYLER, ONE of the security officers withdrawing—retreating—from the grounds back to the main building, paused in front of the rear door to give his comrades some covering fire as they reentered the building. He concentrated his fire on some vast, heaving black bulk that approached from the darkness. He had no idea what this thing was, he simply knew that there was some vaguely humanoid thing, twenty or thirty feet tall, lurching in his general direction. Walt feared he might be going crazy or had perhaps been dosed with some kind of hallucinogen, but he kept firing anyway, even though the bullets didn't seem to be having any effect on the thing coming his way.

Tyler never even noticed the flying things that swooped down upon him and pulled him apart with pincers, beaks, and talons in a matter of seconds. The creatures soon began to squabble among themselves over the morsels they pulled from his frame.

Over the next few minutes, the vast bulk that Tyler had been shooting at reached the rear of the main building and began shoving itself against the building, shattering windows and shaking the whole building with its efforts. Several more things like it—they had no independent wills or identities beyond what the Mother wanted—joined it, seemingly trying to open holes in the building so other creatures could enter more easily. They knew that it would only take another minute or two before large breaches had been battered open, if half the building didn't collapse first.

***

Mark almost shot Pete as he passed Pete's room. The door flew open suddenly and Mark swiveled, his gun pointing at Pete's head. "Don't startle me like that, man," Mark said, lowering his weapon.

"Sorry. What the fuck is going on? First the lights, then that gunfire. Are we being overrun?"

"No idea. It's bad though. Get your gun, come on! I'm heading down to the detention cells."

"Okay, I need to throw on some pants first, then I'll be ready to rock and roll. I'm not going to run around LAPIS with my schlong hanging out. I'll be right behind you."

"Okay. Meet me at the detention block. I want to see what the situation is first, but no way am I letting those fuckers escape LAPIS."

"Do you think this is some kind of AQ rescue attempt? It can't be, right?"

"No clue, brother. Meet me downstairs!" Mark started running.

***

Dave Franklin was drunk. Not merely the low-level but constant state of drunkenness of the functional alcoholic. Not just the sloppy drunkenness of frat boys gone wild with daddy's money, a kegger, and girls to impress. Not simply the drunkenness of a wino living on the street who had given up everything to feed his addiction. Dave was *heroically* drunk at a level where his vision was blurred, his gait halting, his mouth unable to form coherent words, and his mind unable to form coherent thoughts.

Dave had retreated into the bottle over the course of the last two months. Always one to rely on hard drinking to ease tensions whenever work or home life presented problems, the downturns of the last couple months had sent him careening over the edge. A few weeks ago, his wife's attorney had contacted him to let him know that she was divorcing him. Their daughter Lisa, once a bright-eyed college sophomore at Bowdoin, was dying of Stage 4 cancer in a cancer ward. He knew that he had failed as a husband, a father, and an intelligence officer. His life—all aspects of it—were ending in failure. Dave was sufficiently self-aware to have given up hope of his career ever recovering; he half-expected to be recalled to HQ every day when he stumbled into his office, and was surprised when that call never came. Dave knew that he was responsible for fucking up every aspect of his life and that all hope was lost. Hence, the vodka. Vodka, he liked to think, had never let him down, though somewhere deep in his subconscious, he knew that alcohol had *always* let him down.

Dave had been only vaguely aware that the power had gone out, but even he wasn't quite so drunk that he failed to recognize the growing cacophony of gunfire—a real firefight out there, it sounded like—on the grounds. Bleary-eyed, and fortunately unarmed, Dave straggled out of his quarters, still clutching a two-thirds empty vodka bottle, and began shouting questions as he staggered down the hall. Though nearly killing himself while stumbling down the stairs, he finally managed to make his way to the ground floor.

Of the half-dozen LAPIS staff members Dave encountered along the way, most rushed past him or ignored him. He tried to grab one security officer as the man ran down the hall and demand answers. The security officer shook Dave off him and ran on, not looking back. This unbalanced Dave and he landed flat on his ass, arms and legs flailing.

Worst of all, the vodka bottle shattered, showering him with what little was left of its contents.

Dave saw the mess he had wrought and began to weep, ugly sobs almost covering the sound of gunfire outside.

***

Deborah Sullivan had been in and out of consciousness for the last three days. During her brief periods of consciousness and lucidity, she wondered what had happened to her, what was still going on in her body.

This was undoubtedly the lowest period of her life, and she could conceive of no way it could go on. How could she live with herself with what had happened? And what was going on with her still?

Deb knew that she had been pregnant. She realized it when she missed her period a couple weeks after she and Mark had had sex. She was always very regular, her period arriving exactly on time each and every cycle. She knew it had been a mistake to have sex with Mark at the end of April but...things had just gotten out of control. Things had a way of doing that when she drank, so she avoided it when possible, but sometimes she just needed a drink. Or two. And then she got those inescapable cravings. Deb had confirmed it with a home pregnancy test kit she bought in town. Never had any intention of telling Mark it had happened before she took care of it. No muss, no fuss. She had done it a couple times before. It wasn't great, but it happened. Deb had never wanted to be a mother. She had no illusions about some happily ever after with Mark and their baby after he divorced his wife and left his child. No. Mark had been an easy, convenient lay, available and willing when she needed it. But she knew it had been a mistake the next day—they had to work together too closely and things had gotten awkward for a while, though they had been getting back to normal.

Before something strange started happening. Uncontrollable vomiting in the mornings. Nausea throughout the day. The feeling of movement within her abdomen. No way it could be the fetus. No way. It would be, what, six weeks along?

That's why it was so bizarre when her stomach began showing. At first she just thought she had put on a few pounds, but eventually it was undeniable: she was getting bigger every day, visibly larger. She had retreated to her room, telling Mark and Pete that she was sick. Eventually she looked like she was full term. Then the agony felt like it was splitting her apart. After it eased, then happened again, eased, then repeated, Deb realized that she was experiencing contractions.

Then they took her downstairs to the infirmary and Richards took a look and immediately knew what was going on. He had told Mark and Pete it was some kind of parasite, but after Mark...took care of it, when it was just Richards and her alone, he had told her it was some kind of hideous mutant baby. Some warped monstrosity that had crawled out of her womb. Richards had blamed her, told her that she must have some kind of terrible genes to conceive such a *thing*.

She had lost a lot of blood and still felt traumatized by the whole experience. The last three days had been one long nightmare. Richards had given her tranquilizers at first, but now she was locked into a cycle of sleeping a few hours, then having some terrible nightmare of blood and animals rutting and cannibalizing each other or something equally awful, then waking up, gasping and screaming, only to drift back to sleep a few minutes or hours later. Lather, rinse, repeat. Over and over again.

For the moment, Deb felt more coherent than she had in a long while, her mind now fully clear. For now, at least. She knew something was wrong with her, something terrible. Deb cast off her bedsheets so she could take a good look at her body. She couldn't see her feet for the enormous mound of her belly. It was back, bigger than ever.

Deb began weeping uncontrollably. "Not again. Not again. I can't go through this again. What the fuck is happening to me?"

***

Ernie Riggs and Grant Petrie were manning the communications vault in LAPIS. This was normally a pretty cushy post, though both men found the backwater black site to be less interesting the longer they stayed in rural Poland. Until tonight. In addition to the main power system and backup generators being down, the site's satellite link was unresponsive. This would normally merit checking out immediately, but neither man favored climbing up onto the roof at night in the middle of a storm to investigate. By mutual agreement they decided to leave that chore to the morning, when they hoped that a sense of normalcy would be restored. Even the local landlines seemed to be down.

"Bad storm, huh?" Riggs asked. He and Petrie were operating via a battery-powered lantern they pulled out of storage.

"Yep. No messages going out tonight except by satphone, I guess," replied Petrie as he walked over to the charging rack to pull a satphone out so they could notify the ops center at Langley of the situation.

"Well, guess I'd better seal us in," Riggs said as he approached the door to the vault. Security protocols required the comms section to seal itself off in the event of an emergency until the exact situation could be sorted out. The comms shack, as it was called, was the equivalent of a bank vault inside a completely secure facility. This was where all the cryptographic and secure communications equipment was stored, along with the computer servers and the safes where the bulk of the classified records were stored. The room had an independent, battery-powered air supply so the men were in no danger of running out of oxygen.

Petrie needed both hands to close the vault door, so he left the lantern on the desk, which meant that the hallway outside was in pitch darkness, and the area by the door was heavily shadowed. As Petrie approached the door, he smelled something like raw sewage, then spotted just a hint of movement in the doorway.

There was someone—something—standing in the doorway. Not a *person*, but maybe someone in a costume, some kind of monster suit: all black, with insectile plates of chitin that shifted as it moved. Petrie stood stock-still, utterly dumbfounded by what he saw. Its mouth opened, a horror show.

Petrie opened his mouth too, to scream.

***

The Engineer—what was left of him—could hear the other Al Qaeda detainees howling in their cells. He hadn't been allowed to speak with any of them, but he'd seen one of them once in the hallway when the guards accidentally tried to move him and the other prisoner at the same time. But that didn't matter; he had been able to sense them nearby for weeks. It felt like a pleasant itch, a tingle that felt like friendship and warmth whenever he thought of them. But more importantly, for weeks now he had been able to feel the Mother's seeds quickening within them, just as he could feel one quickening within his own body. He knew that it signified growth, completion, the culmination of what he had wanted and been working toward for years. Nothing had ever felt as good as this, for he knew he was doing Her bidding, and he knew that She was well pleased with him.

As the Engineer made his way from the infirmary to the cell block, he encountered a security guard who ran around the corner and blundered straight into him. He casually grabbed the man, wrenched his arm out of its socket, tossing the arm and the rifle it had been holding aside, then pulled the man's head off before continuing on his way. The man had barely had time to scream before that possibility ended abruptly. The security doors leading to the cells presented little more of an obstacle. He made his way inside as bad memories of the place dimmed and began floating away. Those were his old memories. They had no place in his new life—the life of a loyal servant and consort to the Mother. He tore the doors to the other three detainees' cells off their hinges in rapid succession.

He roared in triumph when he saw what they were becoming.

***

The surviving LAPIS personnel were in a near panic. Security forces had managed to barricade all the points of entry to the building, but they also knew that the entire structure was being battered, possibly with vehicles or construction equipment. Visibility outside was poor—with no lights and no moon, and with a fierce thunderstorm still raging, they couldn't tell exactly what was happening outside.

All night, the people inside LAPIS had been acting erratically, out of character. They were tense, anxious. Some felt numb, disconnected, or depressed. Others felt almost giddy with anticipation of something they couldn't articulate. Few were making clear-headed decisions. All were feeling off-kilter, though they didn't know why. Once the attack began, panic rose. When it became clear that LAPIS was under attack by unknown forces, their panic spiked. It would have turned to sheer terror if they knew that communications with the outside world had been cut off, and that no help was forthcoming. The surviving staff members of LAPIS were on their own, though they didn't yet know that.

The remaining security personnel followed the procedures that they had prepared and trained for. They armed themselves, bringing out as much firepower and ammunition from the armory as they could carry, and busied themselves barricading and reinforcing the old manor house's doors. A few of them, those who had been outside, or who had caught glimpses of...*things* peering in the windows, fell into despair.

Some of those inside LAPIS found themselves weeping uncontrollably, or laughing, or both. Some began to scream, or gibber, or run through the hallways until they encountered something that had entered through a broken window. More than a few threw down their weapons and began to strip their clothes off.

Two of the men assigned to guard the front entryway spontaneously and with no words passing between them began to kiss and grope each other. Then, while still kissing, the two started stabbing each other with combat knives, over and over again, never uttering a sound. Their fellow guards could only gape at the spectacle.

The three elderly Polish women who worked in the kitchen at LAPIS emerged from their hiding place in the pantry and approached the men at the rear of the building. The women were nude, their eyes bloody pits. Their wails filled the building, but still they walked steadily toward the men, who found themselves uncontrollably drawn to the women, despite the butcher knives they clutched. The guards, those who still held onto their weapons, threw them down and began tearing their clothes off.

The smells of blood and sex began to permeate the halls of LAPIS.

***

As soon as Mark got downstairs, he knew that LAPIS had been lost. It was only a matter of time before the place was completely overrun by whoever—whatever—was trying to get inside. Based on periodic screams he heard, it sounded like enemy forces were probably already inside.

Perhaps even more disturbing, Mark could tell that his colleagues, those not already unconscious or dead, were freaking out. He had come upon several who were just staring catatonically off into space or crying inconsolably. He tried to shake one man out of it—a man he knew to be a retired Marine with combat experience—but quickly gave up when he saw it was useless. These people were professionals, or were supposed to be, but here they were in a sorry state. Mark couldn't make sense of it, but knew he still had a duty to perform.

Mark made a beeline for the detention area. There was no way he was going to let the prisoners escape. He'd rather kill them, especially the Engineer, than allow that.

Mark's heart sank when he saw that the main doors to the prisoners' area were wrenched off their hinges.

June 17, 2004
Stare Kiejkuty, Poland
CIA Site LAPIS
11:50pm local

THE MOTHER'S CHILDREN knew that LAPIS was now theirs, or soon would be. There were a few more humans remaining, but they would soon be Hers—to kill, to devour, to fuck, to impregnate as she wished.

Only about half the total number of LAPIS staff were still alive, and most of that number were wounded, insane, or dying, if not outright transformed into additional slaves of the Mother, their bodies no longer recognizable as the people they once were. The survivors alternately wailed, or trembled, or wept, or screamed in ecstasy and/or agony. Few were still capable of defending themselves, or even aware of their surroundings. Several piles of people (or what had been people) who had been rutting with each other uncontrollably now found their bodies had fused together into shapeless masses of flesh and sex organs; their minds were now as one, capable only of experiencing sexual bliss and worship of the Mother. She was nearby—coming soon, Her servants could tell—and with Her came a warping of the very fabric of reality that mere mortals thought they understood.

***

Though still feeling sorry for himself, Dave had finally stopped sobbing. He had been vaguely aware of strange noises—stranger, that is, than gunfire and the roar of unknown animals—somewhere in the dark hallway near him, but he hadn't paid any attention until he felt something touch his leg.

After a moment, he looked up, wiped his eyes, and took a few moments to reorient himself and what he was seeing. The hallway remained shrouded in darkness, but there was just enough light to see something black perched on his left thigh. It was an odd shape, and it took additional time for him to realize that he didn't know what he was looking at. He had never seen anything quite like it. It was almost two feet long, but very spindly. It only weighed a few pounds. More than anything, it reminded him of a giant black praying mantis, but that didn't quite capture the malign intelligence he thought he perceived in the thing's multifaceted eyes. Was he imagining that? And were praying mantises covered in spikes and what looked like razor-sharp blades on their bodies and limbs?

The thing seemed to look him in the eyes, then raised its head, emitting a long loud hoot or shriek. Dave heard similar calls—responses?—from down the hallway in both directions. He reached out to touch the thing and it chittered a warning, but he was undeterred. He stroked the thing's back as he tried to wrap a hand around it, but it hooted again and swiped at him, faster than his eye could catch. Dave wasn't in pain exactly, but he was aware that something had happened, so he pulled his hand back and saw long razor slices on his palm and on the back of his hand where the thing had touched him.

What the fuck? he thought.

Dave felt something on the back of his neck and swiped at it with his left hand. He brushed against something and pulled his hand back. More blood. More chittering and screeching too, this time much closer.

Then the back of his head and neck erupted in fire, an absolute blazing pain that immediately cut through the alcoholic fog.

He slapped at it again, trying to stand at the same time, but falling, sprawling on the floor. Dave saw more of the things near him, three or four more at least. Movement down the hallway. More of them?

Then they pounced on him, more of them appearing by the second.

Dave's shrill, whistling screams soon became indistinguishable from the hunting calls of the things that flayed him.

***

Pete wondered how he had ended up in this situation. He'd had a good career in the U.S. Air Force. He had gotten into intelligence early on in his career and found that he had a knack for the work. He had risen through the ranks and retired as a senior non-commissioned officer after serving twenty-two years. His personal life wasn't ideal—he had a divorce under his belt, and two kids he never got to see—but whose life was? He was doing important work as a CIA contractor. No need to be falsely modest, Pete thought, he knew that he was a good interrogator and had great analytic chops. He was doing some real good in the world post-September 11.

So how had things gone so badly?

He had known that LAPIS was dysfunctional almost immediately after arriving; poor leadership will do that, but Pete had had his share of bad bosses over the years, so he just kept his head down and did his job. The place had been in danger of becoming a backwater until the Engineer arrived. Now *he* was a high-value asset, as they say, and Pete was happy to be along for the ride because it was highly likely that he knew some things of real value. Deb was easy to work with, and easy on the eyes, though there was no prospect for romance, or even just sex, despite the fact that both were available. Mark Romero was a good guy, though a novice at interrogation, but he was willing to learn and let the others teach him what he needed to know. Besides, Pete had always thought, if things ever got really screwed up with the Engineer, there were plenty of other people—Mark and Dave among them—who could take the fall rather than him.

But things at LAPIS had gotten weird. Little things at first, but then stranger things that couldn't be explained, something new and bizarre happening almost every day. Then Deb's medical problem. Pete was pretty sure that it was some kind of monstrous birth, but whatever it was, it didn't bear thinking about. Pete had been drunk most of the time since...whatever happened with Deb. Maybe Dave had the right idea after all. If you drink enough, Pete found, you weren't troubled by nightmares and unwanted mental images of monstrous babies with insect faces that had to be killed in a welter of blood and other fluids.

And now this. Whatever *this* was.

Pete had started drinking early tonight, so by the time it became clear that the site was under attack, his head was fuzzy and his reflexes were poor, though he found that he was rapidly sobering up now that he was just wearing a pair of shorts and running down dark hallways with a handgun, hoping he didn't have to shoot any intruders.

After Pete finally made it down to the first floor, he decided that Mark had the right idea and that the prisoners should be his top priority. Secure the detainees, ensure that they stayed in their cells, and hold out until the Poles or someone else could send some reinforcements. That sounded a lot better than trying to repel enemy forces trying to breach one of the outer doors anyway.

Pete was having trouble hearing anything over the din of gunfire, screams, and crashing sounds throughout the building. Whatever was going on, it didn't bode well. It sounded like the defense of LAPIS might even be on its last legs, so he was focused on getting to the detention area as soon as possible. That's probably why it was only at the last second that Pete heard some kind of thundering footsteps—stomping, really, like that of an elephant—behind him.

Despite still being drunk, Pete's adrenaline had kicked in and his reflexes were good. He spun at the sound of these footfalls and could see something large, something dark, heading right toward him.

Pete instinctively fired his handgun as rapidly as he could, certain that he was landing kill shots in the center of mass of whoever it was running toward him. None of that mattered though, once he realized at the very last second that whoever his attacker was, it wasn't human. The thing was some kind of black armored thing, easily eight feet tall, and looking like some combination of a horned NFL linebacker and a humanoid beetle-rhinoceros. The thing gored Pete, catching him on its horns, flipping him in the air, smashing him into a wall, and trampling what was left. Pete mercifully lost consciousness immediately. When the thing became bored with this a minute or two later, all that was left was a red, wet pile of filth on the floor. The creature dripped a watery black goo from the gunshot wounds, but didn't seem much the worse for wear as it trundled off down the hall looking for other survivors.

***

It sounded to Deb like things at LAPIS had deteriorated. She had been hearing more and more gunshots, screams of terror, and crashes and booms throughout the building, but had no idea what was going on. The door to her room was locked, and several times in the last hour someone had knocked on it, loudly, and called her name, but she didn't bother to answer. A few minutes ago she was almost certain that she had heard the sound of someone being murdered in the hallway. A few minutes later, she was sure she heard the distinct sound of two (at least) people loudly fucking in the room next to hers, all while the chaos continued.

Deb wasn't certain any of this was even going on. She thought she was probably imagining most of what she was hearing. A kind of creeping lassitude had begun to creep over her and reality seemed...fuzzy. Uncertain. Wavy around the edges.

But the bulge of her belly *was* real, of that she was certain. She could feel it with her hands and feel the writhing and kicking of whatever was growing inside her. She assumed it was something like whatever had come out of her a few days ago, or perhaps something worse.

She feared it was something far, far worse.

A few days ago, when Richards had left her alone in the infirmary, she had stolen one of his scalpels, a sterile one still sealed in its packaging. At the time she hadn't known why she had taken it, there was simply some vague impulse she knew that she needed to fulfill, so she had hidden it among her clothes and then passed out again.

She could feel the crinkling envelope the scalpel was sealed in under her pillow. She drew it forth, studied it for a long while, unwrapped it, and sat there just feeling the metal of the scalpel's handle in her hand.

Deb knew what she had to do—there was no choice. Choice had been taken away from her when she had been impregnated with...whatever this thing was.

Deb knew that if she didn't do it immediately, she might lose her nerve, so she did it quickly: she plunged the scalpel as deep as she could into one side of her stomach, then drew it across her belly, creating a wide, red smile that yawned open across her belly.

The pain was beyond agony, beyond anything she *had* ever, *could* ever experience, but Deb knew she wasn't done yet. She could feel things inside her frantically twisting, beginning to emerge from the slice she had carved, splitting it wider as they pulled themselves out.

She reversed the scalpel and stabbed it, over and over again, as rapidly and often as she could into whatever was inside her.

She soon passed out, mercifully, with a smile on her face, knowing she had done all she could, then bled out.

***

Mark heard grunting and great, heaving moans from within the detention area. He proceeded forward cautiously, having almost no light to see by in what had formerly been a bright, fluorescently lit space. He had picked up night vision goggles from a dead security officer and that would have to do. The sounds were coming from within one or more of the cells, which, like the main door, had had their doors torn off the hinges. Mark couldn't tell if the sounds were being made by someone who was dying, or being torn apart or devoured, or if they were being made by some monstrosity in the nightmarish hellscape that LAPIS had become.

Mark headed straight for the Engineer's cell but was disappointed to see that the room was empty, Khattab long since fled or been rescued. Mark dashed around the corner of the doorframe to the second cell, one that had been occupied by one of the other Al Qaeda men, and immediately saw that there was a figure in the room, a prisoner by the looks of the orange jumpsuit that he was wearing. Mark no longer recognized the man—his face was a distorted, open-mouthed scream in the dim light—and he didn't hesitate to shoot the man in the face and upper chest three times as the prisoner lunged at him. The detainee crumpled to the floor of the cell. The man fell face down, though Mark could tell that something was dramatically off about the man's physiognomy.

Mark knew that the gunfire could draw more...things to his location, so he knew that he didn't have the luxury of time to inspect the body. Mark stepped into the cell and half-crouched there just inside the doorway, waiting to see what might emerge.

It didn't take long before the other two Al Qaeda detainees—but not Khattab—emerged from their cells. Mark's night vision goggles were poor for discerning specific facial details in absolute blackout conditions, but he knew that he was right to have come here as soon as humanly possible. These two detainees looked as though they were further along in some unspeakable process that was transforming them into something other than human. Their faces looked half-melted, their jaws dislocated and their mouths stretched open in silent screams. Their arms were likewise stretched, their fingertips now elongated into needle-like talons and reaching past their knees. Their faces and exposed skin were covered in fruiting bodies and other stranger kinds of fungal growths emerging from somewhere inside their flesh. They reminded Mark of the soft and wet unbirthed horrors he had seen once as a boy when he broke open a wasps' nest he had found on the eaves of his house.

They immediately lunged at Mark as soon as they saw him, claws outstretched, and he fired as fast as he could, blowing large, stinking, wet holes in their faces and chests. As soon as their soft flesh was opened, a black ooze started flowing, and with it came a horrifying odor that was somehow a combination of rot, sex, wet leaves, and shit.

They, too, fell in a heap before Mark, splattering him with their foul-smelling fluids, but not before raking him in the face, neck, and left hand and forearm with their talons. They seemed to be dead, though Mark sent additional rounds into their heads to be sure.

Mark's heart was hammering as he ran a hand over his facial cuts. They burned like fire, and he knew that he had to get those wounds cleaned out. He didn't want to be infected with whatever had done...this to the detainees.

Mark swapped in a fresh magazine and cautiously poked his head into the hallway to see if Khattab was nearby.

June 18, 2004
Stare Kiejkuty, Poland
CIA Site LAPIS
12:05am local

THE CHILDREN OF the Mother were triumphant. They owned LAPIS, for Her, as they knew they were destined to. The building itself was a shambles, with most of the windows smashed inward, the doors shattered, and gaping holes torn into the exterior of the building where some of Her larger servants had bludgeoned their way inside. Parts of the building had now collapsed. A few small fires had gotten started, but none were yet out of control. The Children strode, crawled, and flapped down the remaining hallways of the building, ensuring that they had dutifully searched each room for survivors, leaving trails of blood and other more viscous fluids as they clamored through the wreckage.

***

Though he didn't realize it, by this point Mark was the last person still alive inside LAPIS who was neither mortally wounded, nor hopelessly insane, nor transformed into some unrecognizable and monstrous form.

He was bleeding from several cuts, but the blood loss wasn't too bad; there were no spurters, so no arteries had been nicked, and he knew he'd be fine if he could apply some direct pressure and get his injuries wrapped. He'd been hurt worse before, many times, and come out just fine. That said, he wasn't feeling great, and he worried that maybe shock was starting to set in. His temples were starting to pound, which worried him, because Mark rarely got headaches, and his abdomen was starting to churn with acid. Waves of pain and some kind of movement rippled through him periodically. Not good. He was definitely going to need some medical care, sooner rather than later.

While binding up the tears on his forearm, Mark's nostrils were assailed by the smells of shit and something sickly sweet and treacly, something like syrup that had gone over. He had just enough time to mutter, "What the fuck?" before something slammed into his back.

Mark was propelled into the wall, seemingly enveloped in something that had wrapped itself around him. Mark just managed to catch the wall on his shoulder rather than being slammed face-first into the wall, though he struggled to free himself from whatever was grasping him. At least he retained his grip on his handgun, though the arms or python-like tentacles that gripped him didn't allow much movement.

Mark dropped to one knee suddenly while also jerking his arms free. He managed to get his right hand up long enough to fire three rounds over his left shoulder into the thing. He heard a kind of whimper and felt frantic shuddering behind him as the arms withdrew, finally allowing him to extricate himself from the thing's grasp. Mark spun away and turned around so that he could get a glimpse of what he was facing.

It was unspeakable. The thing he was facing was only vaguely still humanoid. It was a naked mass of flesh, with thick ropy tentacles emerging and flowing from the thing's form, and covered in a blackish carapace that seemed to be thickening as Mark watched. This shell was forming around it as its flesh rippled to accommodate the armored plates expanding and starting to press together on its back. It oozed a grey sap that might have been what passed for its blood—Mark could see that his bullets had driven into the creature in wounds across its front—but could just as easily have been some kind of snail slime it naturally exuded. And perched on top of this shuddering mass of tentacles and exoskeleton was the unmistakable head of Omar Abu Khattab, remarkably unchanged despite the otherwise complete physical transformation. Khattab's mouth was twisted and contorted into a rictus of hate, though his eyes were blank, those of a dumb animal. Mark didn't think that there was any intelligence behind those eyes. Whatever Khattab was now, he was just a mindless beast in service to the Mother.

More tentacles began sprouting from Khattab's chest; the skin stretched and stretched and stretched then burst open like an overcooked sausage as the tentacles stretched out toward Mark. Now more than six or eight feet in length, they showed no signs of ceasing their growth. Mark backpedaled, trying desperately to remain out of their reach, watching in silent horror as they kept coming toward him.

Suddenly Khattab rushed at him with no warning. Mark managed to land another two shots before the thing was on him. It grappled and flailed at him, battering him badly, then threw him backward. Mark's gun went flying. He was cast down the hallway fifteen feet, landing in the lap of a dead security officer sprawled against the wall. Mark made the mistake of looking up into the man's face, but immediately recoiled as he realized that the man was partially melted, or possibly digested, the remnants of his face slumped down across his chest, with long strings of flesh dangling into his lap.

Mark tried to scramble up as fast as he could, but his reflexes were slow, and his movements were hampered by pain. He felt battered and sore all over, with every movement a chore, even though he knew that his life depended on moving quickly. Even his adrenaline felt like it was sluggishly crawling through his veins. Mark suspected that some of his ribs—maybe all of them—had been broken. Now even taking a simple breath was labored and painful. As he pushed himself to his feet, Mark noticed there was a rifle half under the dead man and he reached for it, praying it was still loaded.

As Mark spun toward the thing that had been Khattab, he lined up the rifle and squeezed the trigger, emptying the magazine into the beast. The shots were all good—Mark was certain they all landed center of mass, or what would have been center of mass in a human— but at first they didn't have much of a discernible effect. The entrance wounds oozed a dark, syrupy fluid that drained out of the wounds more like thick sap than blood. Khattab uttered a deep, lowing grunt, almost a sigh. He...it loomed ominously, frozen, then slumped forward and collapsed on the floor of the hallway.

Mark very delicately walked over to Khattab's remains and shoved them with a foot, but he could tell that all life had fled the monstrosity's corpse. It was already starting to look half-melted and seemed to be breaking down. He breathed a sigh of relief.

Mark was half bent over from the pain and trying to keep it together. He forced himself to walk over and pick up his handgun. It was undamaged and still had a few rounds remaining. He knew that he was going to need them if he was to escape LAPIS alive.

June 18, 2004
Stare Kiejkuty, Poland
CIA Site LAPIS
12:17am local

MARK ROMERO WAS in a lot of pain. He was covered in countless scratches and abrasions, some very deep, deeper than he had ever been cut before. He didn't think that any arteries had been cut—if they had been, he would have certainly bled out by now—but he was worried about blood loss and shock setting in. His clothes were soaked with his own blood as well as the blood and other fluids of the things he had fought, the things that had almost killed him. He was also exhausted, panting, gasping for more air, and knew that he needed a breather, some safe haven in which he could hole up, rest for a minute, get his bearings together, then make a plan for getting out of LAPIS as soon as possible without encountering any more of the things that seemed to have taken the place over.

For the time being, Mark was alone and felt safe enough, but he could still hear crashes and thumps in other parts of the building. He realized that it had been a while since he'd heard any human screams or voices. He didn't have a radio, so he didn't have a good means of contacting any other survivors. Mark decided that he needed to acquire a radio as soon as possible, but knew that, sadly, there were probably a lot scattered about the house and grounds. The dead security guard nearby didn't appear to have one. Mark knew he needed to find the corpse of another security officer and he'd likely find a still-working radio. That shouldn't be too difficult, given the carnage.

Mark felt a presence nearby and experienced a clear sense that he was suddenly under intense scrutiny, that feeling he sometimes got when he was being watched. This lasted interminably; then Mark realized that the sounds of LAPIS—screams, crashing, gunfire—had faded away to nothing and all he was hearing was the sound of *silence.*

He looked up and there She was. The hallway had been empty a moment ago, Mark was certain of that, but the Mother, the figure from his dreams and nightmares of the past several months was standing before him, silent, with her face shrouded in darkness, though he was certain that her attention was riveted on him. His throat was dry and he felt paralyzed. Mark drew himself erect, but felt incapable of taking any action. There was a tiny voice in the back of his mind screaming at him to do something, anything, but he dismissed it, and compelled that unheeded voice to fall silent.

She exuded a luminescence of Her own, and despite the pitch darkness of the corridor, She was as bright as day. He slowly peeled off his night vision goggles so that he could gaze upon Her radiance with his own eyes.

Mark stood there, trembling slightly, when she revealed Her face to him.

She was beautiful. Beautiful beyond measure. Indescribable, of course; there was no way that Mark could have told anyone what She looked like—you simply had to see Her to understand—but She was everything and every woman he had ever desired combined into one beatific vision. His own wife Jessica paled in comparison to Her. So did his mother. So did Denise Caroti, to whom he had lost his virginity. So did every woman he had ever fucked, every celebrity, every model, every woman he had ever lusted after, every woman he had seen across a crowded room and desired and known he would never have. They were nothing in comparison with the Mother, unfit and unworthy of her; whatever slim measure of human beauty they might possess was mere ugliness in the face of the Mother's glory.

She was everything he had ever wanted. Mark stepped forward into Her arms, was pulled upward into Her glorious embrace. Why had he ever been afraid? Why had he ever rejected Her, feared what accepting Her might mean?

She bared her breasts to him, pulling open her garments and revealing the perfection and the splendor of them. He couldn't take his eyes off them. Mark saw that Her right nipple was leaking a single drop of black milk. She squeezed her breast slightly and a few more drops oozed forth. She gently cupped the back of Mark's head and drew him to her. He opened his mouth and gently placed his lips around her areola. She pressed him hard against her chest and he began to suckle, almost involuntarily. He tasted Her milk on his tongue.

It was glorious, beyond words, beyond thoughts, beyond human conception.

Mark's mind was blasted by visions of his future, *their* future together. He was transported to a world in which he was Her consort, blessed among men to be allowed to copulate with Her, to enter the temple of her womanhood, to spill his seed inside Her, to impregnate Her, and have Her bear Her children using his seed.

Mark was lost to all thought.

She pulled him inside Her. His penis was so erect it was painful, the skin stretching almost to the point of tearing as She drew him inside Her most sacred temple, the place of Her holiness. The place from which life was created inside Her and from which it emerged. It was fire and water alike, it was the font of creation.

He couldn't imagine ever wanting to be anywhere else but worshipping Her inside Her Temple.

June 18, 2004
Stare Kiejkuty, Poland
CIA Site LAPIS
12:30am local

MARK FELT SPENT, exhausted, out of breath, but sated. There was a part of him, one all too easily dismissed right now, that knew that he was in real trouble. His head spun, but he retained just enough self-awareness to understand that he wasn't thinking clearly and wondered if he was hallucinating. The situation in which he found himself was unreal. Not for the first time tonight, he wondered if this was all just some horrendous nightmare from which he hoped he would awaken soon.

He could smell smoke now, and he imagined that he could hear the crackling of fire in the distance. That bothered him, but he ignored it for now. Everything felt dreamlike, or rather nightmarish, more of a nighttime vision of being trapped in Hell rather than reality.

Mark could feel his body rippling, muscles he didn't even know he had spasming, clenching, bringing momentary waves of pain shuddering through his abdomen and chest that he knew he shouldn't find so delicious, but he did. They were like the secondary waves of an intense orgasm, a painful spasm of ecstasy. He looked down at his body, which was now naked somehow, and he felt the icy grip of terror squeeze his heart. Mark's stomach clenched, and he could sense the fire of the acid it contained, for he could now see that he was becoming an abomination. Something *new* and utterly monstrous, for Her.

Mark knew that he was no longer human, not fully, and would be even less so in a very short period of time.

She still stood before him. He looked at Her lower body, not daring to take in Her face again, though on some level he sensed that She had withdrawn Her face from his view. Mark could sense her eager excitement—though She remained unmoving before him, he could feel the almost quivering intensity of Her attention upon him and what he was undergoing.

Some fragment of Her being entered his mind without warning. No words were conveyed, but he could sense that She was honoring him by standing witness to his transformation into Her new consort.

Something deep within the core of Mark's being rebelled at that thought. He felt his gorge rise; a flood of saliva gushed into his mouth as he almost vomited at the thought of being made—re-made—into something that would be Her consort. He had seen the physical transformations she produced in people, animals, things, and he could only imagine the mental transformations that would accompany the physical changes. He knew that She would remake him into some kind of savage killing and fucking machine, bent entirely to Her will.

He knew he didn't want that. That fate was not for him.

Mark said aloud, "This is a nightmare. Just a nightmare. I need to wake the fuck up." Then he checked his handgun, ensuring it had a round in the chamber and was ready to go, put the barrel inside his mouth, and pulled the trigger.

June 20, 2004
McLean, Virginia
CIA HQ

CABLE # RX410213-04

SUBJECT: After Action Report: Attack on CIA Site LAPIS

DATE OF REPORT: 20 JUNE 2004

1. Overview and Timeline:
- At approximately 11:00 PM, 17 JUNE, local time, CIA Site LAPIS, housing thirty-nine CIA personnel and local support staff and four Al Qaeda detainees, came under attack by unknown forces. CIA personnel on site were quickly overwhelmed and the LAPIS main building was destroyed in a catastrophic fire. To date, the exact circumstances of the attack remain unclear, as do the disposition of all forty-three individuals believed to be present at LAPIS at the time of the attack. Forensic investigations are underway.
- Last transmission from LAPIS to CIA Headquarters received at 9:57 PM local time. Message was routine and indicated nothing unusual
- Polish Foreign Intelligence Agency (FIA) attempted to contact LAPIS multiple times via radio and telephone, beginning at 2:04 AM, 18 JUNE, and on receiving no answer, sent a liaison to LAPIS to re-establish contact after presumed technical problem. FIA liaison arrived onsite at 2:22 AM and immediately notified FIA Headquarters of destruction of LAPIS and no apparent survivors. FIA dispatched a rapid response force and notified local Polish law enforcement. Additional FIA and law enforcement assets began arriving on the scene at 2:33 AM.

- Nearest civilian habitation is approximately five miles away from LAPIS. Civilians reported faint sound of gunfire in the direction of LAPIS beginning approximately 11:15 PM and continuing for next 30-45 minutes. Dogs were agitated all night. Locals did not report potential disturbance, believing the sounds to be either hunters or government officials.
- National technical means/overhead assets poorly positioned over LAPIS between 9:00 PM local through 4:00 AM local and unable to provide relevant imagery.
- No discussion of the attack by known terrorists or foreign intelligence services prior to, during, or after the attack, though additional collection and analysis are underway.

2. Initial Site Damage Assessment:
- The main building of LAPIS has been completely destroyed by fire, with the upper floors collapsed onto the ground floor. Outbuildings, including the building housing the complex's backup power generators and the security post at the main gate, likewise sustained heavy damage, with doors to these structures heavily damaged and ripped off the hinges. Extensive damage from unknown cause to main and secondary backup generators in outbuilding, rendering both systems non-operational.
- Security perimeter fences have been breached at multiple locations along the rear of the site. Fences appear to have been torn down using some kind of heavy equipment. Drag marks of unknown origin/type in evidence, but no vehicle tracks noted onsite or in forest exterior to LAPIS site.
- No survivors found onsite. There were believed to be forty-three individuals housed at LAPIS at the time of the attack, including four detainees, six local hires, and thirty-three CIA/contractor personnel. At least thirty-two partial or full sets of human remains have been located to date, and DNA has been taken and sent for further analysis in each case. All remains are

badly burned; autopsies are underway but are unlikely to yield much information about causes of death due to extensive burns and charring of remains.

- A complete investigation of the building is still being conducted and may yield additional information and sets of human remains. Whereabouts of remaining LAPIS personnel are unknown at this time; they could be missing or their remains could simply be undiscovered onsite at the time of this report.

- Many bullet casings found on grounds and inside the building. Weapons were found in close proximity to some of the human remains. It does appear that many of the dead were armed and actively repelling an assault on LAPIS at the time of the site's destruction.

- No bullet casings or other discarded weapons or other equipment not directly linked to LAPIS personnel have been recovered. This may suggest the attackers had professional military training and sufficient time to police the site before departing (however, see alternative theory, below, for an alternative view).

- Cryptographic equipment in communications vault received superficial damage, but remain functional, and all cryptographic keys are present and accounted for. Though the communications vault was left unsecure during the attack, all cryptographic equipment and classified materials stored in safes are accounted for. No obvious effort by attackers to capture cryptographic equipment or classified materials at LAPIS.

3. Theories on the Attack:
- The identity of those perpetrating the attack on LAPIS is currently unknown; further investigation is currently underway and has been accorded highest priority. Additional collection and analytic capabilities have been surged to this investigation.

- Number of attackers is unknown, as are their capabilities, training, and equipment. Because they overcame 24 CIA security personnel onsite and managed to destroy LAPIS and kill or capture all present, they likely numbered several dozen, possibly as many as 50-100, and had military/paramilitary training as well as access to modern military hardware.

- The attackers may have had insider access to LAPIS, receiving surveillance information, knowledge of the site's security systems and processes, and/or assistance in overcoming LAPIS security forces.

- Likeliest scenario: An Al Qaeda force of 20+ operatives with military training and conventional military equipment overcame LAPIS security forces through good operational planning and surprise, possibly with the aid of one or more individuals with insider access.

- Alternative scenario: One of the Al Qaeda detainees housed at LAPIS (most likely Omar Aby KHATTAB) inadvertently or intentionally released a novel/unknown biological agent onsite that induced paranoia and hallucinations among the personnel at LAPIS, which quickly caused the infected LAPIS personnel to attack other personnel and destroy the site. Though far-fetched, this would explain the improbability of an entire CIA base inside Europe being destroyed by a large Al Qaeda force. KHATTAB could have swallowed a capsule containing the unknown hallucinogenic/incapacitating agent that was never detected during his captivity, re-swallowing it each time it was excreted.

4. Current Status at LAPIS:
- Polish authorities are cooperating fully with the investigation and are searching for evidence of possible Al Qaeda force traveling to/from LAPIS. No evidence has been located to date but searches are ongoing.
- LAPIS has been officially decommissioned as a black site. Site will be turned over to the Polish Foreign Intelligence Agency (FIA) once onsite investigation is complete. FIA has erected a security perimeter around

the site during the investigation. FIA plans to raze all remaining structures onsite and remove all debris. FIA has been fully cooperative.

- CIA investigation at site is underway and expected to take at least another week to systematically comb through all remaining debris. Investigation is slowed because of the need for all personnel onsite to wear MOPP Level 4 gear. No mishaps or exposures to nuclear, chemical, or biological materials have been detected, nor have any such materials been detected onsite.

- In addition to the classified documents recovered at the site, some additional personal papers and at least one personal journal have been recovered and will be assessed.

- DNA samples have been extracted from each set of human remains as they have been recovered, then remaining biological materials have been sent to an off-site facility for incineration in case of contamination by unknown/novel biological agent.

- Counterintelligence investigation is underway; more details of current counterintelligence operations available under separate cover.

- Investigation of LAPIS leadership (focusing on LAPIS Chief David FRANKLIN) and LAPIS interrogators (Peter DABROWSKY, Mark ROMERO, and Deborah SULLIVAN) with access to detainees also underway.

5. Recommendations:

- Forensic investigation of the LAPIS site should continue, with an emphasis on recovery of additional human remains in order to identify all expected personnel onsite and determine if any are missing. Top priority is a determination of the identities/fate of the four Al Qaeda detainees present at LAPIS at the time of the attack.

- Because the attack may have been made possible by insider threat, recommend immediate moves of all current Al Qaeda detainees at other black sites to new facilities, as well as immediate security upgrades at all other detention facilities until these moves can occur.

- Full-scope counterintelligence investigation of all CIA and allied personnel with knowledge and access to LAPIS site and location. Particular emphasis on LAPIS staff and Polish intelligence personnel with knowledge of LAPIS, seeking understanding of possible malfeasance or leaks (inadvertent or otherwise).

Author's Note

IN THE MORE than two decades since the so-called Global War on Terror began, a great deal of information about how these shadow wars and counterterror operations unfolded has become available, much more than one might expect. Surely, some of the first-person accounts that have been published are self-serving attempts to justify or explain away atrocious behavior. But even these types of accounts are useful for gaining insights into the contours of counterterrorism in the twenty-first century and the ethical lapses and complexities that attended those operations.

Magicians may be wise to not reveal how they perform their tricks, but I would like to pull back the curtain on how I came to provide the details of how the CIA might have operated in *Black Site, Black Mother*. Obviously I had to fill in many of the gaps through guesswork and sheer imagination—I have never visited a black site—but I also had a great many publicly available books and other sources at my disposal that provided the foundation for the novel. I wanted to make everything as realistic as possible where I could.

Terry McDermott and Josh Meyer's *The Hunt for KSM: Inside the Pursuit and Takedown of the Real 9/11 Mastermind, Khalid Sheikh Mohammed* (2012) was instrumental in understanding both how a senior Al-Qaeda leader like KSM (or the Engineer) lived and worked before capture, and what their experiences would be like after they were in CIA custody.

I modeled the opening chapters of the Engineer's detention by the CIA after the February 2003 capture of the radical imam Abu Omar in Milan. The circumstances of his capture have become well known by now, but Steve Hendricks' *A Kidnapping in Milan: The CIA on Trial* (2010) is the best account. Stephen Grey meticulously mapped out the global rendition program and how it used (uses?) aircraft to transport detainees to black sites around the world. Read his *Ghost Plane: The True Story of the CIA Torture Program* (2006) for an introduction. Several British scholars—Ruth Blakeley, Sam Raphael, and their colleagues—continued Grey's work in a systematic way as part of what became The Rendition Project; they eventually published a major report entitled "CIA Torture Unredacted," which remains available online.

The CIA black site in Poland was a real place, though I have taken some liberties with the exact layout of the facility. (Oddly enough, blueprints for the site are not publicly available.) You can read more about that site, now decommissioned, in Adam Goldman's 2014 piece in the *Washington Post* ("The hidden history of the CIA's prison in Poland") and elsewhere on the web.

Several first-person accounts by former CIA officers involved in relevant counterterrorism operations were eminently useful. Among the most directly relevant to *Black Site, Black Mother* are: John Kiriakou (with Michael Ruby), *The Reluctant Spy: My Secret Life in the CIA's War on Terror* (2012) and Philip Mudd, *Black Site: The CIA in the Post-9/11 World* (2019). Mudd's book was especially helpful in working through what day-to-day life inside a black site, for both detainees and the people who worked there, might be like.

Mark's experiences with the supernatural are, of course, products of my imagination, though I will admit that several of his more surrealistic experiences in both the dreamworld and in the forest that surrounds Stare Kiejkuty are based on my own experiences. Woods, like my dreams, are strange places where anything can happen. The blending of cosmic and body horror found here probably owes as much to Clive Barker as it does to H. P. Lovecraft, but I would be remiss if I did not acknowledge all who have come before me in the Lovecraft Circle.

I still haven't quite made up my mind if I like Mark Romero and his colleagues. I think I came to know Mark pretty well during the course of writing this novel. I began writing about Mark fairly uncritically, thinking about the many people I have known who are like Mark, in whole or in part, myself probably included. He's not based on anyone in particular—more of an amalgam—but you can read about some of the CIA paramilitary officers with similar roles to Mark in Toby Harnden's *First Casualty: The Untold Story of the CIA Mission to Avenge 9/11* (2021), Gary Berntsen and Ralph Pezzullo's *Jawbreaker: The Attack on Bin Laden and Al Qaeda: A Personal Account by the CIA's Key Field Commander* (2005), and Gary C. Schroen's *First In: An Insider's Account of How the CIA Spearheaded the War on Terror in Afghanistan* (2005).

Now that I've finished writing about Mark, I'm not so sure what I think of him. He's a flawed human being, like the rest of us, I suppose. Sometimes you just have to take the good with the bad.

Acknowledgments

AS WITH ANY author, I have accrued many debts through the course of writing this novel. I will inevitably forget many of the kind souls who helped either directly or indirectly with the novel, but I hope this captures the majority. While it is commonplace for authors to acknowledge that the craft of writing is a lonely one—it certainly can be—I had a great deal of fun writing this book. I was able to get inside Mark's head early on and the words just flowed. I had fun the whole way, but this wasn't a solo journey.

I would like to thank my old colleague Hussein H. for brainstorming with me some of the Arabic words used in the novel. Any inaccuracies or infelicities of language are my own. Thank you to Fahad B. for introducing me to his outlining method of writing (way back in grad school) that I have adapted for my use in fiction writing. That made the process of writing this book so, so much easier and more efficient than it otherwise might have been. I would very much like to thank two very good friends who enthusiastically read and provided feedback on early drafts: Kelsey W. and James S. Your comments helped clarify places in the book that needed work, but even more importantly, your enthusiasm for the project very much encouraged me. I would also like to thank all my many fine writing friends and acquaintances, too many to list here, for encouraging and challenging me, even if only by the strength of your examples of work. No writer will ever feel that they are as good as the writers that they admire, and I am no exception to that. Several of you—you know who you are—also provided expert advice and assistance along the way, and I hope to repay your kindnesses in the future. I would also like to thank Scarlett R. Algee for championing the project at JournalStone/Trepidatio, and Sean Leonard for the expert editing and proofreading. Lastly, I must thank my wife, Elizabeth, who continues to encourage me.

About the Author

Black Site, Black Mother is Ryan Rennik's second published novel. He is also the author of *As Above, So Below* (Uncanny Books, 2013), an occult detective novel set in contemporary Washington, DC, that pairs postmodern magic with ancient Babylonian mythology. His recent stories have included contributions in *Sherlock Holmes and the Occult Detectives, Volume 4* and *The Book of Carnacki* by Belanger Books and a dark fantasy tale published in Side Real Press' *The Dusk: Tales for Twilight*. Ryan writes in a wide variety of genres, everything from cosmic horror to modern crime dramas to technothrillers. He is currently at work on several novellas and short stories, all horror or dark fantasy.